TIE AND TEASE

I dabbed the puff between Melody's arse cheeks and over her pussy, feeling more servile than usual – the beaten maid powdering her mistress's body, allowed to do the most intimate places because she was too inconsequential for it to matter what she saw.

'Good girl,' she sighed. 'A little more on the pussy, then you can kiss my arse.'

I knew she didn't mean just the cheeks. My face pressed between her big, meaty black cheeks; my lips touched her bottom-hole and I was doing it, kissing another's girl's anus. No sooner had my lips found her clit than she reached back and pulled me off by my hair.

'Not yet, girl. Now get your slobber off my pussy.'

Once more I dried and powdered her, then kneeled back, wondering what she wanted. Her thighs were well apart, with every detail on show. I looked up at her, finding her watching me with an expression of lust and sadistic hauteur.

'Watch my pussy, Penny,' she said. 'Watch me pee.'

Why not visit Penny's website at:
www.pennybirch.com

A NEXUS CLASSIC

TIE AND TEASE

Penny Birch

This book is a work of fiction.
In real life, make sure you practise safe sex.

This Nexus Classic edition 2005

First published in 2001 by
Nexus
Thames Wharf Studios
Rainville Road
London W6 9HA

www.nexus-books.co.uk

ISBN 0 352 33987 X

Typeset by TW Typesetting, Plymouth, Devon

Printed and bound by
Clays Ltd, St Ives PLC

One

My anal ring gave, the plug popped inside and it had been done. I was a fox, or rather a vixen, with a long, swishy brush standing proudly over my bare bottom. The game was simple: if they caught me, they could do whatever they liked. I'd be made to suck cock, lick pussy, kiss bumholes. Certainly I'd be fucked, and if I knew them I was unlikely to get away without a cock up my bottom. I was going to be beaten too, first, they had assured me of that, stretched out and thrashed with riding-crops and birch twigs until my bottom was a real mess. There are other tortures a piece of spring woodland can provide: mud for my face, and worse, big, smooth stones for my pussy and bumhole, fresh young nettles for my boobs, gorse too, and holly. If they caught me I could expect all of that and more, whatever subtle and sadistic torment they could think up. I would probably be tied up by the end, in some awkward and vulnerable position, bringing my anguish to a peak. They had to catch me first, and I didn't intend to make it easy. Well, not too easy: that would spoil my fun.

I fixed the slender belt that held the tail around my tummy and stretched, feeling gloriously nude in the warm spring sunlight. Aside from my trainers and socks I had not a stitch on, while the great, thick brush added a lovely touch of erotic humiliation to my exposure. I was ready to run, and to judge by the way the others were looking at me, they were ready to chase. Amber was fingering her riding-crop, with her pretty face set in a wicked smile. Henry was rubbing his hands and looking at me as if inspecting a particularly fine sirloin of beef; Rasputin was by his leg, tongue lolling out and eyes peering from beneath shaggy brows. Vicky had one long leg up on a stump and was limbering up her muscles. Anderson was leaning on the car, cool and poised, idly fingering a vicious bone-handled whip. Ginny was head first in the car, her ample bottom straining her jodhpurs and wobbling slightly as she searched for something, presumably her whip.

'Got it,' she said and drew back, holding not just the heavy riding-crop I had expected, but something else: a fox's mask.

The sight of the thing sent a fresh tremor of anticipation through me. It was so well made it looked real, and as she took a tiny bottle from inside it I realised that it wasn't going to hold on with just a piece of elastic, either. She passed both to Amber, whose smile grew broader.

'Hold still, Penny,' she ordered happily as she held the thing up to my face.

I opened my mouth. I had to, because the interior of the thing held a ball that was clearly designed to go in it, gagging me. My body had started to shiver from the intensity of my feelings of exposure and humiliation, and I could feel the dampness between my thighs as I took the gag lightly in my teeth. I caught the scent of gum arabic as Amber unscrewed the bottle, and at greater strength as she began to paint the edge of the mask and then my face. It was done quickly and skilfully, the result of long experience at turning girls into ponies, pigs and whatever else fantasy demanded.

2

Now it was a fox, with all the trappings of fox-hunting subtly changed to suit erotic fantasy in place of blood sport. As it had originally been my idea, I had the right to be the first victim, or rather quarry. Most of the other detail had come from the others, including the term 'in at the rape', which had terrified me but added so much raw emotion to the game that in the end I'd accepted it.

It was just a game, but that didn't stop my heart racing as I waited for the gum to dry. After all, the chase would be real, my pain would be real and the sex would be real. True, I expected a truly explosive orgasm at the end of it, but that didn't stop me being scared, especially as I wasn't entirely sure why Henry had brought his dog. The mask made it worse, and yet more real. Now I couldn't speak, so there was no chance to use a stop word. Nor could I see very well, with the eye-holes limiting my vision much in the way of blinkers.

'Ready to go, Penny?' Amber asked as she took her hand away from the mask.

I nodded, picturing my vixen's face moving to the action.

'Twenty minutes then,' she said, 'you had better run.'

She didn't have to tell me twice. I set off, with my brush tickling my bottom as I went, its motion drawing a giggle from Ginny.

The wood was a fair size, ninety acres of mature oak and beech belonging to some horsey friend of Henry's. Horsey, rich, respectable, and so seriously gay that he hadn't even bothered to turn up to watch. With farmland on all sides the chances of us being seen were minimal. A single, overgrown footpath skirted the northern border, but it was easy to stay clear of that. The interior was a maze of gullies, thickets, ancient ditches and still more ancient earthworks, the ideal place for me to go to ground. That was what they expected, but it was not what I was going to do.

I was fairly sure how they'd hunt. Vicky and Anderson were fast, and would act as wings, fanning out to the sides. Amber and Ginny, less athletic but young, would come forward inside them, leaving fat old Henry at the middle, along with Rasputin. That way they could chivvy me forward and close the pincers at the far edge of the wood where an area of open ground and a ruined barn provided gorse, nettles and all the other things they would need to bring my torture to the most exquisite peak. All of that was fine, except for the fact that they'd be too pleased with themselves to really take it out on me. Instead I wanted them sweaty, scratched and hot before they caught me, thus guaranteeing that they would really make me pay.

So, rather than make for the sheltered depths of the wood, I ran until they were well out of sight and then turned north, towards the footpath, the one place they would expect me to avoid. My plan was simple. I would hide by the path until I heard one of the flankers coming, wait until they passed, then dash back down the footpath and into the wood behind them. Hopefully the manoeuvre would leave them completely puzzled and frustrated, ensuring that I got punished for my temerity when I finally allowed them to catch me.

It went well at first, and would have worked if it hadn't been for my brush. I found a thick stand of elder right beside the fence and hid in it, freezing to the ground when I heard someone coming. It was Anderson, jogging slowly along and scanning the woods. I stayed perfectly still, sure he would miss me

4

among the thick green leaves. He looked right at me and kept on, only to stop abruptly as he drew level, no more than twenty yards from my hiding place. His face broke into a happy leer and I knew he had seen me, only he wasn't looking at my face but behind me. That was what made me realise that my brush was sticking out of the bush.

I bolted, breaking from cover at a run. He called a view and followed, whooping with joy as he came. Normally I would have stood at least a chance, being smaller and more agile than him. Now it was hopeless, with my bare skin, limited vision and the plug jerking in my bottom-hole making it impossible to get any real speed. I tried, though, jumping logs and dodging around trunks until finally I slipped in mud and went down, sprawling in the mess and slipping as I tried to rise, only for his hand to fasten in my hair, twist and pull my head back hard.

As I was on my knees, the pressure forced me to curve my spine back and lift my bottom, an action that drew a satisfied chuckle from Anderson. I was really shaking, panting for breath around my gag with my heart hammering in my chest, needing what was about to be done to me but also genuinely scared. His grip tightened in my hair, forcing me to bring my bottom into greater prominence. My knees came apart of their own accord, spreading my pussy to him beneath the shelter of my brush.

'Good little vixen,' he crowed, 'that's right, stick it out and I'll fill you, but not just yet. First you have some sucking to do, if it's practical with your mask.'

It wasn't, which I could have told him if I'd been able to speak. With my mouth full of gag it was hard enough to breathe, never mind suck a penis. Vixens don't talk anyway, so I just wriggled a bit as he pulled my head around to inspect the mouth.

5

'Damn,' he swore as his fingers caught at the mouth. 'Oh well, in that case I'll just have to put a couple of lines across your bottom to help me get ready.'

A moment later I felt him take my brush. It was lifted and laid on my back, exposing the full spread of my rear view with nothing hidden, bottom-cheeks flared wide, pussy agape, anus showing with the shaft of the tail disappearing into the little hole. My stomach tightened and my bottom clenched as he gave a chuckle at the display I was making of myself. I heard him shift position and suddenly my buttocks jolted and a line of fire sprang up across then. My arms had gone limp at the shock, and at the second my breasts went into the mud, my muscles jumping at the pain as his crop lashed down on my naked bottom. A third stroke caught me and he laughed to see me as I kicked my legs and cocked my thighs wide in my pain. I collapsed, putting my belly in the mud as well as my boobs, to leave me grovelling in submission as he laid a fourth cut across the crests of my bum-cheeks.

I'd have screamed if I'd been able, but all I could do was make a ridiculous gurgling noise in my throat. He stopped at four, leaving me sprawled in the mud, pathetically grateful to him as I lifted my bottom to offer myself. He gave his dry, wicked chuckle again and I heard the crop fall to the ground. Looking back, I found him pushing his jodhpurs down, taking his briefs with them to reveal a good-sized cock, already half-stiff.

I lay still as he masturbated over my beaten bottom, his eyes fixed to the four red cuts he had put on my skin. They stung; my bottom was throbbing hard, my pussy wide and wet, while my anus was contracting over and over on the neck of the plug. He hardened quickly, his eyes never once leaving my bottom until his cock was a solid bar of glossy flesh, the head so shiny it might have been oiled. I went up a little, offering myself, knees wide and bottom lifted, surrendered to penetration. He came behind me in a squat, careful not to soil his jodhpurs on the dirty ground. That was perfect, with me beaten and filthy with mud, while he wasn't even prepared to dirty his knees while he had me.

His cock found the mouth of my pussy and he pulled me on to himself, filling me and spreading my thighs wide across his front. I swallowed on my gag as he began to fuck me, holding me by my hips and jerking me on to his cock. My brush was tickling my back, my whip marks smarting in the cool air, my boobs rubbing in the mess of mud and leaves: all perfect to take me so, so high. Soon the others would come, and I'd really be used, beaten again, and entered and teased and tortured until at last they let me come myself . . .

No, it was no good. It hadn't been long enough. I needed more of the excitement of being chased, the alarm and desperation, the fear as I was hunted, the final dismay as they caught me and dragged me down. I braced and hurled myself forward, kicking off from Anderson's leg. He gave a startled cry, went backwards and I was gone, darting across the sunlit glade where he had been indulging himself with me.

He must have fallen right into the mud puddle, because I heard him curse, and I was laughing inside as I skipped between two massive beeches and away. I'd taken him completely by surprise, leaping up while he'd been lost in the feeling of having his cock in me. Doubtless he'd imagined me already beaten into submission, and had been enjoying his dominance and the sight of the whip-stripes on my naked buttocks as much as the physical pleasure of fucking me. Now he was sat in a mud puddle with his erection sticking up in the air, rigid in his frustrated lust.

I nearly collided with Ginny, dodging just in time as she grabbed for me. She had seemed to come from nowhere, and the shock brought me back to earth. With her startled yell ringing in my ears I ran on, rushing through dappled sunlight as her view calls rang out behind me. Others answered: Henry's deep roar to the south, Amber's and Vicky's from much further. Ginny yelled again, close on my heels, then Anderson, now well behind me.

Anderson might have been too fast for me, but no girl with a figure like Ginny's was going to catch me: she has just too much flesh. I sprinted, my eyes fixed dead ahead, forcing myself to ignore the stabbing pain of the plug in my rectum. Her calls had been full of glee and pleasure in the chase, but as they changed to frustration I knew I had the edge on her.

Not that it meant I'd got away, as I knew Vicky would be coming as fast as she could, and against her I had no chance at all. If I kept running they would just herd me into the tip of the wood, exactly where they wanted me, gorse, nettles and all.

At the thought of having my pussy tickled with nettles I hurled myself to the side, crashing through a stand of birch and undergrowth. Twigs whipped at my breasts and tummy; stems caught at my legs, but then I was through, only to feel a smarting throb start on my thighs and pussy. I had run into exactly what I was trying to avoid, nettling my sex without them having to bother. My nettle stings hurt, and lent me new energy as I imagined what it was going to be like when they finally caught me.

They wouldn't just whip me with nettles. They'd spread me out, one to each limb, with my legs wide

8

and my breasts and sex completely vulnerable. They'd each take a nettle and work me over, tickling my nipples and pussy, the tender skin of my breasts and the sensitive area under the tuck of my bottom. If they were feeling really cruel they would even do the centre of my pussy and my bumhole, which would probably be enough to make me come, although I'd writhe and scream while it was happening.

Ginny had cried gone away as I went through the brake, but she hadn't followed. For a moment I was invisible to her and I used my chance, turning back to the north and running low beneath the overhanging birches and hazels. A twig lashed across my breasts, leaving a line of fire, then another, lower, across my tummy. I heard Anderson call from some way off to my left and Vicky answered, already to my right.

At that, and with the pain in my body, I panicked. How she had come up so fast I could not understand, but it seemed barely human. I ran full tilt, indifferent to branches, scratched by holly, stung by nettles, tearing blindly through the wood with my head full of visions of my own torture. Henry's phrase came to me, and the piece of fox-hunting parlance he had changed it from – in at the death, in at the rape.

With that all sense, all reason went and I was running blind through the wood in true fright. Their calls seemed to be coming from all around me, five human voices and Rasputin's bass bark, and with that what had been just a dirty thought became certainty. They would give me to the dog. They'd hold me down and let Rasputin mount me. They'd let him fuck me and he'd knot in my pussy. They'd tease my boobs and tickle my pussy while he was inside me. They'd make me masturbate and they'd take photos of him humping me, of when he came, of when I came . . .

I never saw the bank. One moment I was running in blind panic and the next I was sliding and rolling down through mud and wet grass to land in a huge puddle, face first. The shock of the cold water brought me back to my senses and I pulled my face out of the mud, or rather my mask, which had stayed on and was so heavily plastered in mud that I couldn't see at all and could barely breathe. I sat up, aching and filthy but still intending to run, only to find that I had hurt my ankle as I fell. That was the last straw and I collapsed back into the cool slime, defeated, willing to surrender to whatever tortures and degradations they chose to inflict on me.

Already I was lying face down in a pool of dirty water, blind with mud and probably cow dung, naked but for my footwear, mask and brush, scratched, bruised and with four scarlet whip marks decorating my bottom. How much worse could it get?

A lot, especially with the five of them all determined to get their pleasure out of me, making me service them in whatever way they pleased once my own wants had been dealt with. Henry was most likely to make me suck him and come in my mouth, either that or in my face. Vicky and Ginny would both make me lick, down on my knees with my face in their pussies and my bare bum stuck up in the air, one after the other. Anderson would probably bugger me. Amber would queen me and make me lick her bottom while she played with herself: it was her favourite thing and, at the thought of her lovely bottom being lowered into my face, I couldn't resist a little purr.

I felt a hand on my shoulder, not the rough grip I had expected but a gentle pressure, suggesting that it was one of the girls and that she was worried in case the game had gone too far or I'd really hurt myself.

10

I was in a sorry state, but compassion was the last thing I wanted, at least not until I had been thoroughly abused. Intent on assuring them I pushed the gag from my mouth, wincing as the gum pulled from around my chin and lips.

'You've got me, take me, rape me,' I managed, and sank back into the slurry.

'Oh my God!' she answered: a female voice, but not Amber, not Ginny and not Vicky.

It was like having a bucket of freezing water thrown over me. I'd been in a sort of erotic haze, well worked up, with my adrenalin running high and my endorphins higher still, in a deliciously awkward situation from which there was no escape. Suddenly I was in a genuinely awkward situation, with some concerned woman leaning over me and babbling out horror-struck questions about what had been done to me and by whom.

Fortunately, although it didn't seem so at the time, I'd taken a mouthful of filthy water when I slumped back into the puddle, so instead of saying anything stupid I just choked and spluttered. That gave me a chance to collect my wits and ignore her barrage of questions and sympathetic remarks, which ended with a determined statement that she would call the police on her mobile phone.

I tried to answer that one, begging her not to do it, but it was too late. For once the call got through without delay, and before I could stop her she was jabbering out the most frightful stuff about me being assaulted and beaten up and raped and even kidnapped. Then it was too late, and as she went back to trying to comfort and interrogate me simultaneously I tried frantically to decide what to do.

I certainly couldn't tell the truth, as it would lead to all sorts of trouble for my friends, not to mention the man who owned the land. Nor could I run for it as, with my ankle and a squad of police about to descend on us, there was no hope of escape. It was too late to reason with her, and as I managed to get enough mud off my mask to see I realised that it would have been hopeless anyway.

She was small, not much bigger than me, with dyed blonde hair framing her face and an expression of concerned, honest alarm. From what she was saying and the way she kept repeating 'Oh my God', it was obvious that she was not going to believe anything except that I had been brutalised in some awful way. Why she imagined any rapist would put a girl in a fox's mask and stick a pretend brush up her bottom was a question that could wait until later.

I said nothing, hoping she would accept that I was in shock while I sorted my mind out. She was scared too, and not without reason, because from her point of view whatever maniac had attacked me was probably still in the vicinity. When Anderson gave a hunting call from the wood she stiffened and threw a terrified glance over her shoulder, but the chase had begun to move in the opposite direction. With that, and looking around me, I realised that I was not in the wood at all, but on the public footpath.

My only chance was to bluff it out. I couldn't even admit who I was, as if I did the story would be bound to get out. The thought of my colleagues at the university thinking I'd been horribly raped was nearly as bad as the thought of them knowing how debauched my sex life was. The idea of my mother finding out was worse. It would also mean a full investigation, and it wasn't going to take Sherlock Holmes to put two and two together. What the police would then make of my little fox-hunting fantasy I wasn't sure, but I had no intention of finding out.

12

I finally pretended to come to my senses, peeling the mask off my face with considerable difficulty and looking up at my rescuer with what I hoped was a suitably frightened and grateful expression. She immediately cradled my head, muttering soothing words and stroking my hair, apparently indifferent to the mess she was making of her jumper. My head was held tight to her breasts, which were fairly big, and firm too, briefly making me forget how awkward a situation I was in. I let her hold me anyway, and reached back for my tail, which I was determined to get out of my bottom before the police arrived.

She watched me do it, mouth and eyes wide as I pulled the plug out of my bottom-hole and undid the belt. I was pretty sore, and winced as it came out, which drew a fresh spate of sympathy from her. I stood and stretched, still not feeling able to answer, and as she got her first proper look at my body she went quiet.

I have to admit I was a pretty sorry sight. My legs were red with scratches, particularly the fronts, which also had some pretty bad nettlerash. My tummy and chest were scratched, too, less badly, but with two livid welts, one of which ran across both breasts as if somebody had hit them with a cane. My back was less bad, but the four whip marks on my bottom left no doubt that I had been beaten, and well. There were bruises, too, new ones and a few fading marks from when Amber had had to spank me with a hairbrush the week before.

'Oh my God!' the girl said for about the thirtieth time and at that moment I heard the sound of sirens in the distance.

If I'd been lucky the police might never have found us and would have gone back thinking it had been a

13

hoax call. Unfortunately Beth, which was my rescuer's name, insisted on helping me to the road. She gave me her jumper, too, which was big enough to cover most of me. By chance a squad car was passing at the exact moment we arrived. After that it was absolutely ghastly, and took more strength and downright obstinacy than I've ever had to show before.

They started off assuming I'd be happy to help, and when I wasn't they decided that it was because I was scared of my supposed attacker. First it was the doctor, who let me wash the worst of the mud off and then gave me a pretty humiliating inspection that would have had me fully aroused in normal circumstances. I was in stirrups, legs up and open, pussy wide, while he pulled on gloves and gave me a thorough internal, not just vaginal, but anal too. Samples then followed, swabs and fluids, all of which I consented to just to buy me time to think. He asked questions as well, which I was forced to answer so that they accorded with the condition of my body. Yes, I had been beaten. Yes, I had been penetrated. No, nobody had come inside me. He saw the brush and mask and immediately rang for a psychiatrist, but chose not to question me on that subject. Only then did he dress the few minor cuts I'd sustained and give me some ointment for my nettlerash.

A WPC helped me to wash properly, and stood by while I rubbed the ointment into my rash, a process which I'd also have thoroughly enjoyed in any other circumstances. By the time I was ready and wrapped in a police-issue towelling robe, Beth had given her statement, which seemed to have been pretty dramatic. It was now my turn, and as I sat down and took hold of a cup of thin coffee I was bracing myself for what was to come.

They were pretty sympathetic at first, putting my lack of co-operation down to shock, but it wasn't long before their patience began to wear thin. This was especially true of the male officer, a bullish sergeant who seemed to take it personally that I wasn't eager to tell my story in lavish detail. I'd given my name to Beth as Penny Brush, which had been a pretty stupid thing to say but the first name that came into my head. I had to stick with it anyway, and if any of them thought it a bit peculiar that a girl found naked and made up as a fox should be called after a certain well-known children's TV character from the seventies, then they didn't say so.

Only when they asked my address did I clamp down, refusing to give it. They presented me with several good reasons why I should, but I stuck to my guns and eventually they moved on to asking me about my attacker. I said he had been just under six foot, of medium build and dark haired, with no distinguishing features. By then I was beginning to feel a bit of temper, or perhaps hysteria, because I had to bite back the temptation to say he was four foot tall, one legged, bald and with a livid scar running from forehead to chin.

When asked what had happened I kept to the minimum of what the doctor already knew. I had been walking and had stopped for a picnic lunch: ciabatta with chorizo and sun-dried tomatoes washed down with a Valpolicella ripasso. That was true, as it was what Henry has served for lunch before the fox-hunt, and while I doubted they would pump my stomach, the alcohol was bound to show up in my samples. At the mention of the wine the sergeant gave a knowing frown and the last piece of my intended scheme fell into place.

'And what were you wearing, Miss Brush?' he asked.

'A little summer frock,' I answered. 'It was such a nice day.'

'With what underneath?' he went on. 'I'm sorry, but I'm sure you will understand that we have to ask these questions. Your clothing may provide important clues.'

'Well, nothing actually,' I said after a moment's pause. 'It was such a nice day, and . . .'

'A light summer frock with nothing underneath?' he demanded. 'A short summer frock?'

'Yes,' I answered and saw his brow furrow.

I knew what he wanted to say – that as I'd been out walking, alone, in a short cotton dress with nothing on underneath then I shouldn't really be surprised when I attracted male attention, even to the point of being assaulted. It had been quite windy on the footpath and I could imagine him picturing my dress blowing up to show my legs, maybe even my bottom, my bare bottom. Any red-blooded male would see it as provocative, and if I didn't realise that I was stupid. He wanted to tell me, but he didn't dare, not in front of the WPC.

From then on it was quite easy. He had decided what I was, a silly girl who had more or less got what she deserved, and I was happy to play along with the image. The WPC was pretty outraged at his attitude, but in the end rank told. She tried the line that if I didn't co-operate I would be leaving a violent attacker at large, trying to make me feel guilty. As there was no attacker this didn't work either and I just sat there with a petulant expression on my face until they gave up.

I began to worry again when the time came to speak to the psychiatrist. Having read zoology at a university no more than a few miles away I was worried that they might produce someone who actually knew me, which would have been the end of my little pretence. Fortunately it was just some man full of his own theories and much more inclined to talk than listen.

He more or less told me that the reason I had been put in a fox's mask and brush was that my attacker had been a huntsman frustrated by the moves to outlaw hunting with hounds. My light dress, lack of underwear and casual manner had led him to identify me as the epitome of the enemy; urban, left-wing and unrestrainedly female. Thus I was the ideal victim and what had happened to me had had nothing to do with sex whatever but only power, the act of a male powerless in the face of government and so determined to exert himself on weaker members of society. I let him drivel on for a while and then agreed that this was a brilliant theory and undoubtedly true, and really that was that. He left thoroughly pleased with himself, doubtless intending to write a paper on the subject with plenty of flow charts and bad statistical analysis. From his age it was certain he had grown up during the seventies, yet for all his cock-sure assumption of intelligence it never occurred to him that there was something odd about my name.

All the while I had been dreading that they would run into Amber and the others and bring them in. It didn't happen, and at eleven o'clock when the night's drunks and troublemakers started to appear I began to feel I was going to get away with it. Not wishing to end up wandering around Berkshire in the middle of the night I made no demands, and presently went to sleep from sheer exhaustion.

In the morning they had to let me go, as I had known they would if I just stuck to my guns long enough. The WPC made a final effort to get my identity when she brought me tea in the morning, but

17

I resisted and so two hours later I found myself on the street.

My feelings were mixed as I walked away from the station. Most of them had been sympathetic to me, but several, the sergeant especially, regarded me as a complete time-waster. I did feel bad about that, but really I had had little choice. More importantly, it hadn't been my decision to go there in the first place. I must admit to a degree of triumph too, for having led the sergeant's thought processes down his own preferred line and evading the attentions of the psychiatrist.

Not that my troubles were over. Standing in the road in Beth's jumper and an ill-fitting skirt, it was not obvious what I should do, while I had to consider the possibility that I would be followed. My parents' house was no more than a stiff walk away, but that was the last place I wanted to go, while with no money my options were limited. The best bet seemed to be to take a roundabout route cross-country, until I was absolutely sure I was clear, and then to beg the use of someone's phone to call Amber.

So I walked, north along the river and then out across the fields on a footpath, constantly checking behind me. By the time I was certain I was not being followed I was in the hilly country to the west of Pangbourne, which I know quite well. I was starting to feel confident again, and to see the funny side of what I'd been through, and the naughty side as well.

What with the fox-hunt, Beth, the medical examination and the interviews it had been quite a day. The irony of the situation was not lost on me either. While it has never really been my thing, I know more than one girl who has submissive sexual fantasies centred on forcible medical inspections, and police fantasies too, about being arrested and subjected to various sexual humiliations. I'd had the medical bit for real, stirrups and all, and while I couldn't fault the police for their behaviour, there had been a definite element of humiliation about the whole thing.

Vicky, for instance, has a fantasy about being taken to a health farm and deliberately humiliated for being overweight. She is put in a room with a dozen or so other women, all thinner than her, and made to strip while the others keep on their smart clothes. The nurse then gives her a lecture, spanks her across the knee and puts her through a full medical, including being made to provide a urine sample and given an enema, all of it while the other women watch and make condescending and insulting remarks. Normally she comes when she gets to the enema, and in one version she refuses and has to be tied into stirrups before it happens. This is strange, as she is tall, slim and muscular, but that's fantasy for you.

I was looking forward to telling her, as there's no better way of getting over something like that than making a joke of it with friends. Naturally I'd need to embellish it a bit, and as I struck off down another footpath I began to think of what details I should add to turn her on and make her jealous. I doubted she'd believe I'd been given an enema, but I could say he'd watched while I provided the urine sample, which was guaranteed to both horrify her and turn her on. Yes, that would be perfect, saying I'd been made to pee in front of him, on a thing like a potty, still in the nude with him gloating over my embarrassment.

Really I should know my own sexuality by now, but I doubt it will be the last time I work myself up by accident. Thinking about medical inspections and public spankings and humiliations, I had become desperately turned on. There was the frustration of not having come after the fox-hunt as well, an orgasm I had been looking forward to for days. I had to do it.

There was no hesitation. I was walking down the side of a field, with a thick wood ahead, bright green with spring leaves. On reaching it I ran in far enough to be safe, all the while with a lump of tension building in my throat. I adore masturbating outdoors, but I'm always careful not to be caught, however badly I need it.

Having chosen a thick stand of young hazel, I stood still for a moment, listening for any sounds that might indicate a human presence. There was nothing, just birdsong and the distant rumble of the motorway. A moment later and my panties were down under my skirt and I was settling my bare bottom on to a hummock of wet moss, which felt wonderfully cool and soft. I put my fingers to my pussy and closed my eyes, allowing my mind to drift as I started to play with myself.

It was the police station at first, and the way I'd been spread out, thighs cocked wide, ankles high in the stirrups, pussy wide to the peering doctor. I thought of his clinical manner, the calm, detached way he had pulled on his gloves as I lay there with all the most intimate parts of my body on show. He had seen my breasts and bottom, sore with whip marks, my pussy, wet with my own juices, my bottom-hole, still greasy with the lubricant that had been used on the tail-plug. His hand had gone up me, filling my pussy out opening me, exploring me . . .

I could have come, and it would have been good. Good, but not perfect: medical fantasy just isn't really my thing. It would have been better if the grumpy old sergeant had told me not to waste his time and put me across his knee for a good old-fashioned spanking, hard, on my bare bottom while the pretty young WPC giggled over my distress. That was nice, especially the thought of her enjoying watching me being beaten while in fear of getting the same treatment on her own pert bottom, panties down and all. Unfortunately it was too wide of reality to get me there and I stopped, idly massaging my pussy while I searched for the right fantasy.

Just stroking myself was lovely, feeling the soft, furry mound of my pussy and the wet, open centre, with the heat of my sex a wonderful contrast to the cool air of the wood. Too aroused to worry about where I was, I pulled my jumper up and off, exposing my naked breasts, cupping them and bumping my fingers over my nipples. I lay back, kicking my legs high and spreading myself to the wood. My panties came down further, and off one leg, leaving them hanging from my right ankle. Only of course they weren't my panties at all, but a spare pair belonging to the WPC who had looked after me. I pushed off my skirt to leave myself nude but for trainers, socks and her panties, then went back to stroking my pussy, only now thinking of her. Barbara, she was called, a pretty, freckle-faced girl, bigger than me so that her panties had felt oddly loose around my hips. For all her sympathy, there had been something matronly about her, and it would have been great to be spanked across her knee, in the nude, kicking and blubbering as I was punished.

My legs were right up to my chest and wide, too, leaving me just as spread as it is possible to be. I was rubbing hard, my clitty burning under my fingers, my pussy starting to contract. My orgasm started, rising in my head as my bottom clenched and my spine arched. I slid my spare hand down between my cheeks, found my bumhole and teased her open, feeling so, so dirty as my finger eased into the slimy interior of my bottom. I pictured Barbara slapping my bottom, punishing me, telling me off as she

21

smacked my naked cheeks and then without warning she had turned to Beth, holding me tight to her chubby little breasts, cuddling me, stroking my beaten bottom. She'd squeeze my cheeks, let her hand stray between them, spread them, probe my dirty little hole, all the time whispering soothing remarks in my ear. At last she'd lose control and put me face down for a spanking, punishing me, beating me, until I was a snivelling, tear-stained mess at her knees . . .

I came, squealing aloud in a beautiful, long orgasm that had my back in a tight arch and my head swimming in ecstasy. Beth's name came to my lips and I called for her, although even in that moment of pure bliss I didn't know why it was her I wanted.

Two

I made my phone call and Amber picked me up, well away from the wood and the police station. On the way back to her house we swapped stories and I found that things had gone much as I had anticipated. They had lost me completely in the wood, my panic-stricken dash throwing them off so that the pincer movement had closed on nothing. Shortly after that the sirens had started and eventually they had put two and two together and very sensibly kept out of it. When questioned they had simply stated that they were guests on the estate enjoying a walk after riding earlier, all of which could be proved. That was that, to my great relief.

Experiences that are erotic, or have erotic undertones, but which are not actively sexual tend to make me a little obsessive and determined to explore the full sexual potential of the situation. The fox-hunt left me wanting to expand on a number of experiences, including the sense of helpless panic during the chase, the embarrassment and exposure of the medical examination, and the feeling of sexual impropriety that the sergeant's attitude to my story had provoked. All three relied to a greater or lesser extent on me relinquishing control, which always makes fantasy fulfilment difficult. After all, if I create a fantasy I must, by definition, remain to some extent in control of it. Nor would I risk any situation where my partner or partners did not understand my needs and limits, or something might really be done to me against my will. For a female submissive there can be a fine line between perfect ecstasy and utter disaster, and I need time to find a way to get as close as possible to that line, safely.

One other thing has stuck in my mind from that day, as more of an irritation than a need. This was Beth. Not only had I come over her, but the more I thought about the things she had said to me the more I felt I needed to argue with her. Basically she had been unable to see me as anything other than a victim, and it had never so much as occurred to her that I might have been a willing participant in an erotic game. She had used the phrase 'remember you're a woman' several times, obviously intending to comfort me. There had been other remarks, too, all of which indicated a mindset so different from my own that it was impossible not to be fascinated.

Fascinated and antagonistic, not in the sense of wanting to hurt her, but because I found it impossible not to take her attitude personally. I knew it was petty, but I felt put upon by her automatic assumption that I thought and behaved exactly as she did. At the least I wanted to make her understand that I could enjoy things she found dreadful. At best I wanted her to learn to enjoy them herself.

Even so I'd have put her out of my mind quickly enough had it not been for her looks. With her delicate face, chubby little breasts and rounded bottom it was impossible not to find her appealing. Sometimes when I develop a minor crush on an unreachable or unsuitable girl, or a man for that matter, a couple of good orgasms are enough to clear my head. This didn't work with Beth, especially as I knew that although she was undoubtedly unsuitable for me, she wasn't unreachable.

I had her jumper, which had a name tag in it, like the ones we had to have sewn to our clothes at school. She was Elizabeth Diez-Joyce, a name that explained the subtle olive tone of her skin and that could hardly be difficult to find in a telephone directory. She'd had no car and been pretty familiar with the bit of country we'd been in, so the chances were she lived in Berkshire and wouldn't be too hard to find. It wasn't hard at all. E. Diez-Joyce lived in Streatley.

Amber had to be told, and she gave me exactly what I deserved. We were in her kitchen at the time, both feeling pleasantly mellow after a light lunch and a shared bottle of Riesling. She doesn't mind me playing with other girls, so long as it's not behind her back, so I jokingly mentioned that I was taken with the idea of getting into Beth's panties.

A second later I was over her lap, squealing in shock as my arm was twisted hard into the small of my back. I kicked and struggled, but I was giggling too much to be convincing and she's much stronger than me, so I got spanked. My jeans were undone first, despite my protests and efforts to protect myself. With the button popped they came down, tugged off my bottom in a series of firm jerks to reveal my panties, then pulled all the way down to my ankles. The panties followed them, as they always do, Amber firmly believing that a spanking is simply not a spanking unless the victim's bottom is bare. With that done and the knowledge of how my pussy would be showing between my thighs I gave in. That's always the best part of a punishment for me, that awful moment when my panties come down and suddenly it's all showing and I'm helpless, and bare, and I'm about to be spanked.

After the first couple of smacks I was wishing I'd put more effort into my struggles. It was hard, firm slaps to the fattest part of my bottom, delivered with the full weight of her arm. Each one jammed my insides up high and I was soon panting for breath and babbling apologies and pleas for mercy in between my cries of pain and shock. She ignored me, saying nothing as she spanked me and twisted my arm ever tighter to keep me in place. In no time I was kicking my legs about and bucking my bottom up and down in my pain, squealing too, like a stuck pig, and beating my free hand on the floor. One of my shoes flew off, and that leg came free of my jeans and panties, leaving them flying from the other like a flag. Amber laughed at that and stopped, as suddenly as she had begun, leaving me red-bottomed and breathless over her lap, completely subdued and ready to do whatever I was told.

I lay there, passive and defeated as her hand settled between my thighs and a finger probed my pussy. I was wet, just as I knew I would be, and she gave a little knowing chuckle as her finger went up me. For a moment she explored me, then put it to my mouth to make me taste my own excitement. I sucked eagerly, hoping that she would take mercy on me and frig me off across her lap with my smacked bottom stuck high as I came.

Her knee came up, forcing my bottom higher and I purred in pleasure, sure that she was going to do what I wanted. Sure enough, she leaned across the table, and a moment later I felt something warm and squashy between my legs: butter. She rubbed it in, smearing it over my pussy and up between my bum-cheeks. Fingers went inside me again, two in my pussy, then three, then four and I realised she was going to fist me. In it went, the whole of her hand, eased slowly up my buttery vagina to leave me feeling gloriously full. Her hand began to squirm inside me, pressing to the back of my clitty and bringing me fully on heat. I began to squirm my bottom and hips, sure that I could bring myself off if I just got the motion right. Amber chuckled and pulled her hand free, leaving my vagina to close on empty air as a wash of disappointment ran over me.

She cupped my pussy and began to rub at me, her thumb finding the tight spot of my anus. It went in, forcing my butter-moist hole to make me gasp and then sigh. I lay still, letting her work my anus open and wondering what she was going to put in it. Her thumb came out and she gave me a playful smack, and once more leaned forward. I craned my neck around, finding to my horror that she had the wine bottle in her hand. I felt it against my vagina, cool and hard, then the wet feel of the wine, colder still as she filled my vagina. As a trickle of wine escaped to run down between my pussy lips she moved the bottle, touching the neck to my anus and pushing gently. I relaxed my ring, letting the bottle up, then groaned deep in my throat as the wine gurgled into my rectum.

I could already feel the rush of alcohol as my soft membranes let it in, leaving me dizzy and sighing. Twice the bottle eased into my bottom-hole, stretching my ring around the elegant neck, buggering me between my smacked cheeks. I groaned again, hoping that she would finish me off like that, with my ring clenching on the hard, smooth glass. Instead she pulled it free, leaving me frustrated again, with both my holes full of wine and my head spinning in drunken arousal.

Her grip tightened, pulling my poor arm hard up my back and forcing my bottom still higher. A sudden smack caught me unawares, making me squeal and jump and spraying wine across my thighs from inside me. Another caught the back of my thighs, a third the pouted rear of my pussy and I was left gasping again with my mouth wide and my eyes shut in a helpless blend of arousal and hurt.

She moved again and something touched my pussy, ever so gently. Her hand cupped my mound and began to rub once more, vigorously now, making brisk circling motions to splay my pussy out. Her thumb touched my anus and I was starting to come, my pussy and bumhole warming, then starting to burn as I realised what she had done. I screamed as the pepper sauce caught me, turning my sex to a burning, inflamed mush of flesh even as my orgasm rose and burst, making me scream again, thrashing my legs and writhing my bottom and pussy on to her hand.

It was true sexual torture, an unbearable blend of ecstasy and pain about which I could do nothing, my body held tight in her grip as I contorted myself into a series of postures so ludicrous that she was laughing by the time my orgasm started to fade. I really screamed too, but she didn't let me off, waiting until I was limp and sobbing across her lap before taking mercy and upending a bottle of mineral water between my legs, only then letting go of my wrist.

'There,' she said as I slumped to the floor, 'could Beth do that for you?'

I was beyond speech but managed to shake my head.

'Well then, stick to me, and to other dirty girls,' she advised. 'Seriously, Penny, I'm not trying to tell you what to do, but she sounds pretty prudish, so there's no fun in it.'

She was probably right, but I still had to try.

* * *

I had every opportunity, with three weeks until the start of the summer term, so it was just a question of how to go about it. Having given up trying to dissuade me, Amber became helpful, and invited Anderson and Vicky over to discuss the project. Anderson thought it an excellent idea, inevitably I suppose, as it involved attempting to seduce a pretty girl. Vicky was a little more doubtful, but accepted that if I succeeded it would be greatly to Beth's benefit, while if I failed no harm would have been done.

The first thing was obviously to make contact with her again without making her feel threatened. That was easy. At five foot two in my bare feet nobody ever finds me threatening, while if I said I'd tracked her down to thank her for what she'd done and to return her jumper I wouldn't even need to pretend our meeting was accidental. The next problem was to explain why there wasn't a major hunt for the maniac who had attacked me. Putting the blame on the incompetence and misogyny of the police seemed most likely to work, as to judge by some of the remarks she had made in the car she had no great respect for them.

After that I would be able to concentrate on seducing her, for which purpose I intended to get her completely drunk and make a pass at her. Hardly an original technique, I know, but tried and tested, while there would be no aggression or forcefulness and she could reject me if she wanted to. Of course it was possible that she didn't like sex with other girls, but that was a chance I'd have to take. Besides, in my experience it's remarkable how few women are genuinely antagonistic to at least the occasional lesbian experience. If she proved to drink only mineral water and believe in life-long celibacy, then I'd just have to go home.

Assuming that she was likely to work, and probably not in Streatley, I waited until Sunday, then took the train up. Streatley is small, a couple of proper streets and a cluster of houses by the river with a few lanes along which most of the more prosperous houses are set. Beth's address proved to be a flat over a shop, hardly luxurious, but in a lovely setting with a view over the Thames. She was out when I arrived, and so I spent an hour wandering around and running over my plans.

As I stood leaning on the parapet of the bridge and looking down into the river I found that I was enjoying myself enormously. This was fantasy yet also reality, with an adventurous spice I adore but which is so hard to come by. My sense of mischief was running at full throttle, with an added piquancy from the fact that if I was successful I would end up in bed with a beautiful girl.

I was still leaning on the bridge when Beth appeared, walking from the Goring side of the river. I watched her for a while without hailing her, studying the delicacy of her features and admiring her figure. She seemed pensive, even slightly vulnerable in her expression, which seemed at odds with the deliberate confidence of her posture and walk. The contrast intrigued me and I was positively bubbling inside as I hailed her.

She saw me, looked puzzled for an instant, and her face broke into a big smile. A string of questions followed, which I answered as best I could, handing her the jumper and explaining how I wanted to thank her for her help. She accepted everything, happy that I had sought her out and agreeing heartily that the police were worse than useless. I offered dinner and she accepted, and after a brief detour to her flat we ended up at a table by the riverside, sipping Chablis and chatting as if we had known each other for years. I only realised how badly I was overplaying it when she suddenly stopped talking and said that she thought I must be the strongest woman she had ever met.

With the effect of the wine and my general excitement it took me a moment to realise what she was talking about, and then I remembered that I was supposed to have been raped and brutalised by a sadistic maniac only the previous week. I back-pedalled hastily, giving a heavy sigh and looking at the ground. Her hand folded around mine and when I looked up I found her eyes full of sympathy.

'It's not as simple as it looks,' I said, making my voice seem tired and drawn. 'Do you really want to know?'

'You can talk to me,' she promised, 'but I don't mind if you'd rather not.'

That was a lie for a start, as she was obviously desperate to hear my story. Unfortunately I didn't have one, other than the truth and I was pretty sure she wasn't ready for that. So I nodded, and sighed and filled our glasses, then sat staring out over the river with an expression of vacant sorrow, all the while frantically constructing my story. She held on to my hand all the while, stroking my fingers, which was enough to make it hard to keep my mind on what I was trying to do.

I gave her hand a little squeeze and tried a weak smile, hoping that I wasn't hamming the whole thing up too dreadfully but really having too much fun to care. The story was evolving in my mind, a nice blend of the prurient and the alarming, which I hoped would both shock her and secretly turn her on. I drained my glass, refilled it and took another sip, checked that nobody else was within earshot, and began.

'I told you a little lie earlier,' I said, borrowing a leaf from the horrible Dr Goebbels, 'and I lied to the police as well. You see I know the man who did it. He used to be my boyfriend.'

'Oh my God!' she answered. 'I knew that. I was sure of it! Oh, Penny!'

That was another lie: she was nearly as bad as me.

'Yeah, my ex-boyfriend,' I went on. 'He was so jealous, you see, and he kept wanting me to do all these really kinky things ...'

'And you refused?' she interrupted.

'No,' I answered, 'I let him.'

'Oh, Penny!'

'I know, Beth, but I loved him. What could I do?'

'No, you shouldn't have. As a woman you have to take control of your own life!'

'I couldn't. I'm not strong, you see. I'm really weak.'

'Oh, but you are, inside. You are, all women are.'

I didn't want to get into an argument about feminist philosophy: I wanted to tell her my dirty story, so I sighed and shrugged, then went on.

'It wasn't so bad at first, just little naughty things like wanting to spank me ...'

'Spank you! Oh my God! Penny, that's not a little thing: that's awful! The bastard! How dare he! How could you bear it?'

'He used to hold me over his lap, with my arm twisted up behind my back. Then he'd pull up my skirt or take my trousers down, leaving my knickers showing and hold me like that for a bit so I could really feel the humiliation of it, held down with my panties on show and knowing they would be coming down too. That was the worst bit, having my panties pulled down and not being able to do anything to stop it. He'd always do it really slowly, too, letting what was happening to me sink in.'

'Bastard!'

'Once everything was showing he'd take them down properly, but only as far as my knees. That was because he liked to see them on me, especially the way they stretched taut when I kicked about during the spanking.'

'What a pervert! That's men all through, obsessed with panties! Do you know why? It's because they're scared of what's underneath!'

'Mark wasn't; he loved me to have my pussy showing . . .'

'Don't say that, Penny, it's an awful word, one that's been forced on women by the patriarchal society in order to sexualise us. Say privates.'

'OK, he'd have my panties down with my privates showing, not because it hurt much more on the bare skin, but just to humiliate me.'

'The bastard.'

'Then he'd spank me, hard, so it really stung!'

'Oh you poor thing, it must have really hurt!'

'Like crazy, but he didn't care. The more I kicked and struggled the more he liked it. I'd lose control with the pain and thrash like crazy, sticking my bum up so the cheeks opened and everything showed, and I mean everything. He loved that and would tell me what I was showing to make me feel worse. Sometimes he'd feel me between the legs to see how wet I was getting, because you do, you can't help it . . .'

'I wouldn't.'

'You would. It's just a physical reaction; it doesn't mean you like it, although he always said it did.'

'Typical man.'

'By the end I'd usually be crying. He always tried to make me cry, because he liked to see the tears running down my face while I sucked his cock afterwards.'

'He made you do that?'

'Nearly always, with me kneeling on the floor in front of him so he could see my red bum.'

'Typical male power fantasy, wanting a girl kneeling at his feet. Why did you let him do it to you?'

'I couldn't help it. Like I said, I was in love with him, and it did make me wet, and after a while I got to like it . . .'

'You're joking! No, you're not, are you, and I understand. There was an article about it in *Metropolitan* last month, no, the month before. If a victim is abused enough she will come to regard the abuse as normal, even to accept it. That's what must have happened to you. Oh, poor Penny!'

'It got worse too. At first he would do it occasionally, maybe once a week, and only at bedtime. Then he started to find excuses for punishing me, such as telling me I hadn't done the housework properly, or that there wasn't enough sugar in his coffee. He made it more humiliating, too, doing it in the living-room so that a passer-by might see me getting my spanking, and even on the beach once, bikini pants down and everything, with some other people no more than a hundred metres away!'

She was speechless, which was just as well, as it had been really hard to get the story right when she kept interrupting. I went on, now cruising neatly towards the crucial line.

'He took me into the dunes after that and made me suck him, knowing full well there was a chance we might be seen. Normally he'd make me swallow his stuff, but not this time. He came in my face and made me walk back to the car like that, with his mess in my hair and all over my nose and chin. I've never been so humiliated, but he loved it and started to invent ways of making it worse for me. That was when it started to get really bad.'

She was still holding my hand, in between taking nervous gulps of her Chablis. I'd certainly horrified her, although I wasn't sure if I was turning her on or not. I was turning myself on in any case, as my story was basically my favourite spanking fantasy tailored to the circumstances. All I could do was hope she didn't notice the way my nipples were straining against the fabric of my top, or that if she did she wouldn't put two and two together. I finished my glass, asked a passing waiter for another bottle and went on.

'He was really pleased with himself over the way he'd got me, and he wasn't content to keep it to himself. I didn't know he'd been boasting to his mates, not until a whole load of them came back from the pub with him one evening and started teasing me about how I liked a good spanking. I was so cross, and when Mark told me to get some beers from the fridge I answered him back. That was a big mistake. He did me in front of them, panties down, everything, across his lap with my bare bum wobbling about and all seven of them laughing at me and making dirty remarks. I really fought, kicking and screaming and scratching, but it just made them laugh all the more. He put a finger in me and showed them I was wet, holding it up so my juice glistened in the light.

'The spanking went on a bit more, just to subdue me before he pushed me on the ground, got out his cock and demanded a suck. I did it, Beth; I sucked his cock in front of his friends, and when he'd come in my face he said I'd turned them on and ought to show some respect by sucking them. I did that, too, Beth; I sucked seven men, one after the other, and to make a joke of it they all came in my face. I was covered in it by the end. It was in my eyes and my hair; my mouth was full of it and so was my nose. It was all down my front and on my neck, even in my ears.

'After that night things started to get weird. It was as if whatever happened he needed more. He started to make me wear humiliating clothes, school kit with a skirt so short my panties showed when I bent, a ridiculous little nylon nurse's outfit, even a Girl Guide's uniform! I remember that one, serving dinner to him and another couple in my little baggy green shorts. I knew he'd do me afterwards, and I was trembling so hard I dropped a plate. He spanked me then and there, hauling down my little shorts and the tight white panties he'd made me put on underneath to get me bare. The guy did it, too, sharing me and laughing at me as I kicked and wriggled in my pain. The girl tried to help me and her boyfriend threatened to spank her too if she didn't shut up. Then . . . then they made us do this little act for them, striptease together, then down on the rug in front of the fire, all the way, and I liked it, Beth; I liked it, being made to kiss and lick another girl . . . Do you think that's bad? Do you think I'm a pervert?'

'No, no,' she answered instantly, 'gay sex is OK; there's nothing wrong with it at all. It's a life choice a woman should be able to make without criticism from society. For the men to force you to do it, that's what's wrong.'

'Thank you, Beth,' I answered, squeezing her hand and forcing a weak smile while fighting down the urge not to grin like an idiot.

'Go on,' she said, and I'll swear there was a catch in her voice.

'From the uniforms he got into this business with animals, no real ones, thank God, although I wouldn't put it past him. He'd got the idea from a

36

picture in a dirty book, of some wicked-looking guy driving a little buggy pulled by naked girls. We bought the gear in a sex shop, which was embarrassing enough, but nothing compared to wearing it. I had to go nude, in a little leather harness, bridle and reins, with nothing covered at all. He'd run me around the living room on the reins and use a long riding-whip on my bum, then put me on all fours and have sex with me while I still had the harness on. That kept him busy for a couple of weeks, but then he got bored because he didn't think it was humiliating enough for me. That's what really turns him on, you see, sexually humiliating girls.'

'That's a sign of sexual inadequacy,' she cut in. 'I've read an article on it. Did he have trouble getting . . . you know, hard.'

'Never,' I told her, 'even in front of other people. You see at first, before the kinky stuff started, we were really passionate together. Anyway, the thing with the ponies lasted a bit, only he decided I was getting used to it, so he made me do it outdoors where we'd get seen. Not just the pony-stuff either, but sucking and fucking, even going into a pub in a thong bikini with my bum all red from spanking. Then there was the pig fantasy, with me in nothing but a little rubber snout and a curly tail, rolled in muck, beaten with a stick and mounted from behind. Even in the car I would go nude under a thin cotton dress, with my snout and tail on so lots of people saw, the first time anyway. The second time he brought me this little pink bikini and I thought he was being nice until I realised it was just so that he could show me off in public without actually being arrested. He took me into the woods, made me roll in dirt, whipped me, fucked me on my knees and left me there, miles from home! That was just too much; I left him.

'He wouldn't have it though, and started threatening me and telling me what he was going to do to me . . .'

'You've got to tell the police, Penny,' she said suddenly. 'He ought to be locked up!'

'I can't! If it all came out my family would find out, and at work! My life would be unbearable!'

'No, Penny . . .'

She stopped, because the waiter was approaching with the Chablis and our plates. As the conversation had been going exactly where I didn't want it to I was grateful for the interruption.

The pause was welcome anyway. I was tipsy and aroused and had been starting to let my fantasy run away with me. I knew what mattered, that she wasn't actually against girls having sex together, and with luck I had turned her on, even though I was sure she would be hating herself for it.

I meant to go on over dinner, but by bad luck an elderly couple took the table right next to ours, despite there being several others vacant. They could hear every word we said, so I could hardly expect Beth to express herself and stuck to small talk as we drank our wine and nibbled at prawn salads.

She did most of the talking, which was just as well, as my pretence couldn't have survived any searching questions. One thing came out very quickly, and made me realise where she had picked up all the girl-power tag lines. She was an avid reader of women's magazines, *Metropolitan* in particular, the editorial line of which she followed with almost religious devotion. She was Portuguese-Irish, as her name suggested, and had been brought up a strict Catholic, attending a convent school in Cork. She had rebelled, and filled the gap left by her rejection of the church with millennial philosophy, as preached in the glossy pages of her magazines.

She now felt herself to be the last word in liberated, free-thinking femininity, although really she had just replaced one set of restrictive mores with another. A dozen times during the conversation I could have argued back, but I held my peace, sure that I'd never get my wicked way unless I stuck to my role of worshipful little mouse. Inevitably she was obsessed with diet, although she was slim by any reasonable standards, and she picked at her food, but punished the wine until by the time the bill arrived she was giggly and bright-eyed.

I paid, assuring her that it was the least I could do after the way she had helped me, and we set off for her flat with the sun sinking behind the downs in a blaze of scarlet and egg-shell blue. There's always something wonderful about a sunset before a night of good dirty sex, and I couldn't help but smile, with my excitement rising at the prospect of playing with Beth; also my apprehension, at the prospect of making a pass at her. As we crossed the road I took her arm, which seemed safe enough, and she didn't try and pull away.

'Do you want to hear the rest of the story?' I offered.

She nodded, eager now that the drink had dulled her inhibitions, as she fumbled the key into her door-lock.

'So what happened with the fox thing?' she asked. 'You said you left Mark.'

'I did,' I answered. 'The fox thing was when he caught me, but I still don't really know if he did it to hurt me or to try and get me back. You see, he really thought I liked all the dirty things he did. Sometimes I did.'

'No you didn't,' she said. 'It's important to remember that.'

'Oh I don't know. I don't even know what to think any more.'

We walked up the stairs, which were steep, leaving my face at the same level as her bottom. She flared beautifully from her trim waist, and the cheeks looked so inviting under her dress, full and round and girlish, spankable, kissable and just so lovely that it took a real effort not to reach out and take a handful.

It wasn't the right move, not with her, so I held back, but I knew that now was the time, and as she steered me into her living room I was steeling myself to make my pass. She began to play the hostess, setting coffee up as I sat on the settee.

'I was walking,' I said, addressing her through the open door, 'just trying to get my head straight really. He had followed me, and I never knew he was there until he grabbed me. I saw it was him, and I suppose I could have struggled more, but I don't know, I just felt so weak. He dragged me into the bushes and stripped me. I thought he was just going to fuck me, and I don't suppose I even minded that much, but instead he held me down so that he could put that mask thing on me. When it was stuck on he rolled me over on to my front and put the tail in me, up my bottom. He hung me up by the hands and whipped me, on my bum and across my boobs. It hurt so much and I would have screamed like anything but I was gagged by the mask, so I couldn't. He laughed at me as he did it, describing how I looked dancing on tiptoe in my pain with my fox's brush bobbing about over my bare bum. Six strokes he gave me, four behind, two in front, but it hurt more than any of the spankings.

'Then he took me down and fucked me, on my knees in the grass. I could feel the tail bobbing on my back and my whip marks really throbbing. He started to frig me, with his hand under my tummy to get at my pussy . . . sorry, my privates. I came, Beth, I had an orgasm; I couldn't help myself . . . Oh God, Beth, it was all so utterly humiliating, hold me, cuddle me . . .'

She had come in, a cup of coffee in either hand, but she put them down and came to sit beside me. My arms went around her waist and I buried my head in the soft pillows of her chest, fighting to stop myself grabbing them. For a while she held me, stroking my hair as I plucked up my courage.

'Beth?' I asked, my voice barely more than a whisper. 'When you said it was all right for two girls, did you really mean it?'

She nodded, nothing more, and I took that as assent. My mouth met hers a moment later and her resistance lasted about a second and broke, her lips opening under mine and our tongues meeting. It was a lovely kiss, gentle and soft and long, with her body pressed tight to mine, but I was still holding back, sure that I would only get what I wanted if she felt in control.

When we finally broke apart she stood and took my hand, leading me into her bedroom without a word. She didn't turn the light on, but pulled the curtains shut, leaving the room in almost total darkness, with only the faint orange glow of a street light to see by where it came in over the top of the curtains. We began to kiss again, standing, holding each other, very tentatively beginning to explore. Her hand was on my neck, stroking the nape to make my skin tingle and send little thrills down my spine. I returned the favour and began to inch her dress up behind, keen to get her round little bottom bare.

I wanted my hands down her panties, between her cheeks and on her bumhole, but I had to hold back, letting her stay in charge. Contenting myself with pulling her dress to her waist so that her taut panties were showing behind, I let her explore me, working on my neck and back until I was in a lather of frustration. I didn't know if she was teasing, reluctant to get to grips with me or if she normally went for endless foreplay in the dark, but before long it was more than I could stand. Stroking and cajoling is fine, but I needed my nipples kissed, my pussy touched, and most of all I needed my bottom smacked. It was the story I'd been telling her, with the imaginary Mark punishing me and humiliating me in front of his friends, and I had to have it.

'Spank me, Beth,' I urged. 'Put me across your knee and pull down my panties and smack my bottom, please.'

'No, Penny, that's not right; that's what you've been made to want.'

'Please, Beth, just a little spanking, please.'

'No, Penny, that's not how to make love. I'll show you. Let me teach you.'

She was breathless, and genuinely turned on, but she wasn't going to go for it. I knew that if I pushed it might break the moment, so I gave in and let her have me the way she liked. It was nice, slow and gentle and feminine, but with none of the raw energy and control I prefer. The only order she gave me was to undress, which I did, standing in front of her so that she could watch, even though we could barely see. She waited until I was bare before starting herself, and that was the only touch of dominance I got, with a subtle submissive pleasure in removing my panties as she stood by me, fully dressed.

After that it was all cuddles and kisses, with lots of attention to my hair, neck and back. When I first lay on the bed, face down in the fading hope of a smacked bum, she began to stroke my hair and neck, then to kiss, brushing my skin with her lips. She moved down my back really slowly, making my muscles jump and setting my pussy on fire as she kissed the full length of my spine, ever closer to my bottom. I really thought she was going to do it, to keep on kissing until she reached my bumcheeks, then my crease, burying her face between them to lick my bumhole and the rear of my pussy, which would have given me a glorious orgasm, spanking or no spanking.

It never happened. She just stopped at the base of my spine and gently turned me over, then began the whole process again, starting on my forehead and working slowly down my body, over my face and neck. Her mouth lingered on my breasts, sucking my nipples until they were straining with blood before going down to my tummy and finally to my pubic hair. By then I had her head in my hands, my fingers tangled in her hair and my thighs wide open, spreading my pussy for her tongue. The little bitch ignored the offer, giving me a single kiss on my pussy mound and then starting on my legs. I almost lost control and pulled her head into my crotch, but I managed to resist and went through the whole agonising process of having my legs kissed from ankle to knee, then up the insides of my thighs and finally, at long last, she began to lick me.

I came almost immediately, despite her best efforts to tease, kissing my pussy lips and burrowing her tongue into my vagina. As she tongued me her nose was pressed right to my clit, and it was just too much. Taking a firm grip on her head, I squirmed myself into her face, rubbing my pussy on her nose as it all came together in climax.

She came up to kiss me, her face sticky with my juice. Our mouths met and we stayed like that for a while. I was in the rosy afterglow of my orgasm, but keen to return the favour. Amber likes to masturbate sitting on my face, with my tongue up her bottom. I offered Beth the same, but it shocked her and she refused, asking instead for the same treatment she had given me. I obliged, enjoying her plump little breasts and soft, smooth contours, but resisting the urge to kiss her bottom after what she'd said. In the end, with my face buried in her pussy, she came with a sigh and a sweet little whimpering noise, all the while stroking her breasts.

We cuddled afterwards, before showering, which was fun, as I at last managed to get a proper look at her body. She was slim, but by no means scrawny, and full enough at chest and hips for my taste, if less than voluptuous. I told her, and she replied that she needed to lose weight and described her figure as 'English pear', which wasn't really fair although I could see it as an excellent phrase for the future humiliation of somebody who would appreciate it.

She made a big fuss over my fading bruises from the fox-hunt, although they weren't really all that bad, and the ones from the twigs were worse than those Anderson had given me. Fortunately she didn't know enough to tell the difference between a riding-crop mark and a lash from a branch. She let me soap her breasts and back but was shy about her bottom, which I badly wanted to explore. Not wanting another lecture I held off, and contented myself with another session of kissing and stroking when we went to bed. It was nice, and it made a change, but afterwards I was wishing I'd had my bottom smacked, or really done anything a bit rude, so I couldn't resist mentioning it.

'It is nice to be spanked, you know, Beth,' I said, speaking quietly and snuggling up to her. 'It doesn't have to be hard, or nasty.'

44

'No, Penny, it's wrong. It's taking power over another human being.'

'But what if I want it?'

'You don't, really: that's just the way your mind has defended you against Mark's abuse. You've got a lot to learn, Penny, but I'll be here to help you.'

I bit my lip in frustration but made no resistance as she pulled my head on to the soft pillows of her chest.

Three

I've lost count of the number of women I've had sex
with, although I think it's somewhere in the twenties.
Beth was nowhere near as experienced, for all her
assumption of confidence, and I wasn't surprised to
learn that I was the second. She was pretty insecure
about it in the morning, which is always a giveaway,
much more so than somebody's behaviour in bed.
I've known girls to get into spanking and even peeing
games in the heat of the moment and then be sullen
and withdrawn in the morning, all because it was the
first time and they felt guilty.

With Beth it was more a question of justifying
herself, pointing out that she wasn't a lesbian but that
the empowered modern woman should be able to
make her own sexual choices, escaping the moral
boundaries set by the paternalistic society. For once I
agreed with her, although in my experience women
try and set moral boundaries on other people as much
as men. She went on to explain what she wanted in a
man, and although she didn't express it that way,
basically she was waiting for Mr Right, with her
concept of male perfection based on the editorial slant
of *Metropolitan* magazine. Unfortunately Mr Right
was as much a fantasy creation as the sadistic Mark.

He had to be a strong character, yet willing to
follow her line. He had to be attractive and passion-

ate, yet show her a puppy-like fidelity. He had to be well paid and in control of his own finances, yet willing to let her spend his money more or less as she pleased. Inevitably she had never met such a paragon, but it didn't seem to occur to her that this might be because no such man exists.

So she had drifted through a series of unsatisfactory boyfriends, none of whom came close to her impossibly high standards, and had sex with a girl because she didn't want to miss the pleasures of lesbian sex she had read so much about. She had felt guilty about it, and gone to bed with me because I so obviously needed comforting. I almost laughed at that, thinking of the care and effort she had put into making love to me, kissing and caressing with textbook thoroughness.

I had had the same thought while she was doing it to me, but had put it aside in the heat of the moment. Now it came back, and as she made coffee and toast for us I made a hasty survey of the magazines she had laid out on the living-room table. Sure enough, in the previous November's issue of *Metropolitan* there was an article on how to satisfy a woman by concentrating on the less obvious erogenous zones.

It didn't take much to bring the conversation round to the magazine, and after coffee and a gentle parting kiss I left with it under my arm. Other than the odd idle moment in waiting rooms, I never really read women's magazines, or magazines at all for that matter. Amber takes *Horse & Hound*, which I sometimes read in bed, so I expected a deliberate editorial slant, but *Metropolitan* amazed me. It was like reading a synopsis of Beth's character, although of course it was the other way around.

The tone was absolute, dictating opinions with a forthright and moral certainty that amazed me. Gay sex was OK, even actively encouraged, between men as well as women, although always within the confines of safety. Anything that smacked of exploitation, or of one person surrendering control to another was out, including spanking, bondage and fetishistic role play. Male submission to women was an exception, just about, although it was expressed as more vengeful than sexual. Rubber was all right, and leather as long as it wasn't used to express male dominance.

By the time I reached Paddington I was feeling slightly sick from my efforts to read on the train, and badly in need of something to reinforce my own sexual choices. The tone of *Metropolitan* was just so strong, so absolutely certain of the moral high-ground, and both aggressive towards and contemptuous of anybody who disagreed. I could understand how Beth was influenced, and sympathise with it, although I was determined not to go the same way. I knew I would get over it, but as I worked my way through the underground system I was feeling less secure about myself than I had for years.

I knew the answer, which was to have an afternoon of good, naughty sex that broke every one of the magazine's rules. My first thought was to suggest a pony-girl session to Amber, with me harnessed up and fully under her control, bit in my mouth, tail plugged up my bottom and all. However, one of the major annoyances about the magazine was the way it put men down, especially anyone unfortunate enough to be poor, short, past the first flush of youth or of less than statuesque beauty. Aside from her kinky behaviour, Amber was everything they thought a woman should be, strong, independent and success-ful, also young, attractive and middle-class.

What I needed was someone with all the vices that they most disapproved of, or qualities from my point of view. It would have to be a man, preferably getting on a bit, old-fashioned, lecherous, perverse in his sexual tastes, just the sort of man they felt should crawl quietly into a corner and wait for the grim reaper. He'd also have to be clean, friendly and at least reasonably intellectual, suiting my private limits to deliberate self-degradation.

Henry was the obvious choice, with his fatherly manner and outsize cock: in many ways the perfect spanker. He was good at pony-girl fantasy and most of the other things I like, too, but I knew it would upset Amber if I went to him without calling on her first. If I did that it was going to take ages to get to Hertfordshire, explain things to Amber, persuade her and find Henry. I wanted a quicker solution.

The dreadful Morris Rathwell was another choice, and although he always scared me a bit he could be guaranteed to drop his work long enough to subject me to some fairly vigorous abuse. He'd certainly spank me, and hard, then probably make me go down on his cock under his office desk. If he had the time he would try and bugger me, which I had never given in to, so far. There was also a chance of his wife Melody or her sister being there, which would be even better. Unfortunately it would upset Amber if I went to him, so I was forced to drop the idea.

That left Percy Ottershaw among my London friends: fat, dirty Percy with his obsession with tight white panties and caning girls. He lacked Henry's impressive genitals or Morris's ability to frighten me just enough to be sexy, but he had all the other qualities, in abundance. The editor of *Metropolitan* would have hated him. He was also a wine writer and a serious gourmet, so could be counted on for a decent lunch after taking the edge off my lust.

I turned back on my tracks and made for Warwick Road tube, praying Percy was in and not at a wine tasting or abroad. He was out, leaving me standing on the steps of his block of flats in a welter of frustration. I had really worked myself up, imagining how pleased he would be to have me visit him for sex, and the glorious mixture of shame and pleasure I would feel offering it. I even had white cotton panties on, which he loved, and it was just so annoying to think I was going to miss out.

It was lucky I lingered, because as I finally turned to leave there he was, his portly figure unmistakable as he plodded along the pavement. He was every inch the dirty old man: dark suit, blue bow tie, face red and puffing, great belly swaying beneath a fancy waistcoat. I smiled and waved, to which he responded with a beaming grin and a gesture of one podgy hand.

I knew him too well to need to dissemble, and had broached the subject of needing a punishment before we were even in his flat. He laughed aloud as I explained things to him, and then said I ought to be caned for wearing jeans, as women ought to be in skirts, preferably dresses. That was perfect, and I could just picture the editor of *Metropolitan*, speechless with outrage at his chauvinist attitude. There had been a letter in my issue complaining about those few remaining institutions that refuse to admit women in trousers, and the response had been pretty uncompromising. The suggestion that girls in trousers ought to have them pulled down for a half-dozen strokes of the cane on their bare bottoms would have caused apoplexy.

I wear what I please, and always have, but that wasn't the point. Percy nodded thoughtfully and reiterated his opinion that a caning would teach me to behave like a lady. I apologised meekly for being unsuitably dressed and accepted the justice of the coming punishment, hanging my head and folding

50

my hands in my lap, all remorse and misery, anything but assertive or in command. Caning hurts, and my tummy was already fluttering, while if my lower lip was stuck out and trembling then it wasn't all show.

'Good,' he went on, 'I'm glad you have chosen to show suitable contrition, but you realise I still have to do it?'

I nodded miserably.

'Bare, of course. Shame is an important part of the punishment.'

'Yes, sir.'

'Right, you had better pop your jeans and knickers down I think, Penny. You can bend across an armchair, as I have no wish to make your experience unnecessarily uncomfortable.'

'Yes, sir.'

My hands had already gone to the button of my jeans, fumbling it open with my fingers trembling. I had to swallow a lump in my throat as I pulled down my zip, and I turned my back to him looking over my shoulder as I began to pull down my trousers. He watched, his little piggy eyes fixed on my rear as my jeans slid down, displaying the seat of my panties beneath the hem of my top.

Holding my jeans around my thighs, I waddled awkwardly over to the armchair and climbed into it, kneeling so that my bottom stuck out towards him. I reached back, eased up my top, tweaked my panties up tight between my bumcheeks and I was ready, exposed and unprotected for my punishment.

'Knickers down, I said, Penny,' Percy remarked in a horribly reasonable voice. 'Do you think you'll feel a proper measure of shame without that little fanny showing behind?'

His words put a shiver the length of my spine as I shook my head. My hands went back, delving beneath the waistband of my panties, starting to pull, easing them off my bum, feeling the cotton pull from my crease and I was bare, showing it all to fat Percy.

'Very sweet,' he remarked. 'I do love the way a girl's fanny lips pout in that position. You're showing your anus, too. You do know that, don't you?'

I nodded miserably. My sense of humiliation was beginning to cut in, and the thought that he could see the tiny puckered hole between my cheeks really added to it.

'I trust that brownish colour is your natural pigmentation?' he said, ever so casually, and I found myself calling him a bastard under my breath.

He chuckled and stood up, leaving the room to return immediately with a long, yellow cane with a crooked handle. I braced myself instinctively, clenching my cheeks, only to let them apart again because I just had to be showing my bumhole when he hit me. The cane came up, high over my naked bum, then down with that horrible swishing sound and a line of agony sprang up across my cheeks. I squealed and kicked out, biting my lip in my pain. Percy gave his dirty little chuckle.

There's always a moment during a hard punishment on cold skin when I wonder what the hell I am doing offering my naked bottom to some maniac with a stick or whip. It doesn't happen with hand spankings, or when I'm thoroughly turned on first, but it did now, with no more than a few minutes between accepting the idea of being caned and ending up bent over with my bare bum stuck up for Percy's attention.

It was my sense of humiliation that stopped me getting up, the choking, pussy-wetting knowledge that I was kneeling for a dirty old man to put a cane across my bare bottom, kneeling with my pussy pouting out between my thighs and my bumhole on show. I got back into position, bum stuck out and knees a little bit apart, with my back pulled in to make the best of my shape.

Percy waited until I was ready and brought the cane down again, sending another jolt of pain through my body. The strokes were hard: no playful cuts, but given just as if I was being punished for real. They stung crazily, and with two stripes decorating my bottom I could feel them throbbing and the sting where the cane tip had caught my hip.

I find it impossible to hold still under a proper caning, and had jumped again, but got quickly back, posing my bottom for his attention and getting it immediately. The third stroke came low, only just above where my cheeks meet my thighs, and it stung even more than the others. I was gasping as I settled back into position, but the pleasure had begun to come in earnest, with my whole bottom feeling plump and warm and blatantly sexual.

The fourth stroke came down and I heard the pleasure in my own cry, ecstasy despite the fact that I was close to tears. I was sobbing faintly as I resumed my position, pain and humiliation blending in my head, only for Percy to suddenly reach out and tweak my top up, then my bra, spilling my naked boobs out to leave them hanging under my chest. I'm not big, but they felt huge, and utterly exposed, adding to my woes.

Percy stepped back, brought up the cane and whipped it down across my bottom, jamming me into the armchair and setting my breasts swinging. I hung my head as the shock died, groaning openly as I waited for the last stroke. It came a moment later, hard and accurate, and as the stinging pain shot through me the last of my reserve went and I burst into tears. Percy waited for just one moment, long enough for me to stop it, but that was the last thing I wanted.

'Stop snivelling, you little brat,' he said. 'Yes, you can get up, but you are to take off those absurd trousers, and keep your knickers down.'

I obeyed, climbing off the armchair to remove my jeans, socks and shoes. The tears were streaming down my face and I was sobbing badly, but it was more from relief than anything. I kept my top high, tucking it into my bra, and my panties down, so that everything was showing as I stood for his inspection with my hands on my head.

'Good girl,' he said as he came behind me to inspect his handiwork. 'I see you know your place. A properly humble attitude is very important in a woman: gentlemen so appreciate it.'

A hand closed on my bottom, squeezing the hot cheek, then another, pulling them apart. I bent, touching my toes and swallowing hard with my tears coming faster as he made a minute inspection of my anus. It occurred to me that he was going to bugger me and I knew I'd let him. Not that he'd do it standing up, as he'd never make it. Instead I'd have to sit in his lap with his prick up my bottom, doing all the work until he came up me.

'I trust that taught you a lesson?' he asked, stepping away. 'If not, we can always apply another six lines to that delectable little behind. Do you think it will be needed?'

'No, sir.'

'Very well. Now, I confess to having become a little aroused. You will take my penis in your mouth.'

'Yes, sir.'

He sat down, making himself comfortable in his armchair and spreading his heavy thighs to show off the bulge in his trousers. I got down on my knees, feeling the cool air on the wet patch between my thighs as they came apart. Percy laid his hands on his ample belly, leaving me to do the work. His fly buttoned, and as each one popped open my sense of being about to do something really dirty grew. I'd been caned, bare-bottomed, by a dirty old man, and now I was going to suck his cock, suck him until he came, in my mouth.

I freed his cock from his underpants, a slim shaft of pale meat, already near erection. He was past sixty, and fat, but with a girl in white panties to cane his cock reacted like a teenager's. It came hard in my hand. I leaned forward, opened my mouth and took it in, sucking like the meek little thing I was supposed to be, beaten into submission and sucking the penis of her tormentor.

As soon as I'd got the rhythm of sucking I sneaked a hand back between my thighs to masturbate. My pussy was soaking and it would have taken only a moment, but I was in no hurry. Instead I explored my bottom as I sucked him, feeling the lines of roughened skin where the cane had bitten into my flesh. They stung, a hot, sharp sensation, sexy now that I was fully aroused. Reaching back between my cheeks I touched my bumhole, feeling the tight ring and thinking of the moment my panties had come down to show it off in a vulgar, dirty display of my most intimate secrets.

Percy watched me touch myself, his eyes flicking between my beaten bottom and my lips where they were pursed around his erection. I wanted to come with him still in my mouth, or perhaps immediately after him, with his come in my throat or splashed across my face. He was likely to take a long time, though, and I was beginning to get urgent. I forced myself to complete my exploration of my bum, stroking and fondling myself while I thought about my beating, the pain, the humiliation and the way I had cried.

I began to imagine how the magazine editor would have felt watching me being punished: her outrage as I obeyed Percy's instructions, adopting a pose of blatant submission, exposing my bottom for beating, blubbering my way through the caning, bending to have my anus inspected and finally sucking his cock. That was too much and my hand went to my pussy, two fingers opening my lips, another beginning to rub at my clit.

Percy took me by the hair and started to fuck my mouth. I rubbed harder, hoping to get the moment right, thinking of the editor and Beth staring at me, horrified at my grovelling obedience to a dirty old man, staring at my whacked bottom and Percy's stiff little cock, my bulging cheeks and eager lips, my wrinkled bumhole and gaping, sodden pussy, my fingers working frantically in wet flesh . . .

I came, a long, glorious climax better by far than either of those I'd had with Beth. Even as my muscles clenched and my back pulled in I was thanking myself for being such a slut, for enjoying my beating, for enjoying my own humiliation, for being dirty, and rude and so, so free. I was still coming when Percy's cock jerked in my mouth, slipped out, bumped my lips. He ejaculated, full in my face. My mouth came open and I took him back in, sucking the come up as my ecstasy died slowly down, rose to a second, lesser peak and then died again.

My face was a mess, with sperm in one eye and hanging from my nose as well as in my mouth and on my lips and chin. I ran for the bathroom, and couldn't help but laugh when I saw myself in the mirror, sideways on with my cane marks showing and one eye glued shut by a big blob of sperm, top up, panties down, a classic image of a used girl and a thoroughly happy one.

I felt a lot better for my caning, with my self-confidence restored and a familiar warm glow behind. After a lengthy session rubbing cream into my cheeks in Percy's bathroom I emerged to find him reading *Metropolitan*. His normally ruddy face was going purple, so I took it away from him and suggested lunch, to which he agreed with enthusiasm.

He listened to the full story as we ate, tiny steaks and fluffy potatoes washed down with something called Irancy. The fox-hunting amused him, although he admitted it all sounded a bit active for his taste. The episode with the police had him fuming again and going on about the abuse of personal freedom, so I quickly switched to what I'd done afterwards, which delighted him. My seduction of Beth had him grinning like the wicked old satyr he was, but at the end he said that two dozen strokes would have been a more appropriate punishment for me if he'd know the whole story in advance.

When I left I was in a thoroughly good mood, albeit slightly uncomfortable when I sat down on the tube. Until then I hadn't been sure if I'd see Beth again. Now I knew I would, telling myself it was for her own good, but knowing underneath that it came from a determination to impose my own will over that of the wretched magazine. The fact that I'd lied to her and she thought I was a filing clerk from Reading didn't seem to matter, I just needed her joyfully dishing out a spanking or with her own bum bright red and a big smile on her face.

It was one thing to think about introducing Beth to the delights of kinky sex, quite another to do it.

Anderson and Vicky were at Amber's when I got back, and although all three of them were delighted with my story, only Anderson agreed that I ought to see her again. Vicky couldn't understand why I'd bother when I had plenty of dirty-minded girlfriends to play with. Amber agreed, and might have wanted to point out that I was her girlfriend, but could hardly justify the stand when she had spent the morning driving Vicky as a pony-girl.

I assured Amber of the depth of my faith with a hug and a kiss, by which time Anderson had started on a deliberately melodramatic spiel about how it was our duty to save the unfortunate Beth from the twin monsters of prudery and repression. This involved standing on a chair and waving his arms about, which made Amber and Vicky laugh, more or less winning the argument.

They took turns to read my magazine while he drank tea. It annoyed Vicky much as it had annoyed me, for denying her enjoyment of bondage and punishment while preaching self-expression. Amber was less fussed, pointing out that we were in no way obliged to pay any attention to it. Anderson reacted much as Percy had done, principally complaining about the way real men were denigrated while the readers were invited to strive towards a phantasm of male perfection. I pointed out that if only he would drop his perverse behaviour and do as Vicky told him he himself would be pretty close to the ideal, which drew a contemptuous snort and a threat to spank me on the spot. I'd already shown them the state my bottom was in, and pointed out that for the time being I was off limits. He shrugged and went back to the magazine, turning to the article about rubber as street wear.

'The knack,' he remarked after a while, 'would seem to be to take one of the fetishes they consider acceptable and follow it to the logical conclusion.'

'How so?' I demanded.

'Well, rubber for instance,' he went on. 'These dresses are pretty, but nothing like as rude as some of the rubberwear around. You could try a rubber skirt, see what she thinks; try something a bit naughtier, perhaps at a nightclub with a mildly risqué dress code. Have you seen Vicky's one with the lacing at the back from neck to hem?'

'Yes, but it might take ages, and it would be a pretty expensive process.'

'Leather then. Have you got any clothing-grade hides in stock, Amber?'

'A couple,' she admitted, 'a black one and a zebra print I got in a bundle by mistake.'

'Excellent!' he answered. 'Use the zebra print to make up a cavegirl outfit, indecently short with plenty of tummy and back on show. Naughty, but nothing to raise an eyebrow in a modern club.'

'How's that going to get me spanked?' I asked.

'Easy,' he said. 'You enjoy the club, get drunk, go back to her flat, start playing silly games like being pulled by your hair, that becomes play wrestling, you slap her bottom, and before you know it she'll slap yours back. Giggle and stick it out and you'll have your spanking in no time.'

'You're thinking of Vicky,' I pointed out. 'Beth wouldn't go for it.'

'Would she go as far as the play wrestling?'

'Maybe.'

'Then surely she'd spank you, if only to get back at you if you did her? I mean your bottom, in a leather mini-dress, how could anyone resist smacking it?'

'You couldn't, that's for sure.' Vicky laughed.

'Beth could. I begged her for it, and we were drunk, and we'd been kissing. She told me I didn't really want it.'

'Didn't want it? How could she know what you want or don't want?'

'She thinks the evil Mark has brainwashed me into enjoying abuse,' I explained. 'According to *Metropolitan*, all sadomasochistic games are abuse and as such unacceptable. Men dressing up as maids or taking the odd smack being the exception. You can't genuinely want a spanking: you just think you do.'

'Eh? I've wanted to be spanked ever since I learned how to come!'

'I know, I know, me too. In fact the first time I ever came was after a spanking, from my aunt as it happens. Beth would say that enjoying it was my mind's way of dealing with the trauma.'

'What a load of crap! That's like saying you only enjoy driving a fast car to cope with having had to pay for the thing. It's the other way around: you pay for it because the pleasure is worth the cost, just like the pleasure of a spanking is worth the pain, but you can't get that pleasure without the pain! Explain that to her.'

'You could borrow a nice car, or even pinch it. Besides, the threat of a spanking is enough to come over sometimes, or just having my panties pulled down in preparation, so the pain isn't strictly necessary.'

'Don't be awkward, Penny, that only works once the fantasy is established in your head, and you know it. You have to have at least one spanking to be afraid of what you're being prepared for.'

'Sit on her and spank her pink,' Anderson cut in. 'Once her endorphins kick in she'll be putty in your hands, or wobbly red bottom-flesh anyway.'

'That's not consensual, Anderson, and anyway, she's bigger than me, if not by much.'

'Get Vicky to do it, or Amber, or Ginny. Why not all three of them?'

'Don't be silly; the poor girl would be terrified. The only reason that I managed to get her to take me to bed was because I'm so completely unthreatening. She called me her little kitten at one point.'

'Next time she does that, scratch her, start playing kitten games. With luck she'll get off on it and it can't be too hard to get from one sort of erotic pain to another.'

This was Amber's suggestion, and better than anything Vicky had to offer, let alone Anderson. I wasn't sure about it, though, and in ways I'd spoiled my own bid by going into such lurid detail about the way Mark had used me. Like Vicky, I was so used to spanking as a turn-on that it was hard to imagine someone being scared of it. If Beth hadn't been before she probably was now. The dress was a nice idea though, even if I didn't think Anderson's plan would work. At the worst I'd end up with a new naughty dress, and if I combined it with the kitten idea it had to be worth a try.

'Do you feel like doing some leather work, then?' I asked Amber.

She nodded, drained the remains of her tea and stood up. In nearly five years I'd gained a pretty good understanding of how she thinks. Being in her dress while I played with Beth would go a long way to making up for any bad feelings she might have about me doing it. It was like being Amber's pony-girl but under someone else's control. They might be driving me, training me, even having full sex with me, but I was still in her harness; I was still her pony-girl. Of course, there was another thing. She knew full well that if I did successfully corrupt Beth, she would be the first to benefit, and she does like a new filly to train.

We crossed the yard to the old forge that is now her workroom, a high, red-brick building that I still can't enter without a shiver of pleasure. It was the first place she caned me, and more besides, while the walls are hung with things designed for the restraint and punishment of girls, and men for that matter, including a boss of chains at the centre of the ceiling. When she's been working the smell of leather is almost overpowering, and if it didn't do much for me at first, over the years it has come to be associated with sex.

Now was no exception, with the rich tang heavy in the air. Vicky took a deep breath as she came in and let it out with a long sigh. Anderson chuckled, much in the way Percy always did when faced with a well-fleshed female bottom in tight white panties. Only Amber seemed indifferent, but being a saddler the scent of leather is everyday to her.

She pulled out the zebra-print hide, a smallish pig skin with a particularly strong scent to it, perhaps from the white dye. Holding it up to me I could see that even on me any dress made from it would be barely decent. She tutted, and suggested I strip, so casually, as if it was nothing for me to go nude in front of the three of them. It wasn't the first time, and all of them had seen me do things that would have had Beth open-mouthed in shock, but I still feel vulnerable naked, and I hope I always do, because it's a major spur to my arousal.

I did as I was told, and not just down to my panties but stark naked, without even shoes or socks. Anderson licked his lips and gave an appreciative nod as he sat down on a workbench. Vicky settled on to his lap, deliberately wiggling her bottom, and as I hung my panties on a convenient nail Amber turned back to me, acknowledging my obedience with a pleased nod.

She looked up my measurements in her work-book, only to decide to take them again. In five years I'd put on an inch on my hips, nothing on my bust and waist, which I couldn't help feel pleased with even though personally I like girls to be a little plump, or at least muscular. I suppose that's just the submissive in me, because helplessness acquires a whole new meaning after having your face sat on by a fifteen-stone girl, which has happened to me.

Things quickly began to get to me: the gentle touches of Amber's fingers and tape measure, the all-pervading smell of leather, the sight of the harness and whips. Being naked while the three of them were dressed was strong too, as always giving a sensation of vulnerability and showing off. I smiled at Vicky, who was bright-eyed and beginning to look expect-ant, with her arm around Anderson's neck and his hands folded over her tummy.

Suddenly, with two swift motions, he had pulled up her jumper and bra, spilling her breasts out. It took her by surprise and she gave a little gasp, but made no move to cover herself, leaving them showing, bare and round. He took them in his hands, moulding gently and rubbing his thumbs over her nipples to make her eyes close in bliss. She was in a moderately short skirt, which was already rucked up to show most of her long, elegant legs, and as he teased her breasts she let her thighs slip apart, exposing the silky black crotch of her panties.

Amber smiled and shook her head, moving to the bench where she had spread the hide. Vicky stood, crossing her hands over her front to take the edges of her jumper and pulling it off, and her bra with it. Skirt, shoes and stockings followed, then her sus-pender-belt and lastly her panties, removed in a casual strip to leave her as naked as I was. Anderson smacked her bottom, a playful pat to send her over to me.

'Vicky wants to be strung up on the boss,' he said.

Amber was drawing lines on to the back of the leather and didn't stop, nor did Anderson get up. That left it to me, but I was in no mood to dominate Vicky, not that I don't like being in control now and then, but she's six foot and pure muscle. It just doesn't feel right, except when she's helpless.

Knowing more or less what I wanted, I went to the racks and selected a double pair of wrist cuffs. After lowering the chains to my own head height, I cleated them off and strapped her offered wrists into the cuffs, then my own, closing them with my teeth. Anderson had watched all this and finally condescended to help, taking the pulley rope and raising the chains. Being in bondage is always strong, and I began to feel it as my arms went up over my head, drawn by more force than I could resist. My body went against Vicky's too, not quite face to face, but so that our boobs were pressed together and my pussy was against her tummy.

I squeaked when I found myself on tiptoe, but Anderson ignored my protest, giving the rope a final pull to leave my feet clear of the ground. The pain in my wrists was immediate, along with the awful frustration of having my toes barely an inch clear of the ground but not being able to take my weight on them. Vicky was still standing, and I wrapped my legs around her hips because it was the only thing I could do to relieve the strain. That spread my pussy out on to her belly and left my bottom open, adding blatant sexual exposure to my difficulties.

Anderson laughed and tied off the cleat, leaving me strung helpless from the boss. Vicky had her eyes shut and was moving her body gently against mine, obviously enjoying being nude and powerless enormously. So was I, although my position was just that little bit too awkward and painful to really get off on. Still, my bottom was well spread, and I could feel the air on my vagina and bumhole, making a superb contrast to the heat where my flesh was pressed to Vicky's.

Amber glanced around, smiling to see the predicament I had been put in, then going back to work. Anderson was considering pony-girl harness, and I wondered if he was going to put us in some sort of strap system until he reached out for a head-dress and pulled an ostrich feather free of its mounting.

I felt my guts and bumcheeks tighten instinctively. He was going to tickle me, and I knew where, right between my spread cheeks. I'd lose control, I was sure of it, but if I closed my legs to protect my pussy I'd be swinging from the ceiling by my wrists. My breath began to come in little pants, just from knowing how it would feel. I was panicking, and he hadn't even touched me.

He laughed and the feather touched my skin, at my side, making me shiver and tighten my legs around Vicky's waist. It tickled but I could take it, only I knew that he wasn't going to spare my more sensitive areas. The feather moved up, tickling our breasts where they were squashed together. Vicky began to giggle and squirm, her flesh writhing against my pussy. I could feel her tummy muscles moving on my clit, a really weird sensation, and one that might even have eventually given me an orgasm if I hadn't been in such a tricky position.

I clung tight as he tickled her, drawing the feather gently across her skin, her middle, her bottom and her thighs. She squirmed and wiggled and jumped on her feet, gasping and swearing at him but never once calling out her stop word. With every little wriggle her tummy rubbed my pussy, and I was getting more and more out of control, until I was squirming myself on to her. The anticipation of my own tickling was rising too, and turning to fear from the way she reacted. When he finally stopped we were both wet with sweat and I could feel my pussy juice on her belly. I could hear it too, little wet sucking sounds as we moved together and parted in our distress.

My whole body was shivering as he began to tickle me, first my boobs and side once more, then my neck and back. Unlike Beth he had no compunction about my bottom-hole, tickling my spread cheeks in circles that moved ever closer to my anus. My ring began to pulse even before he touched it, and I was giggling pathetically, clutching Vicky with my legs and writhing my bum in a futile effort to escape.

As the first tiny featherlet touched my anus it just happened: I wet myself. I felt the pee coming and screamed for him to stop, calling him a bastard and a sadist. He just laughed, and ran the wretched thing along my squirming bumhole. It was too late anyway: my pussy just exploded, the piddle gushing out on to Vicky's tummy and spraying from the sides. I cried out in an agony of utter, helpless frustration, shame too, made worse by Vicky's gasp of shock as my hot piddle sprayed against her flesh and ran down her body.

It was everywhere, mostly down her legs, but splashed right up on our boobs and it was still coming. I could feel it dripping from my bumcheeks and around the hole, and only then did Anderson stop tickling, not to save me further distress, but to stop the ostrich feather getting spoiled. My reserve was broken, and I let it all run out, down Vicky's tummy and legs and on to the floor. I was sobbing and squeezing my thighs around her, high on a dirty ecstasy, soaked in pee and desperate to come while still in pain and distress.

It was Amber who took mercy on me, and Vicky, too. She had been watching, and as the last trickle of pee splashed to the ground from my bumcheeks she gave a knowing sigh and pulled up her top. Stripping in front of a man, even if it's only Anderson, means a lot to her, but she took off her bra as well as her jumper, which wasn't really necessary to keep the pee off her clothes.

She masturbated me with a clinical thoroughness, sliding her hand down between Vicky's tummy and my pussy, finding my clit and starting to rub with practised expertise. Her other hand came up between my dripping cheeks and fingers and slid up my pussy, her thumb pressing to my bumhole. I relaxed my anus and the top joint of her thumb went in even as my orgasm hit me, rising and bursting to make me scream with ecstasy.

Once I had finished she undid my wrist cuffs and helped me off Vicky. I sat down in my puddle with a squelching noise, too far gone to care that I was stark naked and sitting in a pool of my own pee. As Amber began to masturbate Vicky the thought came to me that the experience had been far stronger and far dirtier than I had expected. With that came a further, wicked, thought.

Four

When a girl is being spanked, let alone caned or whipped, you can feel her pain and her arousal. Leastwise anybody with the slightest sense of empathy can, especially if they've been through the same experience, which is why I prefer to be punished by those who know how it feels. Restraint is different, with more of the experience in the head, although what the victim is thinking is crucial for any physical erotic punishment, from a meaningful pat on the cheek to a full-blown flogging.

A smack is a smack, and while I've known spankers to pat my bottom to test my reaction, you can hardly pretend it didn't happen. The target is too obvious, for one thing. A smack also creates a clear imbalance of power between the people involved, and a big one, as to accept someone's right to smack you is effectively to surrender your right of control over your own body. That was the root of Beth's objection to spanking, that it was wrong for a woman to submit her will to a man, and by extension for her to punish another woman.

The same would doubtless be true if I asked her to tie me up, and while her slow kissing technique would have been far better with my wrists tied to the bed post, I couldn't see her accepting the suggestion. What I could do was make it seem accidental, and surely she would discover the extra pleasure to be had from having me helpless while she brought me slowly to orgasm. Setting it up was going to be tricky, but an entertaining challenge.

I checked as many back issues of *Metropolitan* as I could find in case there was some long-winded article on why completely free physical movement was morally vital during sex. There wasn't, but there was plenty of other stuff, and it struck me that the editor was basically making her best effort to be the arbiter of what was and what was not acceptable. It was illogical by any rational standards, hypocritical even. Gay men could do as they pleased, although it was far too coy to actually mention what it is gay men like to do, beyond a little cock-sucking. Women, by contrast, could never take a submissive role, and preferably never a passive one, even in lesbian relationships, although I was glad to see that the idea of girls having sex together was actively encouraged. For two girls to have sex in front of a man was out though, as it was supposedly surrendering their bodies for his voyeuristic pleasure, and anything that smacked of male voyeurism was out.

That had me scratching my head in puzzlement, but one thing made me laugh out loud. There were occasional articles on wine, food and so forth, usually with a dietary slant. One of these was by Natasha Linnet, discussing the calorific value of different wines. Natasha was a colleague of Percy Ottershaw, and occasionally a playmate, with tastes not so very different from my own. Her favourite thing was to be spanked, preferably bare-bottomed and across the knee just like me, but ideally by somebody who thought they were giving her a genuine punishment. I'd personally seen her upended, panties off, while Percy whacked her bum with a shoe, and to think of

69

the sight and compare it with the picture of her in the magazine, cool and poised with a glass of white wine in one hand, was just superb.

Both naughty clothing and body jewellery were acceptable, to a point. The argument was that a woman had the right to display her body in any way she pleased without interference. I had to agree, in principle, although I considered the idea dangerously naïve, rather like demanding the right to eat a raw steak in a lion enclosure. That made my leather dress acceptable, in any case, although undoubtedly daring. It was basically a halter top and miniskirt joined by carefully placed strips that left my back and most of my tummy showing. The edges were deliberately ragged, including the skirt hem, which was so short that even bending forward a few degrees left my panties on show. Anybody coming upstairs behind me was going to get a fine eyeful. It was shaped around my breasts, too, with carefully designed little bumps to make it look as if I had permanently erect nipples.

I spent the week working out the details of my plan, then rang Beth, who was delighted with the idea of going out together. She accepted my reluctance to go anywhere in Reading because of the supposed risk of running into Mark, and happily agreed to London as the better place to be. I had chosen the club carefully, seeking advice from among more extrovert friends. This was Geezer's, which sounded pretty awful but had stalls selling body jewellery and so forth, including little bondage bracelets that could be linked to make delicate, playful handcuffs. With those, and a little flattery for Beth's skill in bed, I felt I had a fair chance.

Unfortunately things started to go wrong when we were still on the train. Beth was full of enthusiasm, for me, for going clubbing together, for life in general, and I began to feel bad about deceiving her. It had seemed so easy discussing it with the others, not greatly different from the other games we played, but faced with Beth in the flesh my conscience had begun to get the better of me. By the time we got to Paddington I had decided that at the least she deserved to know who I really was. It wasn't going to be possible to maintain the deception for ever anyway, as what had been intended to be a brief naughty adventure had become something more.

Not that it was easy, with Beth chattering happily away, hinting of the pleasures we might share in bed and speculating on whether this was the night Mr Right might come along almost in the same breath. It was more than I could resist to offer to join in for a threesome if he did, which nearly earned me one of her lectures. I managed to laugh the comment off and suggested we have a drink to change the subject.

I had a long coat on over my dress, and as we had met at Reading Station she didn't get to see it until we got to the club. She was both pleased and a little shocked, as if determined to approve but not really sure about it. Personally it left me feeling exposed and vulnerable, at least until we got through the inner doors and I found it was only a little more daring than what the other girls were wearing.

Geezer's was hot, smoky and deafening, not really my sort of place at all, but Beth seemed to like it, so we drank and danced and had shouted conversations with the various men who approached us. By the time we managed to get to the jewellery stall we were both fairly tipsy, and with Beth giggling over the body jewellery it was easy to buy the bondage bracelets. I put them on, feeling pretty pleased with myself and well in the mood to be fixed to her bedstead and teased slowly to orgasm.

I put my arm around her as we went back to the bar and she made no resistance, but when I took a handful of her bottom and gave it a gentle squeeze she patted my hand away, smiling but evidently not up for a cuddle in public. She was ready to play, though, I was sure of it, and pretty sure that if I played my cards well I'd end up cuffed to her bed. Telling her the truth had been postponed, at least until the morning.

We went into what was called a chill-out room, where the music was less unbearably loud, and settled down to chat and drink. Our arms were around each other's shoulders and I was feeling ever more ready for her when a girl came into the room, handing out flyers. She was black, really dark, beautiful too, with a bold, impudent face and muscular curves, just the sort of woman I like to be dominated by. About a second later I realised I had been: it was Melody Rathwell.

There was no way out. I was sitting in full view, wearing a deliberately provocative dress and bondage bracelets, with my arm around a pretty girlfriend. Melody could not fail to see us, and when she did she was certain to want to chat us up. Being Melody, she would probably offer to take us into the girls' loos and have us bend over the bowl for a double spanking. I could just imagine Beth's response.

Worse still, if Melody was handing out flyers they could only be for Morris's club, and her sister Harmony, and even Morris himself, were likely to be around. I tried to make myself look small, then, on sudden impulse, grabbed Beth and kissed her hard on the mouth, hoping that Melody would not recognise the back of my head. It was a stupid decision, because she was bound to look at two girls snogging and think us ideal material for their club. Sure enough,

Beth met my kiss, responding nervously, only for a hand to close on my shoulder.

'Penny?' Melody's silky voice sounded, right in my ear. 'Put her down a minute. Hi, you're cute. I'm Melody.'

'Beth,' Beth answered.

'You've got to come on afterwards,' Melody went on, smiling and full of enthusiasm. 'There'll be about twelve of us, at my place. You two can come in the Rolls. Amber around?'

'No,' I admitted.

Her mouth curved into a smile that would have put a crocodile to shame.

'Catch you later then,' she finished and left with a playful smack to my bare thigh and a flash of her teeth.

She didn't leave a flyer, which was just as well, as I'd caught of glimpse of them and the picture showed a girl on a lead between the feet of another girl, Melody herself. As she went on she bent to hand a flyer to a couple and her tight shorts pulled right up her crease, giving the most gorgeous display of ripe, muscular bottom. I remembered the same view, only naked, the last time she had sat on my face. A shiver went right through me.

'She's nice,' Beth chirped up cheerfully. 'How do you know her? What's this about a Rolls? Who's Amber?'

'Hang on, give me a chance.' I laughed, frantically trying to decide what to do. 'I've known Melody ages. She's married to this property developer, Morris Rathwell. He runs a club as a hobby and he's got a Rolls, a gold one, he's really . . .'

I'd been going to say vulgar, then go on to enlarge on the disadvantages of Morris Rathwell, other than what he liked to do to pretty young girls, that is.

73

Unfortunately Beth interrupted me with a delighted squeak at the prospect of riding in a gold Rolls-Royce.

'. . . rich,' I finished. 'Amber's a friend, a very close friend actually. Look, Beth, I haven't been as truthful with you as I should have.'

I was going to tell her, I really was, all the details and then beg for her forgiveness and explain it was only because I fancied her so much. She would probably have run out, maybe even slapped my face, which would have been ironic, but she never gave me the chance.

'She's been your lover, hasn't she?' Beth said, her voice full of understanding. 'It's all right, Penny, I know it can be hard to accept your feelings for other women, but you must rely on your inner strength. When did it happen, before Mark?'

I shook my head, still meaning to tell her the truth but with a big lump in my throat.

'While you were with Mark!' Beth gasped. 'Did he know? Did he . . .'

I knew what she was going to ask – had Mark forced us to have sex together. It was actually quite a nice image, although I've yet to meet the man who can force Amber to do anything, but it would have been just one more complication, so I shook my head again.

'Behind his back!' she went on. 'Why did you stop? Did he find out?'

It was pointless telling Beth anything: she just made up her own version according to her imagination. I'd given up on trying to tell her the truth, as I wasn't even sure she'd believe it if I did. The sort of relationship I had with Amber was just too far outside her experience for her to accept, particularly the way I chose to be kept under discipline. Melody was worse, what with threesomes with her sister and the appalling Morris Rathwell into the bargain. That brought my mind back to the more immediate problem: how to dissuade Beth from her Rolls-Royce ride and escape the club without Melody catching us.

'Let's not talk about horrid old Mark,' I chirped up. 'I want you to kiss me all over like you did before, on my neck and down my spine, on my tummy and on my boobs . . .'

'Penny!' she interrupted.

She'd gone red and several people were looking at us, but that was fine: anything for a hasty exit.

'Let's go,' I urged, 'or I'm going to want you to take me in the loos.'

'Penny! You're drunk. Anyway, what about the party?'

'Never mind the party: I want you.'

'Please? At least let's ride in the Rolls; we can get out near a tube station.'

I should have told her that once in Rathwell's Rolls it wasn't so easy to get out, at least not before you'd sucked his cock. That might have put her off, but the point became redundant as Rathwell himself shouldered his way into the room.

'Hey, Penny,' he greeted me. 'Mel told me you were here. You must be Beth? Hi, Morris. Say, this place is a dump, isn't it? You're coming to the party, yes?'

That was it. He put an arm around each of our shoulders as we stood and began to steer us towards the door, indifferent to my explanations of how we really needed to get back. Beth was no help, giggling and simpering for all her supposedly feminist views, and once we were in the main body of the club it was hopeless anyway because nobody could hear what I was saying.

I know I give up too easily in social situations, but it was truly hopeless. Beth wanted her Rolls-Royce ride and if I complained too much I was going to look like a complete spoil-sport. I half expected Rathwell to grope Beth, which would doubtless have saved the day, but for once he showed restraint.

The Rolls was outside, a huge gold thing parked on a double yellow line. Harmony was in the driving seat and waved cheerfully as we approached, blowing me a kiss and then sticking her tongue out in an unmistakably lewd gesture. Beth either failed to understand or ignored the implication of a tongue tip pushed slowly out between pursed lips and Rathwell hustled us into the back, taking a good squeeze of my bottom as he did so, but not Beth's. His hand had gone right under my dress, tugging my panties into my crease, and I was forced to adjust them as I sat down.

'Keep them on, Penny, there's no rush,' Melody's voice sounded from beside me as she swung herself in, a comment which Beth fortunately missed.

'It's great of you to give us a lift,' I tried. 'Paddington would be best, but any tube will do.'

'I thought we were going to the party?' Beth pouted.

'We are, little lady, we are,' Rathwell answered. 'Hey, Penny, where's the spirit, girl? You're usually well up for it.'

'It's not that,' I answered him. 'Beth lives in Streatley; we'll miss our train.'

'Hey, this is Morris you're talking to,' he answered. 'Would I leave you on the streets? Would I? No, party tonight, stay over, and tomorrow who knows? Maybe a chauffeur-driven ride back to the sticks. What do you say, Beth?'

'Look, Morris, I'm really not sure it's her type of party.'

'Hey, Penny, any girlfriend of yours has got to like my parties. Am I right or am I right?'

'Come on, Penny, let's go; I'm in the mood for a party.'

Whether she was in the mood for one of Rathwell's parties was another matter. Being expected to do striptease and suck cock was the least of it. I could do nothing, and when Beth found that Rathwell and the girls spent half their time in New York that was the end. For some reason the US fascinated her, New York in particular, and within minutes they were chatting about shopping while I looked out the window and contemplated the future.

It had begun to rain, and Camden Town looked wet and black, with the people huddled down as the pubs spilled out. As Beth chattered happily on my sympathy began to decrease. After all, she was a grown woman and I'd done my best to shield her. I knew I'd still try, but if she got shocked then I had done my best.

We weren't going in the direction I'd expected and I realised Rathwell must have moved. Sure enough, we ended up somewhere to the north of Hampstead, at a large house with a Greek portico and high, black security gates. Beth went into raptures over this, much to Rathwell's delight, and he offered to show us around, which finally gave me a chance to speak to the girls.

'I'll join you later,' I offered as his arm closed over her shoulder. 'Mel, can I have a word?'

'Sure, as long as it's in the loo. You can watch me piss.'

Beth was in earshot, but not paying attention, staring in wonder at the incredibly vulgar chandelier. I took Mel's arm before she could suggest anything worse and steered her towards the stairs, only to be pulled towards one of the doors leading from the hall.

'You're eager, not getting what you need from little Beth?' she asked as she pushed the door shut.

'No, I mean yes. Look, Mel, she's innocent; she can't handle what you're into . . .'

'Sure, and that's why you were snogging her in Geezer's, with twenty guys watching you and wishing they could get their cocks in there.'

'No, seriously, she's never even been spanked.'

'Leave her to Morris; she's already eating out of his hand.'

'Morris!'

'Calm down, girl. She's getting the tour. No one else is coming till midnight. Relax.'

'Please, Melody, at least tell him to go easy, not to grope her or anything.'

'Jealous, eh? Wanted to smack that little round butt first? I know your game, Penny, you just want first go. Don't worry, you can give us a floor show, then we'll do you together, side by side with your lily-white bums stuck high in the air.'

'She couldn't take it, really, Mel. Look, OK, I have been trying to get her into spanking, but she thinks it's abuse, always, like when a drunk beats up his wife or something.'

'Easy, let her do you first.'

'She won't go for it, even when I beg her. Look, speak to Harmony, please?'

She had been undressing as we spoke, peeling off top, bra, shorts, and a tiny thong without the slightest self-consciousness. Nude, she was even more impressive than dressed, a real Amazon, all firm, dark flesh, but feminine beyond the slightest doubt. She shrugged, took two quick steps to the door and called for her sister. Harmony appeared, fortunately without Beth, and they spoke quickly, much of it out of my hearing.

'All done,' she said as she pushed the door closed again. 'They'll take it easy, at least until the party gets going.'

'Thanks, Melody.'

'So what's with the dom kick? And what's Amber got to say about Miss Clean anyway?'

'I'm not being dominant; I want Beth to take charge of me. She's so sweet, and so bloody self-righteous. I just want to see her with a cane in her hand. Amber knows. She's used to me.'

'Yeah, right. Coming in?'

She had stepped into the shower and I stripped off and joined her. I was quite drunk and my mind was in a whirl. I was worried about Beth, but cross with myself for it and even a little pleased. In the world according to *Metropolitan* the sort of depraved orgy that was going to start in a short while just didn't exist. People like Melody did, and were extolled as icons – the black girl from the East End who had married rich and now lived in a mansion and jetted between London and New York. Personally I didn't care if Melody lived in a mansion or a hut, but the smell of her skin and the way her muscles moved as she soaped herself was really getting to me.

I took the soap and began to wash her, with the water cascading down our bodies as I rubbed lather into her gleaming brown skin. Unlike Beth she took the washing as an act of submission, and unlike Beth she made no fuss about where my fingers went. I was soon on my knees, working soap into her tummy, then the rich growth of crinkly black hair that covered her sex.

'You're going to kiss that later,' she said from above me. 'You're going to lick cunt with everyone watching and I'm going to come in your face. I'll make you lick my ass, too, with your tongue right in the hole.'

I kissed her pussy in response, just a peck, but enough to get the rich, aroused scent into my head.

She laughed and turned, pushing out her bottom to be washed. My fingers were trembling as I lathered her cheeks, feeling their plump, meaty texture, so girlish yet so strong. It was almost in my face, with her cheeks open enough to show a little of the rear of her pussy lips, which I always feel is the rudest view a girl can present, especially if her bumhole shows. Melody's did, a dark star of wrinkled flesh, almost true black in colour. I wanted to lick it, to stick my tongue up in a gesture of utter surrender, but contented myself with a kiss to each firm brown buttock, saving the treat until later. Not that I held back from washing her, even sliding a soapy finger into her rectum. After all, if I was going to be licking her anus later I wanted it nice and clean. She complained at the sting of the soap, but sighed when I wiggled my finger in her bottom.

'Let's do it now,' she said.

'What about the others?'

'They'll be ages, and if your prissy friend's going to spoil the fun I want it now.'

I didn't argue. After all, I'd been getting more and more worked up all night, but there had always been that uncertainty of success. With Melody there was no uncertainty. I was quite happy to lick her in the shower, but she turned it off and climbed out.

'Stay on your knees,' she ordered. 'You can dry me and powder me.'

I obeyed, taking a huge, fluffy towel from a hot rail and using it to dry her body, all the while kneeling, dripping wet, and nude except for my bondage bracelets. With her towering over me and her firm flesh under my fingers I was feeling more and more submissive, even wondering if I dared take a spanking despite the noise it would make, both from the slaps on my bottom and the howls I would undoubtedly produce.

Once she was dry she gave me a tub of some scented talc and a powder-puff. I dabbed her down, powdering every inch of her body from neck to feet, enjoying her breasts and bottom the most, but getting the biggest submissive kick out of her feet. It was just right for my role of body servant, powdering her toes while I grovelled naked on the floor with my bum stuck out and my dangling boobs dripping water on the floor.

'When were you caned?' she asked from above me.

'Last Monday,' I admitted.

'By Amber?'

'No, by a man, Percy Ottershaw. You don't know him.'

'Yes I do; Morris got him to do our cellar. He's grossly overweight, about sixty and a dirty old bastard. You're a slut, Penny Birch, a filthy little slut. Now get on with it.'

She had left her sex until last, and as I dabbed the powder-puff to her pussy the urge to push my face in and just lick and lick was close to overwhelming. I held back, not wanting to make her come too soon. With the front done, she turned and bent, putting her hands on the toilet seat and parting her legs. I shuffled closer, swallowing at the sight of her open pussy, the centre wet and pink. Her anus was a little open too, with bright pink flesh showing in the middle and a little soap bubble over the actual hole. I dabbed the puff between her cheeks and over her pussy, feeling more servile than ever – the beaten maid powdering her mistress's body, allowed to do the most intimate places because she was too incon-sequential for it to matter what she saw.

'Good girl,' she sighed. 'A little more on my pussy, then you can kiss my arse.'

I knew she didn't mean the cheeks. I love kissing other girls' bumholes: it's so wonderfully rude and so

81

wonderfully submissive. What better way to acknowledge a playmate's dominance than to kiss their anus?

I feigned reluctance anyway, because I knew she'd like it. With my lips puckered up I leaned forward, slowly, letting what I was about to do really sink in. My face pressed between her big, meaty black cheeks; my lips touched her bottom-hole and I was doing it, kissing another's girl's anus to show to her just how far beneath her I was.

'Slut,' Melody told me as I began to explore the wrinkles of her bumhole with my tongue.

She let me do it, using my tongue tip to lick her bottom-hole and the flesh around it, then the hard bar of muscle between pussy and anus. I probed her vagina, tasting her juice as it mixed with the flavour of the powder in my mouth. If she had let me I would have licked her like that, from the rear, with her lovely bum in my face as I lapped her clit and masturbated my own pussy. It would have been good, but no sooner had my lips found her clit than she reached back and pulled me off by my hair.

'Not yet, girl,' she told me. 'Now get your slobber off my pussy.'

Once more I dried and powdered her, then kneeled back, wondering how she wanted me if being licked from behind wasn't enough. My knees were set well apart, more or less of their own accord, offering my pussy in case she wanted to feel me or push anything up me. Instead she lifted the lavatory seat, sat down on the china rim and clicked her fingers, pointing at the floor between her feet. I shuffled over, my mind full of the humiliation of licking her out while she sat on the lavatory. She might pee while I did it, over my face and in my mouth, doubtless laughing while she soiled me.

Her thighs were well apart, her pussy swollen and open, with every detail on show: the pink flesh around her lips and between them, the darker crests to each inner lip, the glossy nub of her clitoris, the tiny depression that marked her pee-hole. I looked up at her, finding her watching me with an expression of lust and sadistic hauteur.

'Watch my pussy, Penny,' she ordered. 'Watch me pee.'

As she spoke she let go, her stream gushing out to splash in the bowl beneath her. I watched, entranced, wishing it was in my face or over my breasts. I was expecting her to grab me by the hair and force my face in between her thighs, having let me see her pee start before I was made to take it in my mouth. She didn't, but just let it run, filling me with an odd blend of relief and disappointment.

The gush died to a trickle and stopped. Melody dabbed her pussy with paper, not one sheet but several, luxury thickness and pink, in keeping with the décor. I licked my lips as she dropped it, wondering why she hadn't taken proper advantage of me, but sure the moment had come. She reached out and took my hair, twisting a handful into her fist. It hurt, but all I could manage was a little mewling sound in my throat. I was pulled down, face to the floor, and she took my arms, one by one, lifting them into the small of my back. I held them there as she clipped my bracelets together, depriving me of the use of my arms. I'd been going to masturbate while I licked her and felt a flush of frustration and disappointment, yet I knew she'd make me come in the end.

As she got to her feet I again wondered what she was doing, only to realise as I was dragged towards the bowl. There was nothing I could do. She is far stronger than me, and I could only give a little gasp of misery as my head was pulled over the toilet bowl and pushed down into it. I now realised why she had lifted both seats: to get my head deeper into the bowl. My bottom was up high, my breasts pressed to the lavatory bowl when she stopped, holding my face an inch clear of the yellow water. I could smell the pee and her strong, feminine musk, while my heart was hammering in anticipation of what was about to be done to me.

'This is it, Penny,' she said. 'How does it feel with your face down a lavatory bowl? Now stop wriggling while I flush you. Here we go, one, two, three, and away!'

I heard the rasp of the plunger and shut my eyes an instant before the water erupted around my head. My mouth had come open to cry out in protest, only to be filled with water and piddle as I was flushed. She held my hair tight, laughing as the mess rose up, swirling around my head, soiling my face and hair, going up my nose and in my ears while I drummed my feet on the floor in helpless frustration.

She kept my head down until the last of the water had gone. I was sobbing with reaction, gasping for breath and shivering, completely overwhelmed by what had been done to me and ready for more, or worse. The watery pee was dripping out of my nose and off my chin, while I held my eyes tight shut, both to stop it going in them and in an agony of humiliation. I'd been flushed down a lavatory, which had to be about as bad as it gets, while I didn't even have the dignity of clothes.

Melody was still chuckling to herself as she pulled my head out of the bowl, dragged me to my feet and over to the sink, where she held me in front of the mirror. I was like a drowned rat, my face dripping wet and my hair plastered to my face and full of bits of pink lavatory paper. Looking at myself my main feeling was of self-pity, but the sexual arousal behind it was really strong and I was shivering with need.

'And now it's time to lick pussy,' Melody told me, 'and as I'm such a nice girl you can frig off while you do it.'

'Queen me,' I answered, as she undid my bracelets, 'and talk to me.'

She nodded and I got down, lying full length on the floor. I was shaking hard and eager for my orgasm, equally eager to give her one. She came to stand over me, smiling as she looked down, then turning and presenting me with the full glory of her bottom. I opened my mouth as she sank slowly into a squat, her cheeks spreading wide above my face, then touching, her pussy to my lips, her anus on my nose. She wiggled, making herself comfortable on my face as I began to lick her. My legs came up and open, spreading my pussy to the room as I began to stroke my body.

Melody began to squirm her bottom into my face, moving so that I could alternately lick her pussy and bumhole. She had spread her cheeks, giving me the fullest possible faceful of meaty black bottom, and was squatting, just as if she were going to pee. My mouth was full of the taste of her, and I was thinking of how I would feel in the same position out in the woods, with her squatting over my face to pee in my mouth. I had began to feel my breasts, intending to take my time, but with the thought of her using my mouth as a toilet I could hold off no longer. One hand went to my sex and I began to rub, teasing my pussy just as I was teasing my nipples.

'That's right, girl, you frig off,' Melody said. 'Frig off with my bum in your face and your tongue up my hole. It's what you deserve, Penny, your head down the lavatory before your tongue goes up my arsehole.

That's right, girl, lick, good and deep, taste me. Now lick this.'

She shifted her weight, spreading her pussy in my face. I obeyed, lapping at her clit and all the while rubbing at myself. My fantasy was growing: I was imagining myself on a picnic with her, her sister and several other girls, all big, strapping black girls, full of swagger and self-confidence. I'd be the maid, carrying their things and serving them. They'd start to humiliate me, making me strip and serve in the nude, smacking my face and breasts, Melody giving me a good hard spanking across her lap to leave me red-bottomed and snivelling. As they got more drunk it would get worse. One of them would put a flower up my bumhole, leaving it sticking out between my smacked cheeks. I'd have to crawl, on my knees in the mud and leaves, all the while with them laughing at the way the flower bobbed and wobbled behind me. Melody would say that it would be funny to pee on me, that I deserved to be the toilet, and she'd do it, squatting over my face, peeing right in my mouth while the others watched and laughed at my degradation.

Her weight shifted, her clit pressing to my mouth and my nose into her anus. She began to grind herself into my face, gasping as she rubbed, then coming in a long, drawn-out scream of ecstasy. I had been close myself, but concentrated on her as she came, licking as best I could until at last her orgasm broke and she lifted her bottom. I grabbed her thighs and pulled her firmly back in my face, probing her bumhole with my tongue. That was best, my tongue up her tight bumhole, her big cheeks spread on my face.

My hands went between my legs and I rolled myself up, sliding one finger up my bottom-hole, which was slimy with my own juice. My thumb went into my pussy as I found my clit and started to rub, almost immediately feeling the first pulses of my approaching climax. I thought of the way I was, licking my friend's anus with my mouth full of the taste of her pee and my hair sodden and filthy with piddle and bits of lavatory paper. The fantasy had gone when she'd come, but I tried to get back to it, only for her to start talking, as I had asked.

'That's the way for you, Penny,' she began. 'Your tongue up a black girl's bottom. Yeah, lick deep, rim me out, taste me. I'd piss in your face if I could, all over your tits and in your cunt. You'd love it, wouldn't you, Penny, you filthy little slut, you dirty tart. Deeper, you little bitch, get your tongue up my dirtbox. Yeah, that's what I ought to do to you: I ought to dump in your mouth . . .'

That was too much for me, but I didn't care; I was already coming. My vagina and anus began to pulse, locking in ecstasy, as did my thighs and just about every muscle in my body. I'd have screamed if my face hadn't been buried in Melody's bottom, and my feet were hammering on the floor in an abandoned frenzy. It was beautiful, really superb, as only an orgasm built on mingled physical submission and submissive fantasy can be, but only when I started to come down did I realise that Melody had stopped talking.

The next thing I heard was a gasp of shock, and as Melody's bottom lifted off my face I saw Beth, running away beyond where Harmony stood in the doorway. I was weak with reaction from my orgasm and could do nothing for a moment, only gasp for air. Melody had been pretty well suffocating me, but it hadn't been a problem. Now it was. I was panting and trying to speak at the same time, trying to get up with half Mel's weight still on me.

Beth was at the door before I managed to get up, and I heard Rathwell's puzzled question from the hall. I ignored him, rushing out after Beth to find that the gentle rain had turned into a blinding downpour. Rathwell screamed something about not streaking in case the neighbours saw and then I'd gone headlong, slipping in the morass of mud left by the contractors who were re-laying the drive.

It was Rathwell's security gate that saved me, otherwise I'm not sure Beth wouldn't have gone for the police. She was certainly threatening to, banging on the intercom panel and yelling about perverts and maniacs. I caught up with her and grabbed her wrists, trying to calm her down.

'What were you doing, Penny? What were you doing?' she yelled. 'She said . . .'

'She didn't mean it!' I answered. 'We were playing, just playing.'

'She was sat on your face! She was going to do it in your mouth!'

'No she wasn't! She was joking! She just said it to help me . . . No, I mean as a fantasy thing . . . You know, in play, like talking dirty . . .'

'But that!'

'Listen, Beth, she wouldn't do that; she just said it to scare me, to make sure I got the biggest possible kick out of coming. It was too much in any case, but not by far. Look, Beth, I've known them years. Melody's into spanking and to having people as her slave, men and women, but it's all for fun, all pretend. She does it at Morris's clubs, here and in New York, leading men around on collars and leashes. So does Harmony, only she's more submissive. Morris whips and spanks them both, regularly, and they love it. Can you really see Melody being made to do something she didn't like?

'I'm as bad. Mark never forced me; I love being spanked. I love it from men and from other women too, I really do. I love to be done in front of other people. I like it with my panties down and everything showing! If they don't pull my panties down it's not good enough! I like to give it too: it's nice. It's not wrong; just as long as everyone is having fun it's not wrong at all. That's all it is, Beth, fun, and I wish you would join in.'

It was out, all of it, if not the whole truth, then at least the truth about my sexuality. Beth had listened open-mouthed, indifferent to the rain running down her face and my naked, mud-plastered body. When I'd finished I just sank to my knees on the sodden grass and buried my face in my hands.

Five

I really thought that would be the last I'd hear of
Beth, but I was wrong. On Wednesday morning a
letter arrived from her, not direct, but via the
Rathwells, which must have taken a bit of nerve in
itself. It was pretty heavy stuff, about how much she
liked me but that she found it impossible to accept
what I was into. She still wouldn't believe that I
actually liked it, despite what I'd said, but gave a long
spiel about why I should break away from what I'd
been forced into, comparing it with the way she
herself had broken away from the Catholic Church.
She finished by saying that she'd be happy to see me
again once I had put my perversity behind me.

After the first page of the letter I'd been feeling an
absolute bitch, but by the end I was shaking my head
in disbelief. She had more or less written my life for
me, and it just wasn't true. Admittedly I had only
myself to blame if she thought Mark had done
terrible things to me, but from this she made the
assumption that I was in the habit of choosing violent
lovers. She went on about this at length, saying it was
a common phenomenon among women with low
self-esteem. I knew it already; I'd read the article in
Metropolitan.

I wished I could have answered her, because the
truth was almost the exact opposite. As the youngest

senior lecturer in my department I had more trouble with an excess of self-esteem than a lack of it, and to some extent taking undignified and humiliating punishments counteracted this. Only to some extent though, most of the time I do it because I adore the feelings it gives me.

Worse of all was the suggestion that I might have been abused in some way when a girl, leading to sexual insecurity. This was absolutely at odds with my genteel and even somewhat sheltered early years. True, I'd been a bit of a slow starter and insecure about my sexuality during my teenage years, but that was all. My need for spanking had started with guilt for doing rude things with boys, culminating with Aunt Elaine taking down my panties for getting carried away with my cousin Kate and her boyfriend. I'd deserved that spanking, but afterwards I'd come for the first time and I'd never looked back. A smacked bum became the ideal prelude to sex, not indispensable, but preferred.

The letter left me with my head spinning and a desperate need to answer Beth back. I thought of writing to explain my real feelings, but I knew it would do no good. She had decided that I was 'in denial', and that was that. It was pointless for me to do anything. Amber was off at some horse show, so I couldn't talk it out with her, and when I went up to my room in an effort to clear my head by masturbating over some really dirty and painful fantasy I found I just couldn't concentrate.

I ended up driving in to Broxbourne to see a film, something called *Night Over the Volga* which was supposed to be intellectually challenging. It turned out to involve a bunch of morose nineteenth-century Russians murdering each other and hanging themselves. The closing titles announced that it was based on real-life events, which made my own difficulties seem so utterly trivial that I was just about skipping as I left. This earned me a few funny looks from those who had found it either depressing or deeply moving, but I didn't care.

Back at Amber's I went straight up to the bedroom and stripped, stark naked. I promised myself I would stay that way until she came home and that if I felt like it I would masturbate, wherever I happened to be at the time. When Amber got home I'd ask for a punishment, perhaps for playing with Melody, whom she always regarded as a rival. My cane strokes had gone down enough for me to be able to take something quite hard, and when I'd been whacked, taken her to orgasm and come myself, I would forget all about Beth.

It was warm enough for being naked not to be actually uncomfortable, but no more than that, keeping me constantly aware of my nudity. After a late lunch and a glass of beer, taken sitting bare at the kitchen table, I began to think about enhancing the experience. It is nice being naked, but I'm no nudist. If it didn't make me feel naughty I wouldn't bother, simply because clothes are more practical.

Amber is very careful about her public image, and I had no intention of starting rumours about her in the village. The shutters on to the road remain firmly shut and barred, so I was quite safe, yet it occurred to me that if someone did see me they might or might not be shocked. Even if they were shocked they might just think I liked to be nude, and not think of my behaviour as dirty at all. I needed to enhance my nudity in some way that made it blatantly obvious that it was meant as sexual display. That it was for my own benefit was irrelevant: I wanted to feel naughty.

There was plenty in the bedroom to keep me happy. I started with my riding boots, knee-high black leather, which would have been perfectly respectable over a pair of jodhpurs, but were undeniably kinky when they were all I had on. That felt better, pleasantly naughty in a way that drew my attention to my legs and bottom.

Nothing obviously rude goes on in the bedroom, but there were several riding-crops in the cupboard, all of which had been applied to my bottom at one time or another. I took one out, a whip with a particularly thick leather snap, in two layers to give a satisfying smacking noise when it hits. The last time Amber had used it on me I had been made to bend over with my legs well spread and my hands on my ankles. It was a great position, with my pussy and boobs vulnerable as well as my bum. She had worked me up slowly, with little smacks on my buttocks and legs, even a few on my pussy. It hadn't hurt at all at first; there had just been the snap of leather on my flesh and the feeling of utter exposure. By the end I'd been so turned on she had been able to give me a pretty sound thrashing and I'd just soaked it up.

That would be the way to deal with Beth, if only she would let me start. I'd spend hours over her bottom, cuddling her as I eased up her dress and whispering soothing words as I slid her panties down to leave it bare. With her laid out on the bed I would massage her lovely cheeks, squeezing them and patting them until she had begun to sigh and stick it up. Only then would I start the spanking, slapping her rump with my fingertips, never hard, but just enough to make her flesh tingle. When her cheeks started to pink up I'd get firmer, making them wobble and part, showing off the depths of her crease, her pussy and her tight little bumhole.

I'd change to the crop then, and start to beat her, still lightly, working her up gently until at last she began to beg for it, to ask me to beat her properly, to thrash her impudent little backside while she came on her own fingers . . .

Which was exactly what I was doing, rubbing the leather shaft of the whip between my thighs, bottom stuck out behind and legs tight together. I really wanted to whip Beth, to use every technique I knew to bring her up to such a head of ecstasy that she would end up thanking me on her knees for doing it.

I was close to orgasm, and began to think of what might have been at Rathwell's, if only. We could have given them a show, with Beth over my lap to get her virgin spanking. After that she'd be passed around, from one to the next, red-bottomed and kicking across Melody's lap, then Harmony's. They could do her together, the two of them, knees locked, Beth held tight, wobbling pink bum high in the air, thighs cocked open, pussy and bumhole on show, frigging openly as I laid into her with a whip.

My orgasm hit me and I sank down to my knees, jerking and twisting the whip shaft against my clitoris with that glorious thought of Beth's round, red bottom and her fingers on her pussy. There was a wry smile on my face as I came down, and I realised that it was not going to be as easy to forget about Beth as I had imagined.

Sure enough, I failed to put her out of my mind. Not that I wrote back to her, but it was impossible not to feel that our relationship had been left incomplete. It was also impossible not to resent the way she was so certain that she knew how I thought better than I did myself. True, I was as bad myself for trying to get her into spanking, but at least I acknowledged that she could hold different opinions.

I kept myself busy in the hope that I'd stop being so silly, helping Amber in the shop and at shows, indulging in rude behaviour with her and others and generally having fun. By the end of the week I felt it was working, only to get a shock that brought the whole thing back with a vengeance.

Even though it was certain to aggravate my feelings, I had bought the new issue of *Metropolitan*. It was full of the usual stuff: an article on how men should behave, but undoubtedly never would; a questionnaire that allowed the reader to compare her physique with a supposed ideal roughly on the lines of a Barbie doll; a piece on chocolate cake and what a pity it was we weren't allowed to eat any. I read out a bit of this last one to Amber, suggesting that an hour a day's pony-girl training was more than enough to justify the odd slice of chocolate cake, then turned the page and had the smile wiped clean off my face.

It was the agony column, presented by some smart little blonde called Isabel, whose smug-looking photograph was directly above a letter from Beth about me. It even used my name, and I read it in open-mouthed horror. From the date she had to have written it immediately after our night together in Streatley, and it described in vivid detail my relationship with the imaginary Mark and how I'd begged her to spank me. If that wasn't bad enough, the reply was worse, a condensed version of what she had put in her letter to me, basically suggesting that I was undoubtedly the victim of abuse and should be advised to seek help.

I read it three times as the enormity of it sank in. It was one thing for Beth to lecture me in private, but to display my supposed problem for national scrutiny was quite another. I felt invaded, abused even, which would have been a fine piece of irony if it hadn't been at my expense.

After a spate of tears and a cuddle from Amber I began to feel sorry for myself, then angry, not at Beth, but at Isabel and the magazine in general. I decided to write to the editor, only to abandon the idea as pointless for the same reason I hadn't written back to Beth. It didn't matter what I said. If it didn't agree with their preconceptions then it wasn't my own opinion but something put into my head by wicked and manipulative males.

I could see exactly what would happen. They would get my letter. Isabel would tut over it, shake her head, feel sorry for me and then put a reply in the next month's issue saying more or less what she had said to Beth. Doubtless she would end with some advice on therapy. If I used my full title and qualifications, then they might be forced to take my opinions more seriously, but of course I couldn't without coming out to the world, including my university colleagues and my mother. That was not something I was ready to do, and I was stuck.

After my night with Beth I'd needed reassurance of my own sexuality, a good humiliating punishment. Now I was furious, and seething with frustration. A number of juicy revenge fantasies went through my head, all completely impractical. The best was to hire a man of the sort they hated the most. He would be big, say six foot six, fat, too, a total slob but muscled like a bull. In character he'd be a lager-swilling, loud-mouthed lout, the type to whistle at girls in the street and pinch their bums. A builder or car mechanic would be best, perhaps a dustman, something that involved wearing filthy overalls for rough, manual work. He'd be called Daryl or Dave.

I'd let him do whatever he liked to me, even though it probably wouldn't be anything more inventive than a blow-job. I might even pay him, anything, just so long as he did as he was told. After a crash course in spanking and the humiliation of girls, I'd have him waylay Isabel on her way back from work, maybe even at work. He would pull her over his lap, get her tight little bum bare and spank her purple with all her friends and colleagues watching.

Not that it would have solved anything even if it hadn't been completely impractical, because it would just have served to confirm her prejudices, both about spanking and men. Nevertheless it was soothing to think about it and made me feel a fair bit better.

I had to do something, but I was determined not to act hastily, a decision Amber heartily agreed with. Even the idea of going into the *Metropolitan* offices and giving both Isabel and the editor, Amy McRae, a piece of my mind was out of the question. With my respectable job and exotic sex life I could hardly afford to get on the wrong side of a magazine with a nation-wide circulation. Suing them was impractical for the same reasons and wouldn't have worked anyway. So I was forced to swallow my pride and put up with it, contenting myself with imaginary revenge.

We had been invited to dinner at Henry's on the Saturday, along with Anderson and Vicky, Ginny and her husband Michael. This was more or less the fox-hunting team, and I hadn't seen Ginny since the fateful day, so after we'd eaten I ended up telling the whole story, right up to the publication of Beth's letter in *Metropolitan*. I finished with my wicked plot for Isabel, including Amy this time, tied side by side on a desk with their bare bums stuck out to the office.

'It has to be a huge room,' I finished. 'Open plan, so that the entire staff can see them get their spanking.'

'Excellent!' Anderson declared. 'Spanked in front of their colleagues, especially the men. Just imagine how they'd feel!'

'Utterly humiliated,' Michael put in, 'but probably turned on, too.'

'You're no better than they are!' Amber laughed. 'Not all girls get turned on by being punished; you're just putting your own concepts into their heads.'

'As they do to poor Penny,' he answered. 'At least I don't do it in the national press.'

'Public spanking would be good for them,' Henry put in thoughtfully, 'but it would still leave them the chance to be self-righteous about it afterwards. Using force is no good. They'd have to take the spankings willingly and be seen to submit, mentally as well as physically. That would really humiliate them.'

'How?' I demanded.

'Tricky, I admit,' he went on, 'but maybe if offered enough money ... Yes, I have it, imagine this. Someone, maybe even a woman but tough and physically strong, Vicky say, goes to the office and asks to speak to the two of them alone. She has a case, which contains bundles of twenty-pound notes, shrink-wrapped in plastic. After adjusting the venetian blind to block off the view to the main office, she states that the case contains a million pounds. This can be theirs if they simply kneel on the desk, have their bottoms bared and take a spanking each. How could they resist?'

'Great, except that they end up with half a million each!'

'Not at all. Each bundle is in fact paper topped with a single real note, which they are not going to get in any case.'

'They'd be pretty suspicious.'

'Why? The money is there; the offer is there. You make up some story, explain that their editorial attitude has offended some wealthy man and that he considers a million a small price to pay to prick their bubble of self-righteousness. Avarice would prove too much, vanity, too, as the story makes them seem frightfully important. Precious, too, which sounds like them. Wasn't there some film where a man accepted a million pounds for some fellow to bugger his wife?'

'Just to sleep with her, Henry. It was called *Indecent Proposal*, with Robert Redford and Demi Moore.'

'Yes, of course, thank you. Anyway, they'd be bound to have seen it and you could make the comparison, adding a touch of Hollywood glamour. They'd have to accept, and under the conditions you demanded. So, you lock the door, up they go on the desk, hands tied behind their backs, skirts up, knickers down and there they are, fannies on show, ready for punishment. You spank them, taking your time. Being innocent in these matters they won't realise how noisy a spanking can be, especially when you are using a cupped hand to make the slaps as loud as possible. It would get louder still when they started to howl, as they undoubtedly would.'

'Lovely, and then you let the venetian blind up?'

'Exactly, preferably so that they don't notice. In any case the entire staff now has a fine view of their freshly spanked bottoms. You then pick up the case, lock the door as you leave and stroll from the building. Not only have they been punished and in public, but they have accepted spankings of their own free will, and they have been cheated, making them look not only stupid but also greedy. Their humiliation would be complete.'

'Wonderful,' I admitted, 'but I can see a dozen reasons why it wouldn't work.'

'Sadly so,' Henry admitted, 'but it conjures up a pretty picture.'

'The final indignity would be for them to find themselves turned on afterwards,' Michael put in.

'Absolutely,' Anderson agreed. 'That always puts the cap on it.'

'It's why I do it,' I admitted. 'It doesn't matter how often it happens, it's still incredibly humiliating, particularly the moment when my panties come down, and it still turns me on. The greater the humiliation the bigger the thrill.'

'The same for dishing it out,' Michael remarked. 'Knowing what's going on in the girl's head is half the pleasure.'

'That would seem to argue that the more humiliating the conditions of the punishment the more likely the receiver is to become excited by it,' Amber suggested.

'Why not?' Anderson agreed. 'Picture this contrast. On the one hand we have a girl in an imaginary sixth-form Catholic school, not as they are, but as some might argue they should be. Let us call her Mary. She knows she is under the authority of the nuns and that if she is bad she will be punished. For her, punishment has always meant the exposure of her bottom and a spanking, even the cane. She has also been taught that this is just. When it happens it hurts and doubtless it is a little undignified, showing what she has been taught is such a rude part of her anatomy to all and sundry while it gets whacked, but that is the extent of it.

'In contrast think of a girl brought up to believe that she is special, something precious, something untouchable. She is noble, perhaps; her parents are certainly rich and she is called Annabella. To her, punishment is for other people, the gardener's daughter, bare-bottomed over his wheelbarrow, the kitchen maids, lined up along the range with their skirts high and their drawers dropped while the cook belabours them with a wooden spoon. For it to happen to her would be unthinkable. Then someone, her tutor shall we say, finally loses patience with her airs. He upends her, exposes her bottom and gives her exactly the same treatment as she saw the gardener's daughter get the day before. She howls just the same; she kicks just the same, and although she probably imagines her own pain is far worse, it's really much the same. What is different is her humiliation, which becomes a burning, overriding sensation and which I would bet leaves her with a wet pussy and a lot of confusion.'

'Afterwards,' I added, 'she runs to her room in tears, throws herself on the bed for a tantrum, then masturbates until she's sore. I should know, because that's more or less how I got into it. Not quite as bad perhaps, but I can imagine Annabella's humiliation.'

'It's a nice story, Anderson,' Amber put in, 'but I don't entirely agree. Annabella thinks she's above it, but she knows it happens. She had seen the gardener's daughter beaten, perhaps the maids and other girls, too. Yes, she feels superior to them and above such things. So when it does happen she is far more humiliated and outraged than they could ever be. She knows it's possible, though, in the general sense. Punishment is part of her world, even if she feels it shouldn't apply to her. After all, she's got a bottom, just like the gardener's daughter, and a bottom can always be smacked.

'What would be worse would be for a girl to be spanked when the whole idea is completely foreign to her. OK, nobody could actually be unaware that bottoms can be smacked as a form of punishment, but to a modern girl it could be something totally inapplicable to her life, frightening but out of date, like being put in a scold's bridle or ducked as a witch. We'll call her Gemma. She's an absolute brat, and likes making boys fight over her. She's been in a pub, flirting with two boys in the hope that there will be a good fight after closing time. Sure enough, they agree to fight and go into a park where they won't be seen, along with Gemma and others. The boys don't fight, though. Instead they grab Gemma and push her over a swing. One sits on her back while the other pulls down her panties and shorts, leaving her bum showing, then lifts up her top to bare her boobs. All her friends and several men are watching as she's spanked, bare-bottomed, and lectured for being a brat. Her humiliation would be worse than Annabella's.'

'I agree,' Michael said, 'but I think the same situation can be taken a step further. Picture this, a girl having to submit to the cane from a stepmother who is actually younger than her. She, we'll call her Elaine, is twenty-two, in her third year at university, pretty, well educated, very self-confident. Her parents divorced when she was a teenager, and both have thoroughly spoiled her. She has never been spanked, let alone caned, and would be outraged by even a suggestion that any modern woman, let alone herself, could be subjected to such indignity. Like Gemma, she thinks of it as something that used to happen a long time ago in cruder and less civilised times.

'The stepmother is a mere nineteen, called Sue, has dyed blonde hair and wears white high heels. She knows about spanking, because that's what Elaine's father is into. Elaine looks down on her and is always cold towards her. Sue resents this and engineers a way to get a hold over Elaine, blackmail or whatever it might be. Sue then tells Elaine that she is going to cane her. Elaine protests but ultimately has to do it. She is made to bend over a chair. Her dress is lifted on to the small of her back. Her expensive silk knickers are pulled down. She is told her sex is too hairy and that she ought to shave. She is told that before the next time she takes a punishment she ought to wash her bottom properly. Then she is caned, caned by the nineteen-year-old slut her father has taken as a second wife. There is true humiliation.'

'Maybe,' Vicky said, 'but there's no audience, only she and Sue ever know what has happened. I like an audience, and Amber's Gemma sounds like she'd be less able to handle her feelings, so they'd probably be stronger. She wouldn't understand why she was turned on afterwards either, so she'd be really flustered and confused. As you know, my ex-boyfriend, Todd, got me into being a pony-girl before I got fully into CP. Getting the crop across my bum was all part of the fun and I didn't find it humiliating at all. I've always liked being naked and showing off; it's only humiliating if people don't appreciate it. The same goes for having my bum whacked.'

'What about your health farm fantasy?' I put in.

'That's not the same. There I'm being punished for not being good enough. It's like when Melody beat me wrestling and made me kiss her bumhole. It was losing that humiliated me, not kissing her bum in front of all those people. I'll admit it turned me on, but I did get her back.'

'You lot are a bunch of perverts!' Ginny laughed. 'I was an innocent little farm girl until Amber got me into spanking, and pony-carting and the rest of it. If you want humiliation, though, what about this? I let this guy talk me into playing with him. He was this fat old bloke, bald with a red beard, and we got talking one afternoon. He gave me this big story about how lonely he was and how he'd never had a girlfriend and everything. He even said he'd never

103

seen a girl's pussy bare, or anything. I believed it and let him watch me sunbathe. He talked me into stripping, then got me to suck his cock! I even swallowed for him! I didn't even mind so much, because I felt I'd done something special for him, a sort of good deed for the day. Then Katie King told me it was her uncle. He'd been married twice and had seven kids! That's humiliation.'

'No, that's being a slut.' Amber laughed. 'After all, you didn't have to strip off for him, let alone suck his cock.'

Ginny stuck her tongue out at Amber but left it at that, taking a swallow of port. All the talk about how best to humiliate a girl had left me with a wet pussy and a strong need to have my own bottom seen to. I hadn't been dealt with properly since Percy had caned me, and the thought of being stripped and whacked in some thoroughly rude and exposed position was immensely appealing.

In front of them wasn't enough. Amber would have put me across her knee if I'd asked, maybe passed me around so all six of them could warm my bum. It would have been nice, but after thinking of the depth of feeling the various imaginary girls would have experienced I wanted something more.

'I'm inclined to side with Michael,' Henry remarked. 'At least in terms of depth of humiliation. I think Elaine would have suffered the worst. Maybe this is unfair of me, but I can never imagine a working-class girl getting so upset about a spanking, so I can't really picture Gemma being anything more than cross. Annabella's better: just what some haughty little rich girl deserves, a good bare-bottomed spanking, preferably in front of the servants. Sadly the tale belongs to a bygone day. Nowadays the tutor would be arrested for assault.'

'Annabella would still have had her spanking.'

'True, but at what a cost, when really the tutor should be thanked. No, Elaine would have experienced the greatest depth of humiliation, and if she had found she had to masturbate afterwards I imagine she'd have been crying even as she came. Nevertheless, I think I can do better, albeit within a similar context. Michael's fantasy relies on a disparity in age and status, and so does mine. My girl is called Camilla. She is a Sunday-school teacher in some quiet and genteel village, very proper, very well brought up, thirty or so and a virgin. She is pretty in a gentle, rustic way, and has a good figure if perhaps a touch fleshy around the bottom and breasts for modern fashion. Not that anybody really notices this, because her clothing is demure to say the least. When she eventually marries, the display of her body to her husband on the wedding night will be a moment of immense sacrifice to her, and even then it will be conducted in the dimmest of light.

'So, she is in the habit of taking the local children for nature rambles each Sunday. There is some sort of exchange going on, so that instead of her normal polite and well-brought-up twelve-year-olds she has a group of twenty sixteen-year-old toughs from the local steel town. They are less than impressed by the glories of the English countryside, and the fact that Camilla knows a glade where ragged-Robin grows leaves them cold. They begin to tease her, quickly bringing colour to her maiden cheeks. Spurred on by her blushes, they go from bad to worse, suggesting she expose herself for their pleasure. "Get your tits out for the lads" is, I believe, the sort of phrase they might use.

'Camilla's blushes deepen at such rude words, and she is feeling distinctly flustered. In a desperate effort to keep control she threatens to tell their parents of their foul language. This is the worst possible thing for her to do, as it both amuses and antagonises the youths. No longer is she seen as the harmless butt of their jokes, but as an active member of the repressive establishment they all hate. Poor Camilla is dragged to a fence. She is bent across it. Her ankles are tied with bailing twine, wide apart. Her wrists are crossed over her back and lashed together. Her blouse is cut open, her bra too, spilling her large breasts out beneath her chest. Her skirt is pulled up. Her petticoats are exposed, much to the amusement of the lads at seeing such quaint underwear. They are lifted anyway, exposing big French knickers heavily trimmed with lace. After a period of jokes and laughter at the sight of this old-fashioned garment and the way her position stretches the silk across her ample behind, they are pulled down. Now everything is showing, details that even her husband was never supposed to see. They tell her so, too, describing in gloating detail the way her pussy lips show, with the inner labia peeping out from between the outer. Her anus is also remarked on, how pink and tight it is, and how it is bound to be virgin.

'When they finally run out of things to say about her naked bottom and dangling breasts they beat her, with their hands and with twigs, slapping her bottom up to a rosy glow as they continue to tease her. Only then comes the final humiliation: tied, stripped and spanked she can no longer resist the lust that she had forced down for so many years. Choking on her own emotion, she begs to be entered, fucked if you will, not by some gallant swain in between fresh cotton sheets, but by twenty laughing oiks who take turns with her from the rear.

'Her humiliation, at the moment she asked to be mounted, would, I suggest, be beyond anything so far mentioned. Hardly acceptable behaviour, of course, and if I were ever to come across such a scene I would do my utmost to drive the youths away . . .'

'And fuck Camilla senseless,' Vicky interrupted.

'Certainly not,' Henry answered. 'I would release her immediately. Still, for humiliation I think I must claim the prize for Camilla, unless Penny has any say in the matter?'

'I can think of a thing or two,' I answered, 'but just now I'd rather have it done to me, preferably like Camilla.'

'We lack twenty steel-town roughs,' Amber pointed out. 'Why not just come over my knee?'

I rose to go, tingling with anticipation for my spanking, only for Anderson to raise a hand as he tried to swallow his mouthful of port.

'If she wants to have it in public, then she must have it in public!' he declared. 'We may not be able to provide such luxuries as gangs of perverted oiks, but there is a lay-by not so far from here where Vicky and I have occasionally provided the local dirty old men with a treat. How about it, Penny? Amber?'

'Fair enough,' Amber said, 'as long as it's safe. Michael, you'd better drive.'

'I'd be delighted,' Michael answered, 'and may I suggest as an added refinement that Penny be put in a pair of frilly panties or something equally ridiculous?'

'Better still, put her in nappies!' Ginny chimed in. 'We can use towels and big safety pins!'

They did it too, all of it. Amber and Ginny took me upstairs and told me to take off my panties under my dress. I was in red velvet, a full-length dress, and had put on panties to match, grey silk with a lace trim, about the most expensive pair I own. Ginny fetched a big white towel from the bathroom and I lay down on it, allowing her to fold it around my tummy and up between my legs, closing it off with a big safety pin.

My breathing had already started to get fast, and being put in a towelling nappy made it faster. When I stood up the feeling was stronger still, just knowing I had it on under my dress: in nappies, at my age, as if I was in the habit of wetting myself. I put my panties back on, stretching them over the impromptu nappy to add an extra touch of ridicule to my look.

I showed the others when we got downstairs, lifting my dress and twirling to give them all a good show. Then it was outside, to Michael's big four-by-four, the perfect vehicle for what we intended. Seated, we all looked respectable: the men in black tie, the girls in demure frocks. With Michael sober and the police not in the habit of performing panty inspections beside the public roads, we were completely safe, just so long as Anderson and Vicky knew what they were doing.

Experienced exhibitionists that they are, they made no mistake. The lay-by was near St Albans, a pull-off with a high hedge shielding it from the main road. One other car was there, a battered old Ford moving to the motion of the teenage couple humping away merrily inside it. They took no notice of us, and when Michael had parked the car Vicky flicked the headlights. We had agreed everything on the way, and this was a known signal, showing that there would be something worth watching. A moment later a torch beam flashed out from the undergrowth and Anderson declared that we were safe. At his words a knot formed in my stomach. It was still a game, but that torch meant there was a genuine dirty old man out there, maybe more than one, and the prospect of my little bit of exhibitionism had suddenly become very real.

We had already worked out what to do, a little sketch designed to give our audience the biggest possible thrill by making me seem reluctant. The signal Vicky had given meant look but don't touch, with Michael and I the players and the others ready if anything got out of hand. With the lights off Michael and I began to snog, the others crouched low down in the back. It felt odd enough kissing Ginny's husband in his car as it was, almost as if we were being unfaithful, and I have to admit to enjoying it. He soon had my top down over my boobs, leaving them feeling incredibly exposed as a flicker of torchlight from outside ran over their pale, naked skin.

I started to play up, pushing his hands away when he tried to touch my breasts, putting them away, only to have my dress tugged smartly down over them again. He became more insistent, kissing my chest and sucking a nipple into his mouth. Again the torchlight washed over me, illuminating my naked breasts with Michael sucking greedily at one teat. It was getting to me, and I wanted to show my nappy.

Michael continued to kiss and feel, doubtless enjoying himself as much as I was. My nipples were achingly hard; my pussy was soaking, quite ready for a cock or Amber's tongue. As Michael pulled back I knew the time had come, and found myself shaking hard as he opened his door and climbed down. There was a rustle in the foliage and I saw a face for just one instant, a red, leering face with a bushy moustache, faintly illuminated in the beam of his torch. That really set my heart hammering, but as Michael helped me down I managed to give an angry shake of my head. It was quite light, with the big lights from the main road throwing long shadows from the hedge, but the red colours of the car and my dress clearly visible.

'You're a bastard, making me do this!' I snapped. 'We could easily have made it home.'

'That wouldn't be half the fun.' He laughed. 'Anyway, why do you think I made you wear your nappy?'

'To humiliate me at Annabella's!' I answered. 'Can you imagine if I'd tripped or something and my dress had gone up? I'm sure it shows under my dress in any case.'

'Nonsense. Anyway, you loved it, you slut. Come on, pee-pee time, or do I have to spank you first? That's what happens to naughty girls who won't do as they're told, you know, they get their botties smacked.'

'Oh come on, not that.'

'Yes, that. I think it'll do you good, actually. Put your hands on the bumper and stick your bum up.'

'People are watching! I heard noises. I saw a torch!'

'Nonsense, you're just trying to get out of it. There's only that old Ford and they're just a couple having a quickie. Anyway, it'll do you good if they see your bare arse, and probably spice up their sex a bit. Come on, bend, now!'

The last was a sharp command and I did it, giving him my dirtiest look but bending to rest my hands on the bars at the front of the four-by-four. I got well down, making my bum the highest part of my body, gripped the bars and looked back, sulky and resentful as he came behind me.

'Let's put it on show then,' he said and took the hem of my dress in his hands.

I really felt it. We were acting, but the dirty old men were real, very real, and very close. My exposure was real, too, my breasts already bare and dangling, while I really was in a nappy, so as Michael lifted my dress and dumped it on my back I was close to tears

110

in reaction. I was in stockings and a suspender-belt, grey to match my panties, which were now on show, bulging with nappy material, a sight at once lewd, ridiculous and perverse.

He took hold of the back of my nappy and I braced myself, feeling that awful moment of exposure as the ludicrous garment was pulled slowly down off my bottom. I was looking back, and he was grinning as he did it, watching my bare rear view come on display until it was all showing. My legs were far enough apart to make my pussy show, and as he settled the tangle of nappy and panties around my thighs I pulled in my back, spreading my bumcheeks and maybe revealing the little hole between, pink and winking in her nest of hair.

'Good girl,' Michael remarked. 'Such a pretty pose, it's just a shame Annabella and the boys can't be here to see it. Now, my dear, spankies time.'

I gave a little broken sob, which was by no means all fake. Michael raised his hand and slapped me, hard across both cheeks to make me squeak. I tried to rise, only to be grabbed around the waist and held down as he released a volley of hard smacks to my naked bum. It may have been acting, but it hurt. I made a thoroughly undignified display of myself in any case, without having to pretend, kicking about, wriggling and squealing like a stuck pig as he punished me.

He may have given me fifty, maybe sixty, and when he suddenly stopped my bottom was a burning ball of flesh. My pussy was juicing so well it had started to trickle down my legs and into my nappy. I was breathing hard, too, really hard, and would have been happy to take his cock, and all the better for our audience. I could hear a shuffling noise from the bushes as I stood up to rub my smarting cheeks, and

I knew exactly what they were doing, despite the darkness.

'There, now perhaps you'll be a bit more obedient in future,' Michael told me. 'Now, you can go and do your business, over there, where it's nice and light. Oh, and you can take those fancy pants off, but leave the nappy on and down. You're to do it in it and come home with it wet.'

I hung my head as I pulled down my panties, letting them dangle limp from my fingers as I walked to the place he had pointed out. It was the brightest part of the lay-by, illuminated by two areas of lighting, and would give everyone the best possible view. I was shaking inside and acutely conscious of my bare bum as I went over. Choosing the brightest spot, I squatted down, tucked my panties into the front of my dress and lifted it safely clear of any possible splash. With my bum stuck out and red from spanking I felt wonderfully exposed, especially as I knew I had to pee in the nappy stretched taut between my legs. I just had to masturbate, so I bundled my dress into the crook of my arm and put a hand to my pussy.

Peeing and coming at the same time is less than easy, so I frigged a little and then stopped, nicely high as I let the tension in my bladder build, rocking on my heels and squeezing my smarting bottom-cheeks. It came, a trickle, then a gush, and I was filling my nappy, in public, with an audience watching as my pee spurted out beneath me. It wasn't just going in the nappy either, but down my legs and into my shoes, which felt so beautiful and so dirty as I started to rub at my clit once more. With my orgasm rising in my head I let go completely, filling my nappy behind me and revelling in that terrible heavy feeling as it built with my orgasm.

I screamed as I came, my muscles locking in ecstasy. My balance went and I sat down in my own mess with a sticky squelch, but it didn't stop me, I just kept on rubbing, gasping and squealing out my pleasure to the night until it finally began to fade and I sank down in blissful exhaustion.

Six

That should have been enough. They had completely taken my mind off Beth, and given me a dirty experience to rank among my best. It had been so good that I had come twice more back at Henry's, once in front of everybody and once alone in bed with Amber before sleep. It was the best sex we had had in a while, and I went to sleep with my head on her chest, feeling absolutely contented.

We spent the Sunday pony-carting at Henry's, with Ginny, Vicky and I naked and in harness, being put through a dressage routine and then raced. Inevitably Vicky won, but I did manage to beat Ginny, just. Just was enough though: I had the pleasure of making her pose in the yard behind Henry's and whacking her big, wobbly bottom with a crop. I got my own, too, across Amber's lap, leaving me red-bottomed and giggling and just in the mood to give Henry a slow suck before lunch.

I was in an excellent mood on Monday morning and just felt silly for the state I'd let myself get into over the magazine. After all, other than Beth and my friends nobody was going to know it was anything to do with me. As she didn't even know my real name it wasn't worth worrying about. I felt they could spout their opinions to their hearts' content, too: after all, I knew dirty, painful sex kept me happy.

With term approaching and Amber at a show I had decided to go into the library to look up an obscure paper I'd been unable to get hold of in the north. As this meant being in Midland Road I thought of Natasha Linnet and suggested lunch, which she cheerfully agreed to.

We met in a wine bar in Primrose Hill, just yards from her flat, and were soon chatting away merrily. I told her about the Beth fiasco, making light of the bad bits and concentrating on the sex. She found the whole thing hilarious anyway, particularly the way Melody and I had been when Beth walked in. It was typical Natasha, laughing at the most ghastly social disasters, but it was impossible not to smile.

'That's priceless!' she said when I finished with the bit about Beth's letter. 'I can't wait to tell Amy!'

'Amy?'

'Amy McRae, the *Metropolitan* editor. She'll split.'

'No, you mustn't! She's the cause of it all. Beth believes every word she writes! Anyway, she sounds ghastly, not your sort at all.'

'Amy? No, she's great.'

'You're joking. She believes all women think the same way, want to look like elongated Barbie dolls, spend their time either gold-digging or dieting and can't even enjoy a good spanking!'

'Get real, Penny, that's just the editorial line. It's what the readers want to see, so it's what they get. Amy's not like that, well, no more than I am. Honestly, Penny, how can you be so naïve?'

'Easily, when I write a paper I present my facts as clearly as possible, making absolutely certain other people can follow my results and if necessary reproduce the research. Truth, Tasha, ever heard of it?'

'That's science, Penny, it's not the same. Amy commissions polls to see what the women in her target audience want to read about. Then she commissions articles on those subjects.'

'So she's feeding the readers back their own ideas?'

'Yes. It works. Have you seen their circulation?'

'That's so cynical.'

'The real world, Penny dear.'

'Sure, when it's OK to get a tattoo or have your clit pierced but not to ask a friend to smack your bottom.'

'Who says?'

'Amy, there's more than one recent article about how women should never cede control of their bodies to another, especially for physical discipline.'

'That's because she sees it as male violence and control. Be fair, would you like to be smacked around by some yob?'

'No, of course not, but that's not the same. I like to be spanked, and if I want to be I don't see why I shouldn't be. It's my choice.'

'Sure, I know that. Most women don't.'

'Fair enough, but why aren't I allowed to be an individual? What I really hate is being told I don't know my own mind. What gives her the right to dictate to me?'

'Nothing, she just does what will sell the magazine. She's not trying to dictate to people; she's just telling them what they want to hear. Personally she's great fun; I won't have a word said against her.'

'Fair enough, I'm sorry. I'd still like her across my knee, and enjoying it.'

'I'll tell her that, too!'

'Tasha!'

'I might. She'd laugh, after all it's not as if you're a threat to her. Anyway, you couldn't do it if you tried: she's really fit, and bigger than you. That's the thing with her, you see, although I shouldn't really

116

say this. She's tough and fit, but she always wants to be tougher and fitter. You know how she takes the piss out of muscle men?'

'Along with the rest. No, you're right, more than the rest.'

'That's because she knows that however hard she works out she can never be as strong as some men, even ones who don't try but are just big and well muscled by nature. I didn't tell you that, by the way. She'd never commission me again if she knew.'

I nodded and took a swallow of water. After what Natasha had said Amy McRae seemed human, even a little vulnerable, rather than a complete harpy. I still felt a touch of resentment, but understanding too.

'How about Isabel?' I asked.

'Isabel?'

'The girl who writes their agony column. Pert, slim, blonde, twenty-something.'

'That could describe half the female journalists in London. What I will say is that if they got Beth's letter into the last issue then they pulled the stops out to do it. Two to three months would be a more normal period between receipt and publication.'

What Natasha said was true. To get Beth's letter in they must have more or less stopped the press. For a scientific journal it would have been out of the question. It seemed a major effort to get one letter in, especially when they must have had a stockpile of appropriate material for the agony column. Natasha's conclusion was that it could only mean the topic of sexual violence was due for an airing, probably in the next issue, maybe in several. I could only agree. She promised to find out from Amy, and not to reveal who I really was.

Sure enough, the very next afternoon Natasha rang to say Amy was planning a full exploration of what she called hidden sexual violence. Among other things this was going to cover women getting spanked by their partners and would take the attitude that it was inherently non-consensual. Moreover, Amy was delighted to discover that Natasha knew the Penny from the letter and wanted to interview me.

It was impossible to turn it down. I could almost see what was going to be said in front of my eyes and it made me burn inside. Amber was doubtful, saying that it was a bad idea to reveal my true identity and in any case Amy could always twist my words whatever I said. I had to agree with the first point. The second was a chance I'd just have to take, if only because if she did then it would leave me on a clear moral high ground.

I agreed to talk, but only on my own terms, which meant somewhere that could in no way be identified with me and with no camera present. That felt safe enough, as unless she was in the habit of attending genetics conferences she was not going to recognise my face. After a lengthy exchange of telephone calls via Natasha it was arranged for Friday. We were to meet at a pub in Southwold and she could interview me walking along the beach.

Although I was genuinely distrustful of Amy, I have to admit enjoying setting up the interview enormously. It had a thrill of danger, which was not entirely false, and was also a challenge, and from what Natasha had said Amy had a pretty high opinion of her intelligence.

The basic idea was mine, to choose a place that I had no association with at all but where we could stay in control of the situation. Amber had suggested Suffolk, which she knew from childhood holidays, and Southwold because of its location. The pub we had chosen was right on the river front, just yards from the southern shore across the Blyth, but nearly ten miles by road. We arrived early, driving to Walberswick and walking up the river until we were opposite the pub. I was actually hoping that Amy would arrive with a cameraman, but she kept her word.

I still made her go through the whole routine, crossing by the ferry, meeting her and crossing back to be absolutely certain nobody else was with her. She was fairly tall, very sure and poised, with a confidence and strength about her that actually reminded me of Amber. There the resemblance ended. Amber, with her unruly honey-coloured curls and outdoor clothes, is very much the country girl and always looks out of place in the city. Amy was the opposite, cool and poised in her smart suit and cropped blonde hair, but completely out of place on a Suffolk beach.

Not that she was prissy, which I'd rather expected. When I said we were going to walk along the beach she bought a pair of jelly shoes and quite casually peeled her tights off under her skirt, ignoring the various yachtsmen and tourists nearby. The day was fair, and a few people were on Walberswick beach, so it was a while before we could speak in confidence. When we did she came straight to the point.

'So your boyfriend beats you?' she asked, obviously expecting the answer to be yes.

'No,' I answered, 'I haven't even got a boyfriend . . .'

'Hold on, what about the letter? Your friend said you'd been so badly abused by your boyfriend that you'd started to tell yourself you liked it.'

'She wrote the letter, not me. Most of what I said to her wasn't true at all, but never mind that. I'm

119

bisexual. I've been in a stable lesbian relationship for nearly five years.'

'So you're a lesbian? What was all this stuff about being beaten up by your boyfriend then?'

'I'm bisexual; I like men. I just happen to be in a relationship with another woman. The boyfriend doesn't exist; I just made him up to get out of an awkward situation. I got a bit carried away telling the story. Look, it's complicated and not really relevant. Let's just say I told her a dirty story, went to bed with her and when I asked her to spank me she wouldn't. That's what got her on her high horse. What does matter is that I never said the boyfriend beat me up, nothing like it. I said he spanked me and deliberately humiliated me.'

'Isn't it just the same?'

'No! I'd hate to be hit. I never have been. I love to be spanked. I adore it; it turns me on like nothing else, and my girlfriend does it to me all the time.'

'You're losing me, Penny. So you don't mind the violence as long as it's from another woman and done for sexual purposes?'

'More or less, but I don't see it as violence, that's the thing. I want it; I enjoy it.'

'Look, I know about endorphins, but that doesn't excuse the act . . .'

'Why not? If both people want it and no harm is done?'

'But how can you let someone do that to you? Doesn't it make you feel inferior? How can you feel sexy like that?'

'That's exactly it. The feeling of inferiority, of humiliation, is the main turn on. Sure, I need the pain to get my endorphins running, but the real thrill is all in my head.'

'So you like it, I can see that, even if I don't understand. Why do you like it though? Most of what

I've seen on the subject says it's a mental defence against abuse. How did it start for you? Was it because some boyfriend did it to you against your will, perhaps when you were a teenager? Don't take this the wrong way, but you're very small. It wouldn't be difficult. Is that what happened?'

'No, very firmly not. I'm going to be absolutely honest here, and if you choose not to believe me then so be it. I didn't get into it because it was forced on me. If anything it was the opposite. Maybe I don't even need the pain, because I used to get turned on by the idea of being spanked even before it happened to me.

'I was brought up to be quite shy of my body and guilty about sex. I was something of a late developer too, and I did well at school, which may have put the boys off. They used to call me Little Miss Smarty Pants. I used to fantasise though, and it was my sense of embarrassment about my body that turned me on. For instance I'd think about tearing my skirt and having to walk home with my panties showing. That got stronger after a boy persuaded me to show him my boobs and bum so he could wank over me . . .'

'Typical. Bastard. Like I said, you were forced.'

'No, he was wanking over me because I'd talked him into doing it. I'd caught him doing it, and I wanted to see, and when he asked me to strip off it seemed unfair not to.'

'Hmm.'

'He came all over my bum, which I admit hadn't been part of the deal, but he didn't try and rape me or anything. I'd enjoyed it, but I felt guilty and confused. I felt I ought to be punished, and I knew how, by being put over someone's knee for a hard spanking, on my bare bottom, and that just turned me on so much, like nothing before. That's where the link between sex and spanking came from.'

121

'From repression. I'm afraid I've heard lots of similar stories from women our age, mostly with religious upbringings, although none of them handled it quite the way you did.'

'Repression perhaps, but never abuse, everything I did was done willingly, with no force applied. It wasn't just old-fashioned Christian guilt: I've been an atheist since I was twelve. It was guilt though, and some of it because of how strongly my mother would have disapproved. Most of it was because the boy who made me strip was socially unpopular and my friends, especially my cousin Kate, would have been horrified if they'd known I'd been with him.'

'Peer pressure then, which is much the same.'

'Exactly, and what do all your articles on how women should look and what they should eat and what they should do exert? Peer pressure.'

She laughed, a really free, easy laugh.

'Peer pressure,' I went on. 'Guilt for not conforming, just like a slightly less than slim girl might feel after reading your last month's article on chocolate cakes. I think that's more immoral than indulging in a little spanking.'

'It sells magazines: women want to be told they should slim.'

'So Natasha Linnet tells me. Anyway, back in my teenage years, I didn't want to conform; I couldn't conform anyway, but I wanted to be punished for it, and I wanted to be punished by Kate, who was the very image of the popular, conformist girl.'

'You already knew you liked girls?'

'Nothing so clear, I just knew I wanted to be spanked by her. She thought it was funny.'

'Did she do it?'

'No, she tried to get me on the straight and narrow, but all the boys she found for me were spotty little weeds and even they preferred her. My ideal man was a sort of shambling ape who'd put me across his knee, wallop my bottom until I cried, fuck me for ages and then sit and discuss natural selection or environmental problems. What she did do was decide to make a present of my virginity to her fiancé, for my sake too, that's when I got spanked.'

'He spanked you then took your virginity? Jesus, Penny!'

'No, we got caught. My aunt spanked me, across her knee with my panties down. Afterwards I gave myself my first climax, over the spanking.'

'Which was forced on you!'

'Which I deserved! Sharing her future son-in-law, with her daughter? In her eyes it was the next thing to incest!'

'No, it wasn't her right!'

'Try telling her that! I felt it was just, too, afterwards, although I kicked and struggled a bit at the time. It's no different from paying the fine when you're caught speeding.'

'Yes it is!'

'OK, it is: getting a speeding fine doesn't make me frig off with a hairbrush handle in my pussy and my toothbrush up my bum!'

She didn't answer that, but just blew out her cheeks and slowly released her breath. I'd been truthful, but I wished I was telling Vicky's story, which left no room at all for doubt. Mine did, at least from someone else's perspective. I let Amy think for a while and wandered a little deeper into the water, which was cool on my legs with the waves washing up to the height of my knees. I was feeling a bit flustered, both from arguing and from going over my early sexual experiences. Amy was certainly doing some hard thinking herself.

123

'Look at it another way,' I went on. '*Metropolitan* is always complaining about men being so quick during sex. What was the article called, about three or four issues ago?'

'*One-Minute Wonders.*'

'That's it, and I thought it was a bit unfair. Still, on average, how long would you say it is from when a man gets his cock out to when he comes?'

'I don't know. I'm gay, Penny.'

'Oh. A girlfriend then.'

'Girls don't have cocks to get out, Penny.'

'A strap-on?'

She blushed, faintly, and I knew I'd hit a chord. For one moment I had a beautiful vision of her, in a trouser suit, but with a little fake moustache and a monstrous dildo protruding from the fly. Unfortunately the bright green jelly shoes would have completely ruined the image.

'From what the girls in the office say, ten minutes on average for a man. One minute is a bit harsh, just artistic licence. I'm sure five's not that exceptional. Using tantric techniques, an hour, two hours?'

'It would be next to impossible to fit a spanking session and sex into five minutes. Certainly I've never done it. Ten would be possible, if we were rushed. Half-an-hour might be normal, just for a panties down spanking and an orgasm each.'

'Is this with your girlfriend?'

'No, a man. Amber takes her time if she can. She likes to dress up for one thing, and make a ritual of it, maybe lecturing me while I stand with my hands on my head and my panties around my knees or something. A few Sundays back we had the whole day clear. We hadn't seen each other for a bit and badly wanted to play, so I got spanked in the morning, just across her knee in the bedroom with my nightie up. I licked her afterwards but she said I wasn't to come. Now, I could have insisted, or stopped it, but I didn't. All the rest of the morning she made me do housework in the nude, hoovering, dusting, scrubbing the kitchen floor, even cleaning the bathroom and loo. Because I'd been spanked I could see my red cheeks every time I passed a mirror, and a lot more when I was kneeling to scrub.

'By lunchtime I was so turned on that I couldn't stop shaking, but I still wasn't allowed to come. Instead I had to cook lunch, nude except for a pinny, then serve her, standing behind her while she ate. I cleared and washed up, then had my own lunch, cold, out of a dog bowl on the floor. That was too much for me and I had to come, so I used my stop word . . .'

'Stop word?'

'It's what the submissive partner says if she can't handle it or there's a problem. Red is for an immediate stop, say if we're playing with wax and a drop goes on my pussy. I generally can't take that.'

'Ow! I'm not surprised! That's dangerous, Penny.'

'Oh, you've got to know what you're doing. I won't deny that. Amber reckons anyone who wants to dominate another person ought to be trained by someone with experience, and they ought to know how it feels to be on the receiving end, too.'

'I can see that. Go on.'

'Yellow is for slow down, or in this case to bring our play to a peak. She did, and in the most wonderful way. I was on the kitchen floor, which is stone, licking my bowl clean. She came to stand in front of me and reached up under her skirt to take off her panties. They went in my mouth, balled up and pushed inside, then tied off with a piece of string to gag me. She put my face in the bowl, sideways, pulled my hands up into the small of my back and tied my wrists together. I was helpless, utterly completely helpless, stark naked, gagged and tied, totally at her mercy. I could see her, just about, standing over me. I watched as she opened a draw and took out a long wooden spoon. She beat me with it, twelve hard smacks and I couldn't even scream or struggle, just kick my feet on the ground. My bum was burning by the end, which was the joke, because she rucked her skirt up, squatted over me and just peed all over my hot, beaten bottom. She frigged me off like that, with her fingers between my thighs, my bum blazing hot and my whole body wet with her pee.'

'Jesus, that's degrading!'

'My orgasm was so powerful I blacked out for a bit. It was just before three o'clock by then, Amy. My first spanking had been before nine, so that makes roughly six hours of sex before orgasm. Six hours solid of rude, dirty, subtle sex. With her it gets as good as that maybe once every week, when we're together. We've been together five years.'

'So you love it, but it's so degrading! How can you do it?'

'Because it's ecstasy, a whole higher level over and above normal sexual pleasure. By conventional standards the sex is degrading, yes. In fact that's half the fun of it. Like I say, it's mostly in the head. When we're not having sex we're equals.'

'So she doesn't tell you what to do and things normally?'

'No.'

'I thought that's how it worked, with the stronger, dominant partner controlling the weaker.'

'No, anything but. Admittedly Amber's bigger and stronger than me, but almost everyone is. She'd never hurt me or force me against my will.'

Amy went silent and I didn't carry on, letting her think as she splashed through the shallow water. With the beach curving gently away to north and south, we could see for miles, a view spoiled only by the distant bulk of Sizewell power station. I had to offer. I'd made her think; she did like girls and the worst that could happen was for her to turn me down. Besides, all the tension and all the talk about spanking and dirty games had left me badly in need. I could only hope she was thinking how nice it would be to play with me and not that I was an incorrigible pervert.

I waited, feeling shy and rather silly, as I always do in such circumstances unless absolutely certain of the response. Amy was biting her lip, a girlish gesture well out of keeping with her businesslike poise. I told myself I'd ask her when we had gone another fifty paces and counted them, the lump in my throat growing bigger with every one.

'Do you want to?' I managed, really quietly, but not so quietly that she didn't hear.

She stopped, still biting her lip as she looked at me. For the first time I realised that her eyes were blue, a very pale, china blue, big and now slightly moist.

'You can do it to me,' I offered. 'Anything you like, any way you like, just enjoy me.'

Amy looked down at the water and shook her head, immediately giving me an awful sinking feeling.

'No,' she said, 'not that. Would you do it to me? Maybe just gently, maybe just a little?'

She was pleading and she was scared, so very, very far from the tough, immaculate career woman I'd met an hour or so before. I said nothing, but took her hand and began to lead her up the beach.

I wanted her badly, and I wanted her to enjoy it. I was desperate for her to enjoy it, so I had to be good.

As I led her I was thinking how hard it was to be in charge, how much more difficult it was for Amber than me, always having to take charge, always having to know what to do. I was wishing she could tell me, because Amy was trailing after me like a lost puppy, obviously expecting me to make all the decisions, but I had no idea how to handle it.

Not that I let my insecurity show. I led her to the ridge of the shingle bank, which stretched away to north and south, over a mile in each direction, deserted but in full view of both Dunwich and Walberswick. I could have spanked her then and there, made her show her bare bum on the beach, taking the risk someone would see. If I'd been with Amber and she'd been in one of her rare submissive moods I'd have done it, right there, making her expose herself with emptiness stretching away on all sides. It couldn't be right for Amy, though, representing an exposure surely far too blatant for a first-timer.

I only had one choice. I led her down the bank and pulled her gently down among the reeds where the shingle sloped to the river. If anybody came along the ridge of the bank we were going to get caught, but I had to do it.

'Kneel down,' I said, struggling to keep my voice firm and level, commanding without revealing my urgency.

She obeyed, facing me and putting her head to the ground, as I had been when Amber made me feed from the dog bowl. I took her by the chin and gently tilted her head up to look into her eyes. She bit her lip again, but now it seemed more expectant than uncertain.

'Good girl,' I told her. 'That's a pretty pose for you. Now, I think we had better have these showing, don't you?'

I reached under her front, finding the buttons of her blouse and tweaking them open, one, two, three and a fourth just to be sure. Taking her jacket by the scruff I pulled it back, drawing her arms up behind her. Her blouse followed, the remaining buttons keeping it tight around her middle and helping to fix her arms. She was shivering and had closed her eyes, perhaps trying to forget how exposed she was as her breasts came closer to being bared. Her bra was black, a lacy, expensive thing with full cups holding two firm little breasts. I unclipped it and tugged it up, letting them swing free and naked. She gave a little whimper as they came on show and I reached out, cupping one and running my fingers over the nipple. Her whimpering noise came again and I leaned down to kiss her for reassurance. She responded and for a moment our tongues met.

My confidence was growing as I pulled back. There had been a lot of passion in her kiss, although I could tell she was still scared. I pulled her bra over her head anyway, and knotted it across her arms, not really tight but tight enough to give her a feeling of being in restraint. She said nothing, although I couldn't imagine she was comfortable. Still, quite possible that was part of what was exciting for her.

I moved behind her, admiring the way her bottom swelled out the rear of her smart, pinstripe skirt. She was slim, but fit enough not to be scrawny, with muscular cheeks still well shaped despite the taut wool covering them. Bare breasts are exciting and vulnerable, a bare bottom more so, at least for me. I could only hope Amy felt the same.

'Right, Amy,' I told her. 'Listen carefully. I'm going to pull up your skirt and I'm going to take down your panties. You realise that, don't you?'

She nodded dumbly.

'Good,' I continued, 'it's very important for a girl to have her bottom bare during a spanking, and just because it's your first is no reason to let you off now, is it?'

She shook her head, every bit as miserable and contrite as I would have been in her position.

'Just as long as you understand why it has to be done,' I told her and took hold of the hem of her skirt.

I did it slowly, easing the skirt up her thighs and letting my eyes feast on her bare, creamy flesh as it came on view. Her legs were slim and muscular, her skin very smooth and pale, doubtless kept well pampered with expensive creams. That was nice, to have such a well-groomed, urbane woman on her knees for me as I stripped her bottom. It got better when the hem lifted high enough to show her pussy, with the lips tight in black silk and a wet patch at the centre. I paused, knowing exactly how she would feel with her skirt about to be lifted over her bottom in expectation of a spanking and letting the feeling sink in. In my head I counted to ten, then once more began to raise her skirt.

She groaned as I bared her bum, easing the hem up over her cheeks so that she could feel it rise and experience every second of her exposure. Her panties were gorgeous, silk with a panel of lace at the rear to leave her beautiful little peach of a bottom showing beneath, with the crease dark and tempting between the cheeks. They were cut quite high too, disappearing beneath the tail of her blouse but leaving a fair bit of cheek showing to either side. Like her legs the skin of her bum was smooth and pale, and once her skirt was safely up on her back I took a moment to stroke her, feeling the warm texture of her skin. She moved, lifting her bottom to bring it into even more glorious prominence.

'That is hardly a ladylike thing to do,' I chided, 'sticking your bottom up like a she-cat on heat. Still, it won't matter in a minute. One spanked brat looks much like the next. Now then, it won't do to keep you waiting: let's have those pretty panties down.'

I flicked the tail of her blouse up and took hold of her waistband. As I tugged her panties pulled a little into her crease, exaggerating the cheeks. She groaned again as I began to pull them down, a really meek, submissive sound.

'Down they come,' I announced, 'off your bottom, showing your crease, revealing everything, just like a girl who's going to be punished should. There we are, all bare. That isn't so terrible, is it? Yes, because pussy shows? I wouldn't worry about that; it's fine for girls to show their pussies nowadays. We ought to be proud of our pussies. It's the fact that your wrinkly little bumhole is showing that you ought to be ashamed of.'

She started to sob at that, so I left off, although I'd been tempted to describe her bumhole to her in some detail. It was pretty, not brown at all, but pink and very regular, tight, too, certainly virgin. I'd love to have kissed it, but it would have hardly been a dominant thing to do. Just as tempting was her pussy, pale and neat, with tiny inner lips barely showing between the outer and shaved bare save for a tiny triangle of golden fluff.

I had to touch: it was impossible not to. Using a single finger, I drew my nail slowly down her crease, lingering on her anus to make the tiny hole wink and pout before tracing an oval around her pussy. A shudder went through her as I finished my exploration with the gentlest of flicks to her clit and I found myself grinning.

'Very pretty,' I told her, 'and very wet, you little tart. Now I'm going to spank you.'

131

I slapped her bottom as I spoke, using just the tips of my fingers, and gently at that, enough only to make her flesh quiver. She gave another of her forlorn little groans in response and I set to work, slapping gently at her cheeks, each in turn, over and over, each smack just that tiny bit harder. I could really feel for her, getting her virgin spanking with her naked bottom stuck out so blatantly, and outdoors as well.

'Most girls get this in the privacy of a bedroom,' I said as the first delicate pink marks began to appear on her cheeks, 'or maybe across the back seat of a car. Some of them even get to keep their panties up, the first time or two, perhaps. Not you, though, Amy, you're in the open air and you're showing everything.'

Her bottom was going pink and she had begun to squeak. I didn't have to stop: she was tied, and had a straight choice of staying where she was or running down the beach, topless with her hands tied behind her back. I stopped anyway, leaving her panting gently and shivering in response to her punishment, a reaction that set her bottom quivering in the most delicious way.

I began to remove one of her jelly shoes. She had to know I intended to spank her with it, but as a spanking virgin she had no idea how much it was going to hurt. I intended her to find out, but not too fast, just fast enough to let her endorphins build with the pain. With her shoe off, I smacked it against my palm. She winced, her cheeks tightening and her bumhole winking at me. I repeated the action, then put it to her bottom, just hard enough to leave the imprint of the shoe showing on her lovely skin.

Once more I began to spank her, firmer now, each slap making her take a sudden, quick breath. She began to squeak again, but I ignored her, increasing the force of my blows. Her bum was firm, but not so firm that her flesh couldn't wobble and bounce once the smacks started to get serious. All of it was coloured up, both cheeks, with her crease a pale divide between. Her bumhole was winking, too, rhythmically, which happens with some girls during spanking.

She began to pant, her breath coming in great, deep gulps, and I increased the speed and force of her beating, until her bum had began to wobble seriously, the flesh never having a chance to get back in shape before the next smack hit. It was getting hard to keep my fingers off my pussy and my face out of her bottom, but I kept on, determined that she would come in front of me before I showed so much as a boob.

'You may masturbate,' I said, struggling to keep my voice even. 'Come on, get your fingers in that pretty little pussy, deep in, then to your clit and you can come for me while your bumhole winks and your fat bottom wobbles under my smacks.'

It was only then, as I told her she had a fat bottom, that what I was doing began to become revenge. Until then I had been putting everything into making her first spanking a good one, taking it slowly, trying to keep her mental state one step ahead of her pain. As her hand slid back between her thighs I knew I had won. She was going to bring herself off, and if I didn't know what was going on in her head then I could have a pretty good guess.

I had said some pretty humiliating things to her and she hadn't objected, and the last thing I'd told her was that her bottom was fat. It was a lie, but that wasn't important, when so many women are so deeply horrified by the thought of being fat, and worst of all, of having a fat bottom. A fitness fanatic and journalist could surely be no exception.

Watching her masturbate was too much for me. She had slipped two fingers into her pussy and was pulling juice out to rub on her clit, which was deliciously rude, especially with her winking bumhole and quivering, beaten cheeks. I kept going, slapping hard even though my arm had started to ache, but I also adjusted position, spreading my knees and reaching in under my dress. I was soaking, hardly surprisingly, and quickly had two fingers inside myself and my thumb on my clit.

Amy started to come, and as I saw the muscles of her vulva squeeze and heard her cry of ecstasy I brought the shoe down on her bottom with all my force. She yelled and bucked, but kept frigging, screaming for me to beat her harder, to hurt her and punish her. I obliged, giving her other bumcheek the same treatment, then again, spanking her furiously in a frenzy of ecstasy and revenge as her sex spread and tightened over and over on her fingers.

I stopped as she slumped to the ground, but I wasn't finished with her. Finishing her off with a final hard salvo to her crimson bottom, I moved to reach for her head. My hand caught her neck and I pulled her around, pushing her face in under my dress, right on to the soaking gusset of my panties. Reaching in, I wrenched them to the side, forcing her head to my pussy. She began to lick at once, lapping up my juice in abandoned, beaten submission, tonguing me with her reddened buttocks stuck high and naked, her swollen, soaking pussy and tight pink bumhole showing to the sky, puffy and moist with her excitement.

My thighs clamped on her head and I was coming, slipping into a glorious climax as her tongue flicked over and over on my clit. She was good, doubtless better for her beating, and I couldn't hold my pose, but slumped back to the ground, spreading my legs to her as the sky spun over my head and I cried out in pure, perfect pleasure.

Amy McRae and I walked back along the beach arm in arm. She was still asking me questions, but they were different now, and a lot more understanding. I promised to keep what had happened between us secret, although Amber was at Walberswick and knows a spanked girl when she sees one.

Her virgin spanking had lasted somewhat over half an hour. After what I'd said it had had to, and I'd been checking my watch throughout. As is often the case with someone after a new and intense sexual experience, she was keen to justify her actions to herself, and to have me support her. Not that she needed much help, finding a dozen reasons why it was acceptable in no time at all.

I had been partially right about what had been going on in her head, but not entirely. She had decided beforehand that she would let me do it to her if I asked. Not bare, though, that had come because she fancied me and from my own obvious enthusiasm for being punished. She hadn't expected to enjoy it either, but for the experience to confirm her beliefs and leave her in an unassailable position to argue from. Once she had tried it and hated it nobody could have said she didn't understand. She had still been doubtful, even after I'd taken her panties down, and I'd nearly overdone it with my humiliating remarks.

Only once her bum was warm had she really given in to her arousal, and I'd really hit the nail on the head when I'd said she had a fat bottom. With her boobs out and her bum on show as she underwent punishment, it had been the final straw. As she came she had been thinking of how awful it would be to be force fed until her bottom really was big and fat and wobbly, then spanked for getting that way, adding injustice to her distress over her ballooning figure.

That was a new one on me, although for a weight-obsessed fitness fanatic I could see the power of it. What it did mean was that I had to admit that taking punishment could, at least sometimes, be a way of overcoming fears or past tribulations. After all, her worst nightmare was suffering mockery for being overweight, and that was exactly what she had come over, and to deny her the right to her own feelings would have been in total contradiction to my own argument.

We thrashed it out as we walked back down the beach, once more along the water's edge. I had to admit that a lot of my fantasies involved being punished or degraded for things that would have been totally unacceptable in normal life, especially having my ability to control myself taken away. She asked if maintaining an exact control was a normal part of my life, and I admitted I was a scientist. This fitted her rapidly evolving theory, but I had to point out that girls exist who enjoy spanking largely for the physical aspect.

By the time we reached Amber I was completely confident that Amy was genuine. She was being too open to be anything else, and I was sure her request for secrecy had been genuine, if only because she had been blushing so hard when she made it that the cheeks of her face were nearly as red as the cheeks of her bottom. I couldn't see it as a set-up in any case. After all, dedication is one thing, but what editor is going to give her camera team a full spread of her bare pussy and red bumcheeks for the sake of a scoop?

Amber was sitting on the little breakwater at the mouth of the Blyth, which meant she could see the whole of the beach, to well beyond where Amy and I had nipped behind the dunes. She greeted me with a knowing smile, which set Amy blushing again, but we were soon chatting intimately between the three of us.

We ate at one of the pubs, a lobster and salad washed down with Gewurztraminer, which was delicious and all the more so for being on Amy's expense account. I was feeling distinctly cheeky by the end, and couldn't resist ordering a large slice of sticky chocolate cake smothered in cream.

Amy asked how I dared to eat like that, which brought the conversation round to pony-girl play, which she had never heard of. Amber began to explain, first the basic pony-girl fantasy, then about piggy-girls, puppy-girls, vixen-hunting, tack, whips, dressage, everything, talking until long after dark with Amy soaking it all up in baffled amazement.

By the time we got back to the car it was the only one there, with the dunes a black line against the stars and only distant street-lights to show the way. It was lonely, but there was just that slightest risk we could be seen from the village, if not in detail. I was tipsy and thoroughly pleased with myself, so I asked for a spanking and got it, bent across the bonnet of the car with my dress high and my panties down, from both of them, slapping my cheeks in turn to bring the day to a perfect conclusion.

Seven

It was going to be just under two months before the article was published. Amy was going to write it herself, and make it the main feature of the issue, all of which was immensely satisfying. I was absolutely triumphant. The best I had possibly expected to achieve was to make her accept that my viewpoint was valid. To have converted her was better by far, especially in view of the pleasure of dishing out her virgin spanking.

The only pity was that, with so little time before my return to the university, I had very little chance to enjoy my new-found playmate. She had no regular girlfriend, and was keen to explore, coming up for an afternoon and dinner. We introduced her to the pleasures of pony-girl play, first with me in harness and then herself. She enjoyed it, as I had been sure she would, with the blend of sex and sport having a strong appeal to athletic girls, especially when, like Amy, they had once owned a pony. She liked the harness as well, and was impressed by Amber's ingenuity and skill, both at making things for keeping girls in restraint and at inventing erotic games.

We spanked her after dinner, naked over the end of the table, which is set up so the victim can see both her face and bottom while she is punished. I could remember my own first experience in the same place, and the strength of feeling as I watched my bottom stripped and the way my pussy juiced as I was beaten. I'd been caned too, and we did the same to Amy, warming her well first and soothing her in between strokes to calm her down. She took six, despite having been genuinely scared at first, ending up excited enough to use a candle in her pussy in front of us. The night was spent in each other's arms after Amber and I had come together while Amy spanked us, an experience made all the more intimate by our hot bottoms.

Two days later I was back in the north, missing Amber and my other friends as ever, but with an added nostalgia and an undeniable sense of dissatisfaction. This came from events with Beth. True, she would read Amy's article when it came out and doubtless have her eyes opened somewhat, but I had still failed, either to get her to punish me or to tie me up.

When I had first moved north I'd been pretty lonely, a long way from Amber and with nobody who knew about my sexuality, let alone understood it. I had managed to get involved in a particularly lewd affair with a janitor, Colin, but that had been based purely on our compatibility when it came to rough, dirty sex. In any case, he'd been sacked for installing a miniature camera in the female students' lavatory, which had left me with mixed feelings of relief and regret.

Two years later I'd become involved with a group of female students who had formed a coven. It had been fun, with some deeply intense sexual experiences, but at the end of the day their beliefs were complete mumbo-jumbo and I'd found it impossible to fit in. All of them had either left or were now third-years and busy with their approaching finals, and so it had fallen apart. Ella, who had introduced me to them, was in the department, so I saw her occasionally, but that was all.

More lately there had been Wendy, who had been with me in Brittany to set up the previous summer's field course. We had ended up in bed, and she had proved no innocent. She and I had continued our intimacy, which was just as well as she had managed to secure a junior lectureship and now worked in the department. That at least meant I had someone to talk to and an occasional playmate, and if her tastes were rather different from mine there was enough overlap for us to have fun together.

Amber rang me a week after the start of term to say that there had been a development. Amy was having a little difficulty getting her idea of what should now be in the article on corporal punishment accepted. Being pretty strong-willed and the editor, she had managed to get the majority of her colleagues to agree with her or at least accept her viewpoint. An exception to this was Isabel, who, although she was freelance and had no direct say in the matter, was also the niece of a director on the board of the company that owned *Metropolitan*.

Isabel was apparently questioning the authenticity of the piece, not suggesting that Amy had made it up, but that I might be a fake. I could see the logic behind the argument, as could Amy, although she assured us of her trust. If *Metropolitan* published a piece with anything less than a damning condemnation of the whole subject, erotic spanking included, and they turned out to have been set up, it would be pretty embarrassing. The upshot was that Isabel's uncle, Sir Rhys Mintower, wanted to meet me, ostensibly to confirm that I was genuine.

It sounded to me more likely that Mintower was a dirty old man with entirely different motives for wanting to meet a woman who liked her bottom smacked. Amber agreed, and suggested I meet up with him but be careful. She defined careful as not letting him do anything Henry Gresham or Percy Ottershaw wouldn't. This was not what worried me, but that it would be difficult to convince Mintower of my sincerity without risking my professional position. Yet if I refused it would risk damaging Amy, as a degree of her credibility had come to rest on me. Mintower was hardly going to accept my word for it if I insisted on anonymity.

After a minute of cursing myself for getting into such an awkward situation I decided that I had been right to contact Amy. There comes a point when one has to take a stand, but I had no intention of taking it publicly. Instead I needed somebody to introduce me to Mintower, somebody he trusted to tell the truth and who knew me well enough to be relied on.

My first thought was Anderson, whose father had been an important city figure of the same generation as Mintower. I drew a blank, but he pointed out that during Percy's career as a wine merchant before taking up journalism he might well have supplied Mintower. Again I drew a blank. Henry was my next thought, although it was a long shot. He had bred horses, and it was just possible Mintower shared his interest. Sadly Mintower had no such hobby and Henry had never even heard of him. On my fourth telephone call I struck lucky, although it wasn't the word I used when I replaced the receiver.

Morris Rathwell knew Mintower. Not well, but well enough for my purposes. Both were directors in some obscure holding company, based on some almost equally obscure Caribbean island, so I could guess what it was for. They met once a year at board meetings, but Rathwell felt certain Mintower would accept his word. What was required of me in return for this favour was made very clear, in fact so clear that it had the colour rising to my cheeks.

It is true that Rathwell exerts a sort of horrid fascination for me. He is so crude, so direct. His favourite thing is to take a girl's virginity, better still, her anal virginity. Next to that he likes to add conquests to his list, and again he took a particular pleasure if the encounter included buggery. He had spanked me, and a few other things, and I had sucked his cock, but by and large Amber had kept us firmly apart. Now he wanted me properly, pussy and bumhole, and he was not going to compromise. The worst of it was that he was so appallingly arrogant that he would think I'd been angling for it all along and just needed an excuse to let myself go.

I could just imagine it. It wasn't likely to be in my flat: that would be too cosy, too secure for me. More probably he'd do it in the back of his great vulgar car, with me bent over the back seat as his long, skinny cock was worked slowly up my bumhole. That would be after the fucking, which would probably be done on my back so that I got my bumhole greasy with my own juice. Harmony had told me that detail, of how he liked to bugger a girl in her own lubrication.

Undoubtedly he would come up my bottom, or worse, pull it out and finish off in my mouth. Only when he'd had his fill would I be spanked and allowed to come myself, probably with a carrot or something in my bumhole to remind me of what had just been done to me. More likely than not he would bring the twins, so not only would I get watched as I was sodomised but I'd be obliged to do whatever they wanted. After what Mel had said the last time I wasn't sure if she was any better than her husband. I thought about it for a bit, but in the end I picked up the phone and called him back.

I always like to try and understand other people's viewpoints, whether or not I agree with them. Certainly I could see Rathwell's. He was a busy man, giving up time to do a girl a favour that would gain him nothing more than her gratitude. All he wanted to do was be sure of that gratitude by making certain it was delivered in concrete terms, specifically, his penis up my bottom. The fact that social conventions make it utterly outrageous to suggest to a woman that she submits to buggery in return for a favour was neither here nor there. Not that Morris Rathwell ever cared for social conventions. What his family must have thought of him marrying a black girl from the East End and then living in a *ménage à trois* with her and her twin sister I could only imagine.

So I was going to get it, that very weekend. To be fair, he could have made me go all the way to London, but he decided to come north and I was instructed to meet him at a cottage to the south and east of the city. This was obviously hired for the weekend, and he had chosen well. It was at the bottom of a little valley, wooded on both sides with a long track down to the buildings, the cottage, a garage and a jumble of sheds. They welcomed me at the door, all three of them.

I greeted them happily, actually feeling quite reckless about it all, probably because my adrenalin was up. They showed me inside, Rathwell giving my bottom a proprietary squeeze as I went through the door. The interior was cosy, twee even, with lots of polished wood and chintz décor. It had obviously been a barn before, as the roof beams were blackened with age and riddled with nail holes, which showed despite a heavy layer of varnish.

They didn't rush things, but sat me down to a hearty dinner with plenty of wine and Cognac to follow. By the end I was feeling pretty mellow, with only a mild knot in the pit of my stomach at what was coming. The buggery wasn't the problem: I'd always known he would get me in the end. More alarming was the system of ropes that I'd glimpsed as I came in.

I was expecting him to want to humiliate me, perhaps making me dress as a schoolgirl or a cheer-leader, but I hadn't really counted on being strung up from the ceiling, nor on what Harmony brought in to the kitchen area. As I saw it I realised that they intended to completely destroy my dignity, and that they had probably spent hours deciding how best to do it. Rathwell loves that, making a girl feel as ridiculous as possible while she is punished, and as long as it is presented in a sexual way, no piece of imagery seems too extreme for him.

Schoolgirl uniform and maid's outfits are the least of it. Both imply innocence and a low social status, even if the concept is a bit out of date. A Girl Guide's uniform is much the same, perhaps stronger still. When I'd told Beth that Mark had made me dress as a Girl Guide it was Rathwell who had given me the idea. He had made a girl do it at one of his parties, a little green uniform, green tights, the lot, even green knickers. She had been spanked with it all disarranged to leave her bare bum showing in the middle, which had left me feeling sorry for her and jealous at the same time.

Every person is different, and every submissive girl has her vulnerability when it comes to clothes. The image must be meaningful, and as downgrading as possible, but still look cute. That way she can feel humiliated and sexy at the same time. A very serious girl, say an accountant in real life, might be most effectively dealt with in a clown's costume, perhaps with the seat and front cut away to leave her bottom and breasts showing. The converse of this is to punish a girl in an outfit she normally wears in a context of which she is rightfully proud. Thus a barrister might be beaten in her wig and gown, with her smart suit beneath. Expose her bum and boobs and whack her like that, and she will get a far stronger experience than she would taking the same punishment naked.

Morris Rathwell knows all this and often puts it to good use, so I had expected something chosen to suit me. A lab coat was possible, if perhaps over simple. Full academic dress would have been great, but I doubted he knew what I was technically entitled to in the way of fancy gowns and mortarboards. A comic witch's outfit would have been a humiliating and ludicrous parody of my work, or a Salvation Army uniform if he'd wanted to play on my atheism. He chose none of these, but something that demonstrated a refined cruelty and an alarming amount of knowledge about me.

At first I thought it was just a white dress, a typical piece of innocence imagery but no more than that. Only when Rathwell held it up did I realise what he had done. It was a confirmation dress, and not any old confirmation dress, but one with the badge of my old school sewn to the bodice. Pure white, frilly, flared and knee length, it would alone have been enough to send the blood to my cheeks. There was more too. A little white trainer bra, white sandals, white knee socks, white petticoats and a pair of absurdly frilly panties with elasticated leg holes.

How Rathwell had discovered the agonies I had gone through to stop myself being confirmed at school I had no idea. Confirmation had been absolutely standard at my school, something everybody just did. One or two of the most rebellious boys could always be counted on to resist, but they all gave in at the end. Not me: I'd been sixteen and a secret yet militant atheist, for all my normally meek character. I'd refused, and fought off pressure from my peers, from the school authorities, from the chaplain. My mother had thought I was being silly, pointing out that if I didn't believe in it then it didn't matter anyway. Finally my tantrums had roused my father from his perennial daydream and with his help I had escaped.

The memories of my bitter tears as I'd shouted at the headmistress and the chaplain down in her study came flooding back as Rathwell showed me the dress, turning it from side to side so that I could fully appreciate the puffed sleeves and the big white bow at the back. It was symbolic, there was no denying that. Refusing to wear one had been a crucial element of my victory. I felt a lump rise in my throat at the prospect of doing so now. Rathwell waited, gloating over my rising humiliation, then threw it over the back of a chair.

'How . . . how did you know?' I managed as it was pointless to pretend I wasn't affected.

'Easily enough,' he answered, 'a phone call to your old university saying I was a prospective employer who needed to check your references as your school exam results seemed improbably good. A visit to your school, a jolly chat with the chaplain, a little logical deduction. Easy, for a man like me.'

'Bastard!'

'Now, now, Penny, we mustn't have any tantrums, must we? Come on, off with your clothes now, let's have that pretty little body bare.'

I began to undress, struggling not to betray my feelings more than I already had. Stripping still gets to me, whatever I do, and my agitation rose even more as I removed shoes, socks, shirt and jeans. The underwear was worse, with the three of them, all fully dressed, watching in unabashed fascination as I unclipped my bra and let it fall from my breasts. My panties followed, pushed quickly down, dropped to the floor and kicked off to lie close to Rathwell's shoe in a tiny, pathetic puddle of white cotton.

Harmony gestured to me and I followed her from the room, leaving the Rathwells to sip their expensive brandy. She went to the bathroom, which seemed brand new, with sparkling tiles in pastel colours. Somehow that made it worse, the very cleanliness of the place enhancing the dirtiness of what we were doing, with the gloves, syringe and blood bags laid out on the sink making an obscene contrast with the primrose pattern on the china.

I had quickly guessed their significance. In keeping with Rathwell's tastes and the confirmation dress, I was to be a virgin. Leaving me to contemplate my fate, Harmony began to undress, stripping casually to her underwear as I watched. Facially, and in general build, she was so like her twin sister that they could easily be mistaken for one another. Not by anybody who knew them though. Harmony had a little less muscle tone, but only that, yet she lacked all but a shade of the air of dangerous power that never left Mel. She was still a lot bigger than me, and having been put across her knee I knew that her softness was purely comparative.

Her underwear was bright yellow and frilly, very girlish and a pretty contrast to her dark skin. Not that I had long to admire it, because she quickly covered herself, pulling on a nurse's uniform, starched, white and very proper.

'A little bird tells me you've been getting off on medical fantasies,' she said as she pulled on a rubber

glove and let the rim snap against her arm in true
style.

'Not really,' I said. 'I was examined by a police
doctor, that's all.'

'And you didn't frig off over it afterwards?'

'Not all the way. Who told you? Vicky?'

'Anderson. I ran into him in Victoria Street. He
gave me lunch.'

'And you sucked him off in return, no doubt.'

'Is that a wise thing to say to your nurse just before
she takes a sample?'

I shook my head. She had both gloves on and had
picked up the syringe, a five-cc sterile unit I was glad
to see.

'Arm please, Penny darling,' Harmony said. 'Come
to nursie.'

I ignored her, briefly, stepping back into the
kitchen to pinch some of Rathwell's Cognac to act as
a disinfectant. He wasn't there, nor Melody, but I
could hear them in the bedroom. After dabbing my
arm with spirit I held it out to Harmony, finding it a
lot harder to be brave than if I had been at a real
surgery. She took my arm and put the needle to it,
pressing my flesh down, pushing abruptly forward. I
winced at the sudden sharp pain and she smiled,
adjusted her grip and began to pull back the plunger.
My blood filled the syringe, right up to the five-cc
mark.

'Good girl,' she said as the needle slid from my
arm. 'Now, how about a wash while I get this ready?'

'Why the medical bit, anyway?' I asked, trying to
be bold as I stepped into the shower. 'Wouldn't a
schoolmistress be more appropriate?'

'That's Morris's kick,' she answered. 'You know
what he's like about virgins. This is for me. Did you
know I was a student nurse when I met Morris?'

'No. Not Mel too, surely?'

'You know what Mel did. I was the shy one, but when men in the wards used to goose me and make rude remarks I always used to think of getting my revenge by making them lick me. I never did, but that's what you're going to do.'

'Yummy.'

'Hurry up then, slut.'

I washed as quickly as I could, still apprehensive, but less so with the prospect of licking Harmony's pussy before getting into the awful dress. With luck it would turn me on enough to make my sexual feelings conquer my memories.

'Of course you need to be nice and bald if you're to be a virgin,' she went on as I stepped out of the shower. 'Morris likes that.'

'Bald?'

'Your pussy, silly. It might be fun to shave your head, but tonight he'd rather you had long hair.'

'I had long hair at school. Right up until university in fact.'

'We know. We've seen the photo. Now come on, up with your arms.'

She dried me, using firm, brisk motions, then put a little powder under my boobs and arms before telling me to lie down on the rubber bath mat and roll myself up. I obeyed, lying on my back and taking hold of my ankles to leave my pussy spread and my naked bum showing in every detail. If anything the position is more exposed than being bent over, and I could see her as she took a razor and ran the hot water into the sink.

I'm naturally very hairy, with a thick bush of black pubes and a lot between my bumcheeks. Standing, my pussy lips don't show at all, and I like to think I still look neat even in the rudest possible position,

albeit rather hairy, while my bumhole shows as a
pinkish brown wrinkle in a nest of fur. That was the
view I was presenting to Harmony, legs rolled high,
everything showing in detail as she took a can of
spray foam and began to squirt me between my legs.
In an instant my whole pubic area was a mass of
foam, which she rubbed up to a lather, almost
bringing me off in the process.

The shaving was quick and efficient, my hair
scraped away with little flicks of the razor. Occasionally she would adjust one of my legs to get at a
tricky bit, or squeeze my flesh to flatten a curve. It
was incredibly intimate and was turning me on more
and more, until I was wondering if I didn't dare take
an orgasm with her before going to the others. Better
still, I could string out what I was doing with
Harmony to delay the moment Morris's cock went up
my bottom.

Eventually I was done, shaved bald from belly to
bumhole and feeling deliciously naked for it. My
pussy was swollen and juicy, and as Harmony washed
my shaved skin, creamed me and powered me I was
getting more and more eager.

'Sit on my face,' I urged as she tidied up the
shaving apparatus. 'You can pee on me if you like.'

'You'd love that, wouldn't you? Unfortunately
we'd be keeping Morris waiting and I'd be lucky to get
away with a caning. Come on, girl, up on your knees.'

I kneeled up, and as she turned she took me by the
hair. Standing with her front to my face she pulled up
her uniform skirt, pushing my face against the crotch
of her panties. I reached up underneath to tug them
aside, breathing in the rich, female scent of her sex.
As my lips found her pussy I tried to get her fantasy
into my head, determined to be as excited as possible
by the time Rathwell got to me.

Not that it was hard. I could barely see, but I had her scent in my nose and I could feel my own body, naked and shaved at her feet as she stood over me in her uniform, covered and in control, not even deigning to show off the pussy I was being made to lick. It was a lovely image, the cool, dominant nurse standing over the quivering, nude girl whose pussy she has just shaved, using her authority to get her sex licked.

Harmony's clit was bobbing under my tongue and her grip was growing tighter in my hair. She had begun to moan and I knew she was coming. Pursing my lips, I sucked her clit suddenly into my mouth and bit, ever so gently. She screamed and her knees buckled as I suckled at her clitoris, showing no mercy as the hard little bud popped in and out of my lips. It was cruel, but fun, giving her a brilliant orgasm and ensuring that I kept her in the right mood for the rest of the evening.

She called me a bitch as she pulled away and slapped my face, but not hard, and she was grinning as she tidied herself up. I stayed down, knowing what was next. Harmony picked up the two tiny blood bags she had made while I was in the shower. Each was a little dark ball, similar in size and colour to a dark cherry. I lay back on the mat, spreading my thighs in mute resignation to Rathwell's perversity. Making me a fake virgin was typical of him. So was using my own blood, a subtle touch that was not lost on me.

'Spread for nursie,' Harmony instructed and I caught my legs up, pulling them as high and wide as they would go.

Taking the blood bags and a can of liquid skin, she kneeled, easing one into the mouth of my pussy. I felt it go in, then the cold shock as the aerosol sprayed out over my freshly shaved skin. I held absolutely still, allowing the film to dry, feeling a mixture of emotions at my restored virginity, shame, helpless arousal and an odd and totally irrational pride. I expected that the second blood bag was a spare.

'Walk carefully,' Harmony instructed me and offered a hand to help me rise.

We left the bathroom, finding the confirmation dress where we had left it, along with the various accessories. Putting it on was hard, an essay in self-humiliation, and I had to keep reminding myself that when all was said and done it was a game, no more. It didn't feel like one, and an awful sense of defeat had started to well up inside me even before I'd begun to dress. I started with the trainer bra, which was the right size around my back but had AA cups which left my B-size boobs flattened and spilling out around the edges. That was bad, but the frilly panties were worse: long, but absurdly tight, pulled hard between my pussy lips, showing every contour of my bottom at the back and the elastic tight around my thighs to make my flesh rise and bulge. Plain they'd have been awful, but with the frilly leg holes and the great puff of lace at the rear I felt utterly ridiculous. The socks and shoes were less bad, their virgin whiteness and girly design their sole drawback. The petticoats, for all their frills, were actually a relief as they hid my ludicrous panties, even if I knew full well it would be only temporarily. The dress was the worst, with all the personal emotions that went with wearing it. At the end I looked like a fairy from a particularly vulgar greetings card and Harmony was laughing out loud.

In the bedroom Rathwell was standing over his wife, dressed as a vicar, and so well disguised that he could have been in a cathedral without raising an eyebrow, except that Melody had her top open, sitting in front of him with his erect cock between her plump breasts.

'How sweet,' he announced as I came in. 'Well, I'm ready: let's string her up and thrash her. Cover up, Mel.'

Harmony reached for the tangle of ropes that hung from the central beam. I held out my arms and she took them, laying one wrist across the other. Melody scooped her breasts back into her bra and buttoned up her blouse as her sister tied my hands, making herself look respectable if not exactly innocent. Harmony pulled my rope up, raising my wrists to the level of the beam and tying it off to leave me on tiptoe and completely unable to defend myself.

'Right,' Rathwell said as he started to stroke his cock, 'let us imagine that rather than listen to your little tantrum, the good Reverend Allen had lost patience with you and decided you needed a lesson. He has brought you out here, made you dress properly and now intends to beat some sense into you, obliging you to accept his will. Of course, once you've been broken he may well be unable to restrain the lust engendered by the sight of your virgin buttocks squirming as you're thrashed. More than likely he'll want his cock up that pretty cunt. He may even want to bugger you, popping your little rosebud arsehole as you beg for mercy.'

'You can't make me!' I spat.

'Good girl,' he answered. 'I do like a girl who can play, even when she knows it's got to go my way.'

'Fuck off.'

'What sort of language is that for a schoolgirl? You need your beating more than I thought. Still, it would be a pity to spoil that pretty dress. I think we had better do it across the seat of your knickers.'

Harmony pulled up my dress, lifting the knee-length white skirt to my waist as Rathwell watched and nursed his erection. Melody had stood up and was rummaging among their luggage, from which she brought a long, dark-brown cane, thin, but knotted at intervals. Rathwell took it as the hem of my dress was tucked up into the small of my back, beneath the big bow. As my petticoats followed I began to imagine how it would have felt if they'd really done it. Awful, I was sure, although I couldn't see the real Reverend Allen buggering me, or at least not in front of the school nurse and a mistress. With my absurd panties on show Harmony stepped away and Rathwell took the cane from Melody.

'Fine malacca,' he said, 'normally used to thrash malefactors in Singapore, so perhaps a little hard for an English schoolgirl bottom. Still, we shall just have to manage, shan't we?'

I was looking back over my shoulder, watching him heft the cane and clenching my buttocks in terrified anticipation. No cane hurts more, except possibly whalebone, as I knew from bitter experience. He gave me a stern smile, reached out, tapped it across my bottom, all the while tugging at his cock. I winced and shut my eyes, expecting the agony of a cane cut at any second. Nothing happened.

'This is your first chance to surrender,' he said. 'Give in now and you will escape your beating. Sadly you will not be able to escape with your modesty, because the sight of your pert little bottom so nicely exhibited has aroused me past resistance. I intend to fuck you.'

'Fuck off.'

'Mind your language. Very well, if you want to, play it the hard way.'

An instant later my bottom exploded in pain. He'd taken me unawares, bringing the cane back while we were talking and striking to leave me squealing in shock and dancing on my toes. I heard a purr of appreciation from one of the girls as I managed to control myself and stand again, trembling but ready.

Again the cane cut down, harder still, and right over the first stroke. Someone laughed as I did my little dance, and I thought how absurd my bottom must look, wobbling inside my knickers with the frills bouncing. The tears were beginning to start in my eyes, as I'd known they would.

It was impossible to keep the fantasy Rathwell had planted out of my head. I was strung from a beam and I was being beaten by a man with an erection he intended to put up my bottom, but that was nothing compared to being in my confirmation dress. Balanced on my little white shoes, with all the flounces and frills of the dress bobbing to my movements and the back turned up to show my absurd knickerbockers, in my head I was being beaten for wilful disobedience.

Sometimes I don't cry at all. Sometimes I start near the end of my beating. This time the first heavy drops began to roll from my eyes as the cane was tapped against my bottom for the third stroke. Both eyes were heavy with tears, and as the cane smacked down the shock broke them, spattering tiny droplets across my face.

I let it go, starting to snivel and whimper, only for my self-pity to be crudely interrupted by the fourth, fifth and sixth strokes, delivered in quick succession. That really had me jumping, kicking my legs about and hopping up and down on my toes as I wiggled my bottom in a frantic effort to dull the pain. I was struggling to catch my breath too, taking in great ragged gasps of air and choking on the mucus in my throat.

When I finally managed to regain control of myself they took down my knickers. Melody did it, taking hold of the sides and tugging them down as if it was totally unimportant whether they stayed up or not. That was too much for me, just the awful, casual way my bum had been stripped. I thought of how I looked, hanging there in my white dress, tails turned high and silly knickers pulled down, little bare bottom showing and marked with six red welts from the cane. At that I began to blubber openly, sobbing hard and choking on the lump in my throat as I waited for the punishment to go on.

'Don't be such a baby!' Melody called.

'She knows how to stop it,' Rathwell answered.

They beat me like that, crying and snivelling in my bonds with my bottom dancing to the cuts in a border of white frills. I'd soon become dizzy with pain and reaction, hanging limp in the ropes and jerking to the cane-strokes as they came in. My face was wet with tears, my nose running and dribble coming from the edges of my mouth. I know I farted several times, each one bringing a new stab of shame and a chuckle from Rathwell.

I lost count after twelve strokes, but I know I took forty-one when they finally decided that if I took any more I'd start to bleed, they told me. My whole bottom was burning, an overwhelming, throbbing pain that had gone straight to my sex, leaving pussy juice wet between my thighs and in my knickers. They photographed me like that, and promised to send a print, but I was too far gone to care.

The rope was loosened, allowing me to collapse on the bed, utterly limp and gasping for breath. Rathwell turned me over on to my back and pulled my ankles up, leaving my pussy open to his cock, only not open, but blocked by my artificial cherry. I felt his cock touch my flesh, bumping on my clit to make me sigh and tense my legs. The pressure came against my cherry, a stab of pain as the skin broke and a popping noise. The blood dribbled down between my bum-cheeks, warm and wet and sticky from my burst cherry, trickling down over my bum and on to my dress.

It was Rathwell's cock sliding up my pussy as he pushed, but I was thinking of the Reverend Allen, rolling me up in my confirmation dress, my panties around my thighs, my pussy spread and entered, my virginity taken as my blood soiled my dress to mark me as fucked.

He let go of my ankles, leaving my legs kicked high and resting on his shoulders. My bodice was torn open; my little boobs popped out of my trainer bra, all the while with his cock moving in my pussy, fucking me with slow, easy strokes to keep himself hard inside me.

I'd have masturbated if my hands hadn't been tied above my head, put my fingers to my pussy and rubbed off in front of them, coming in a welter of shame and the overwhelming feeling of being used so cruelly and so casually. It was impossible. All I could do was lie there and let him enjoy my body, humping away as he felt my boobs and the others watched, Harmony holding the rope to make sure I stayed under control.

He can't have taken more than a few minutes in my pussy, but it seemed like an eternity. Then he was out and I was being rolled over for the climax of the evening and my final degradation, buggery. My legs were taken and pushed up underneath me, forcing me to raise my bum and stick it out over the edge of the bed. The rope was pulled and twisted off on the door handle, stretching my arms out in front of me to leave my face and breasts pressed to the bed cover. My knees were pushed apart, spreading my thighs until the lowered knickerbockers were stretched taut between them. The dress had fallen as I turned, but he lifted it again, exposing my bare, beaten bum, the wet, bloody hole of my pussy and my tight, pink anus.

I know how I look bent like that, and I could imagine the spick pink skin of my shaved sex and bottom crease, my purple, well-beaten bottom in a froth of lace and my gaping, recently fucked pussy. My crease was wet with juice and blood, into which his cock slid as he laid it between my cheeks.

For a while he stayed like that, rubbing gently between my bumcheeks, his balls slapping my pussy to make my clit twinge in response. His knuckles touched me, down between my cheeks and he began to slide his knob down my crease, rubbing it in the slick flesh. It touched my hole, and he groaned in pleasure at the sight before pushing again.

I couldn't hold back a grunt as my anal ring stretched, gave and filled with cock. The head had popped in, leaving my sphincter to close on the neck before he began to slowly, rhythmically force his way up my back passage. With each push he pulled back, taking me a bit at a time, just as a girl's anal virginity should be taken, or indeed how any considerate person would bugger a girl. His hands were on my bum, spreading the cheeks to let him watch his cock go in and pressing down on my cane bruises. I made a fuss, whining and groaning as he filled my rectum with hard cock-meat and letting out a long, defeated moan as his balls nudged my pussy and his front touched my beaten buttocks.

He began to bugger me, slowly, easing his erection in and out to make my ring evert and push in, over and over until I was moaning, then panting with the breathless ecstasy of it, utterly surrendered and thoroughly enjoying the prick up my bum. Had I been able I would have masturbated, treating myself, and him, to the feel of my ring pulsing on his cock as I came and with luck sucking his sperm into my guts. Tied, I could do nothing, only take it and suffer the twinges of near climactic bliss each time the hair of his balls touched my clit.

I thought he would come up my bottom, enjoying the view and the warm, sticky embrace of my back passage. The last few, hard shoves always hurt a little, although it can be perfect if I'm coming too, and I was expecting them, then perhaps to be made to beg for my own orgasm. He was still the Reverend Allen in my mind, buggering me in my little confirmation dress, and I wanted to finish off that way, coming over the consummate humiliation of the experience.

When he started to pull his cock from my bumhole I was surprised, but as Harmony began to pull back on the rope I knew he had one, final degradation for me. My arms were pulled back, over my head as far as they would go, forcing me to lift my body. My boobs came off the bed to swing free of my trainer bra at the same moment his cock popped out of my anus. I felt the wet, sticky sensation of fluid running down over my bumhole as it closed with a lewd bubbling sound and my head was up.

Quick paces took him around the bed, holding his erection out. I was going to take it in my mouth, the cock that had just been up my bottom, and I couldn't stop myself. The girls were watching, eyes wide in breathless pleasure as I opened my mouth. He pushed his penis forward, not forcing me but making me take the decision myself. I tried to hold back, but my sense of dignity was completely gone and with a last, miserable whimper I lowered my mouth on to his erection and began to suck it.

I could taste myself, rich and female against the male taste of his penis. Kneeling, whipped and buggered with my anus and pussy dribbling goo, I sucked, revelling in his cock and the pain in my bottom, even in my arms. A hand found my pussy, firm, skilled fingers entering the hole and starting on my clit. My hair was taken, hard, controlling my head as he began to fuck my mouth.

They held me like that, masturbating me as I sucked cock. I was in an ecstasy of submission, grateful for every detail of my ordeal, but in my mind I wasn't there but back at school. I was in the headmistress's study, tied up, beaten into submission and then buggered by Reverend Allen, made to suck his dirty cock while the nurse took pity and masturbated my hairless pussy from behind.

I heard a grunt and the cock in my mouth was pushed deep, jamming into my windpipe. It jerked and hot sperm hit the back of my throat. Then I was coming myself, sucking his penis with desperate, depraved need, my back arching and every muscle in my body locking. More sperm erupted in my mouth, right down my throat and suddenly I was gagging, choking on spunk as I came. He pulled back but too late, leaving me coughing and spluttering, my chest heaving uncontrollably as I fought for breath with my orgasm still burning in my head. Bubbles of sperm were coming out of my nose, more from my mouth, spraying out to spatter him with the filthy mess. My senses went black, but the last thought in my head before it all slipped away was that the bastard hadn't broken me.

Eight

My bottom was purple. I was walking bow-legged,
too, but at the end of the day I found it impossible to
regret what I'd done or even to resent Rathwell. It
had just been so intense and, after all, I had given my
consent and they had looked after me when it was all
over.

I'd needed it, too, and that is why nobody without
the sort of skill and experience the Rathwells have
should ever get into anything so heavy. When I'd
come around I'd been on the bed, propped up as
Harmony tended to me. I'd heard the worry in
Rathwell's voice and Harmony telling him it wasn't
as bad as it looked, and then I'd opened my eyes.

The evening had finished with sipping Cognac
and talking as perfect equals as we discussed the
situation with *Metropolitan*. It would have been the
most innocent of scenes, except that I was face
down on the rug with my bottom bare to spare the
bruises. Rathwell had already had Harmony type a
letter for me, vouching that he had known me for
years, that I was a professional woman with no links
to the media and that I genuinely liked to be spanked.
The last was fairly self-evident, with forty-one welts
decorating my bottom. As Rathwell laughingly
pointed out, if I was happy about that then he'd have
to believe me.

I slept with Melody in the smaller bed, and managed to summon up the energy to give her a lick as she had missed out on her share earlier. As I drifted towards sleep I was wondering why I had been so sensitive and I found out when I started my period in the morning, two days earlier than expected. This removed the embarrassing possibility of having to show off for Mintower while I was still menstruating. Rathwell, being Rathwell, joked that if I'd known he would have let me delay the mock virginity taking until morning.

With the letter and Rathwell's assurance of further support if necessary, I felt pretty confident and drove back in a happy mood, although seated on two folded towels to spare my bum. It's one of the standard threats to a girl about to be punished, that she won't be able to sit down for a week, and I rather felt that way. I saw Wendy that evening and showed her, to her horrified delight. As she wasn't really used to much more than hand spankings, she viewed heavy punishment with a mixture of terror and anticipation, to which the state of my bottom added a fresh dimension.

She agreed to come with me to see Mintower, which I felt was wise as I'd never met the man in my life. Not that I really expected to be imprisoned as a sex slave, but moral support is always a good thing. We joked about that as we drove down the following weekend, elaborating the fantasy as we went on. First it was spending a life of drudgery and beatings while wearing revealing and humiliating maids' uniforms. Escape would have been too easy, so we devised a complex system of runners and chains that allowed us to go wherever necessary and to be put in proper bondage at will. We decided we would sleep chained in the cellar and do our work either nude or dressed to show us off sexually. There would have to be someone to keep us in order, and we decided on a gigantic, fat cook who'd do things like stick us upside down in refuse bins while he beat us with a spoon. That was Wendy's suggestion, messy fantasies being very much her thing, with the spanking aspect thrown in for my benefit.

Mintower's place was in Wales, a few miles out of Wrexham, and our dirty conversation kept us amused until we arrived. By the last few miles I would have been more than happy for a cuddle in a lay-by, but the opportunity never came. I was ready for Mintower though, if only because he couldn't possibly be the sort of sadistic monster we had been imagining on the drive.

The house was big, but not the sort of grand country seat I had expected. A drive led between gate-posts of red brick to a typical Victorian villa in a grove of dark firs, private and a little gloomy on a wet spring morning, but entirely devoid of the air of gothic menace Wendy and I had been imagining.

He was more the sort of thing we'd been thinking of, a huge, shambling man who must have been impressive in his youth but had gone to seed. Nor was he alone, but with a tall young woman with dyed blonde hair and improbably shaped breasts. I assumed her to be his daughter, but was not entirely surprised when she was introduced to us as his wife, Cheryl. He was welcoming, effusive even, while she sat at the far end of the living room wearing expressions varying from a cold sneer to a sulky pout. This made it hard to relax, but we accepted drinks and sat down.

'So,' Mintower remarked as he lowered himself into an armchair, 'you're the girl who claims to like her bottom smacked?'

'That's right,' I answered, trying not to blush in response to the dirty look his wife was giving me. 'I have a letter from Morris Rathwell here. I believe he rang you?'

'Yes,' Mintower answered, taking the letter. 'Still, I'm dubious. Can you prove what you say?'

I had been ready for that, and prepared to have to show him my bottom. I'd even worn a dress over loose French knickers, both to make it easier and to spare my bruises. What I hadn't been ready for was the presence of his wife, who sat there scowling with her arms folded across her stomach as I stood up and turned my back to Mintower.

A good many men, and women, have pulled down my panties, and this wasn't the first time I'd had to take them down myself in front of a stranger. The difference was that it had always been done for people who were thoroughly looking forward to what I was going to show them. Certainly he fell into that category. Cheryl didn't, and I found the blood rushing to my face as I turned the back of my dress up and tucked it into my waistband. My knickers followed, pushed down with an embarrassed motion to leave my bare, bruised bum showing to the room. A week had reduced the overall blotchy purple colour to a mixture of bruise shades and sets of tramlines where the cane had landed. Cheryl gasped; Mintower gave an unreadable grunt. Nobody said anything so I stayed there with my bum showing, feeling thoroughly sorry for myself.

'So what do you think, my dear?' Mintower asked after what seemed an age.

'I think it's perverted,' Cheryl answered in a sulky tone.

'No doubt it's genuine, though,' Mintower said, ignoring her. 'So how did that happen?'

'A boyfriend caned me last weekend,' I said as I'd promised not to mention Rathwell's direct involvement.

'And you really enjoyed that?'

I nodded, unable to answer for the lump that was rising in my throat and sure that if I had to stand there with my knickers down any longer I would burst into tears. Mintower went silent, sipping his drink and looking at my bottom as if sure enough inspection would reveal some inner truth.

'Convincing enough, if a little convenient,' he eventually remarked. 'OK, you can cover up.'

Two quick motions had my knickers up and my dress back in position, leaving me to sit down, still blushing but relieved. Mintower reached for a book from the shelf behind him and as he took it down I glimpsed the cover, a line drawing of a tearful girl bending for the cane. I recognised it as a thing about lifestyle domination, entirely unrealistic.

'Let's see,' Mintower said, flicking the pages to a bookmark. 'OK, so your boyfriend is your master, right? You serve him at all times, do everything he says, get beaten when you're lazy, insolent or whatever, and that gets you off?'

'No,' I answered, 'that's a fantasy view of things. Nobody actually lives like that and the few cases I've heard of have all been with the woman in the dominant role. Even then they never last long: it's just fantasy. So is that book.'

'Then how does it work?'

'By consent. I do play games like that sometimes, pretending to be a maid or something, but more often we just use spanking as a bit of foreplay. It's not even all that hard, normally, and most of the pleasure comes from within my own head. I like being spanked, but in many ways I like being prepared for spanking even more.'

'And it's not because you'll get kicked out if you don't let your boyfriend do it?'

'Absolutely not. I do it because I enjoy it, when I like and with whoever I like.'

'There we are, Cheryl dear, it's not just whores who do it. She's an intelligent girl.'

Cheryl sniffed and made a tiny change in the defensive posture in which she was sitting. I'd been blushing throughout my little speech, but I'd imagined he'd ask questions to make sure I could give confident answers and had been prepared.

'What about you, Wendy?' Mintower went on.

'My feelings are similar to Penny's,' Wendy answered. 'It's really quite a common female fantasy, and quite genuine.'

'OK, so what if Cheryl was to get your little tush bare and give you a good smacking? Would you like that?'

'You don't seem very keen on it,' Wendy answered, deliberately addressing Cheryl.

'Cheryl used to table-dance,' Mintower went on as she shook her head in embarrassment. 'She reckons sex is basically something men pay women for, in one way or another, romance excepted. I know different, but then she's nineteen and thinks she knows the way the world works. I did, too, at that age. So, you've convinced MacRae you're genuine, which says a lot in my book. I'm nearly convinced, but I want to see one of you get a smacking and like it. Given the state of Penny's arse, how about you taking it, Wendy?'

'I would,' Wendy answered. 'I often do. Not now, though . . . I mean, it just doesn't feel right. You're obviously not comfortable with it, Cheryl. I do like it, and I might even let Penny do it to me with you watching, but I can't enjoy it in front of someone who thinks it's perverted.'

Mintower said nothing, but reached into his jacket, pulling out a sheaf of twenty-pound notes. After counting five on to the table he looked up at us, his eyes moving between Wendy and I.

'No,' I said, 'that isn't the point at all. I'll do it when I enjoy it, not otherwise.'

Again he said nothing, but spread out the notes and placed a further twenty on the table.

'Look, really . . .'

'Everyone has their price, Penny. Let's see what yours is. A thousand?'

'No, seriously . . .'

'Two thousand, that's this whole bundle and I bet it's more than you see in a month, two months even.'

'Honestly, I don't want any money.'

'I'll write a cheque then. Ten thousand to smack your friend's lily-white arse?'

'No. I mean it. I'd rather be forced than paid. Look, I think we had better leave.'

He had been reaching into his jacket, his cheque book half out of an inside pocket. As we rose he put it back.

'Sit down. Relax,' he ordered. 'OK, I believe you. Now do you know something?'

'If I'd taken the money you'd have refused to let Amy publish?'

'You are bright. Innocent though. I'd have watched Wendy get her smacking then thrown you out. No money. So, I'll probably let MacRae go with it, and maybe you've learned a lesson. Certainly Cheryl has, eh, dear? So, the woman doesn't exist who won't take my money?'

Cheryl shrugged and smiled, the first friendly gesture she'd made. That was it, no lunch, no being obliged to perform lewd acts for his amusement, just the embarrassment of showing my bruised bottom to

167

them. That, and of course victory, or at least probable victory, and as we drove away it was impossible not to feel triumphant.

Despite that the visit to Mintower had left a bad taste in my mouth. There was frustration too, having worked myself up to expect something naughty. Also I felt a strong need to reaffirm my sexuality, just as I had after my initial misadventure with Beth. Wendy agreed, suggesting we should find somewhere safe for a cuddle in the back of the car.

We were driving through farmland, with a grey sky overhead and rain hanging from the clouds on the horizon. On a hot, sunny day I would have wanted to find some quiet spot in the woods and strip off for sex in the open. Being naked outdoors gives such a wonderful thrill, but as it was the weather was simply not on our side. It was going to be in the car then, which would be nicely smutty, if only we could find somewhere safe.

As we drove we began to talk about Tom, the dirty old man I had allowed to have me in Brittany the year before, believing him to have been sent by Amber. He'd not only fucked me, but pissed on me afterwards in what I'd taken for a gesture of dominance but may have been contempt. Remembering the episode brought a blush to my cheeks and a warm flush between my thighs. I wanted cock, and to be taken by some earthy, sex-driven man to whom I represented sex, nothing more and nothing less.

We began to joke about it, stopping some man and propositioning him, then perhaps sucking him off together. Wendy wanted to be made to pose, showing her bum and boobs while I sucked. That seemed unfair to me, as I would end with the mouthful of come. I said she should bring him off between her ample boobs and I'd lick them clean and kiss her while he watched, which set her giggling.

With no hurry, we drove north, talking of muscular farm boys in tractors and road-menders with their big, hard hands and the smell of tar on their clothes. When I actually pulled off, it was not in the hope of sex, but because we were hungry. I had hoped for a decent country pub, but Wendy didn't want to wait, so we pulled over by a tiny roadside café. This was little more than a shack, run-down and seedy, with a leering man serving greasy burgers and watery tea. We bought bacon sandwiches and coffee and took them back to the car to eat.

'He should do you,' Wendy joked as she put her mug on the dashboard. 'A dirty old man if ever I saw one. I bet his cock tastes of bacon grease and ketchup.'

'I'm trying to eat, Wendy!'

'That's funny, coming from a girl I remember eating an apple tart a man had just come over.'

'You watched!'

'I love watching you do dirty things. Come on, go and tell him you'll suck his cock if you don't have to pay for the sandwiches.'

'I already paid. You should go anyway, it's more your thing. Think of it, kneeling behind that counter, nude, with his erection in your mouth, your bum and boobs all greasy from where he's pawed you.'

'I wouldn't dare; I just haven't got your courage.'

'You admit you'd like it then?'

'Maybe, but I just couldn't.'

'Don't ask straight out then. Flirt a little. Say you'd like another sandwich but you can't pay. See what he says. Come on, I'll go with you.'

She would never have done it on her own, and it wasn't easy for me. Propositioning men never is, and it's not something I do often, but now was an exception: I just felt too dirty to let it go. I got out of the car as soon as I'd finished my sandwich, and teased Wendy until she got out too. The man was leaning out of the service hatch, watching us with no more than casual interest and he doubtless thought we were just coming to bring the coffee mugs back.

I don't think I could have done it alone, and I nearly backed out anyway, thanking him and passing the mugs up. Wendy would have teased me and I'd have felt pathetic, as I always do when I want something but don't have the courage to see it through. Another thing was that I felt really insulted by Mintower's offer of money, even though I'd turned it down. Sucking cock in return for a greasy bacon sandwich would be just the thing to make a mockery of his horrid, mercenary philosophy. So I swallowed the lump in my throat, pretended to look at a pattern of petrol colours in a puddle and turned back to him.

'We were wondering if we might have another sandwich each?' I asked in my best little-girl-lost voice.

'Sure, hen,' he answered. 'Bacon?'

'Yes, thank you,' I went on, 'but the thing is, you see, and I know this sounds silly, but we've no money left.'

'No money left?'

'Well, about ten pence.'

'Ten pence?'

'I know, just enough for a slice of bread, but I'd really like that sandwich, I mean a lot. Maybe we could help you in some way.'

That was supposed to be the line he seized on, leering and making some lewd proposition. I'd have pretended to be shocked, protested a bit, then done it, which would have made it all the nicer for him. Unfortunately he was either dense or completely innocent.

170

'I can wash up myself, thanks, hen.'

'Nothing else?'

'Not really, no.'

It was hopeless. With the blood burning in my cheeks I made a quick check up and down the road and turned back.

'Look, in return for a sandwich each my friend and I will suck you off. All right?'

'Two posh tarts like you, suck me for a sandwich?'

'Yes. Seriously.'

'Yeah, sure.'

'No, I mean it, you can even come in my mouth.'

He glanced around and ducked back inside his shack to push the side door open. I took Wendy's hand and led her after me, up the wooden steps and into the inside, which was full of steam and the smell of his cooking. He was working on the catches that held the front shutter up, fumbling in his haste.

'This'd better not be a joke,' he told us.

I shook my head. I was trembling slightly but eager, just in the mood for what I had promised to do. Wendy had bolted the door behind us, sealing us in with a man who expected his cock sucked by us, maybe more.

'How about getting your knockers out?' he said. 'I like a bit of topless.'

Wendy and I exchanged glances. Topless was out in my long dress, besides which it looked as if I might have to kneel on the floor.

'Would you do my zip?' I asked and turned my back to Wendy.

I felt the zip drawn down and the air on my bare back. Reaching down for the hem, I pulled the dress high, showing off my French knickers and bra. He licked his lips at the sight, although I could still see uncertainty in his eyes. I met his look, reached my

171

hands behind my back and unclipped my bra, letting it fall from my breasts.

'There we are,' I said. 'As you wanted it, topless.'

'Nice,' he drawled, 'nice knicks too.'

'They stay on,' I told him, mainly in the hope of exactly the opposite. 'Look, if I'm going to suck you, shouldn't we at least be introduced?'

'Introduced,' he repeated, exaggerating my pronunciation. 'Posh little tart, aren't you? You do this a lot, I'll bet, offering blow-jobs to blokes in transport cafes and such. Get off on a bit of rough, do you?'

'Something like that.'

'Fair enough, just keep your eyes off the till. I'm Joe.'

'Penny. This is Wendy.'

'Well, how about you get your knockers out, too, Wendy? You look like you've got a big pair.'

'I'll take my jumper off,' Wendy answered. 'Not my bra.'

She suited action to word, peeling her heavy jumper off over her head to reveal the plump globes of her boobs in a plain white bra.

'Christ, they are big ones,' Joe said. 'You wouldn't put them round my prick, would you? The wife's are like that, big and fat.'

'You're a dirty old man,' Wendy answered.

'That's good, coming from some posh tart who wanted my cock in her mouth. Come on, down you go, on your knees.'

There was only one chair and he had sat down in it before we could argue, spreading his thighs to stretch out the crotch of his trousers. I did as I was told, kneeling on the dirty floor, acutely aware of being naked but for shoes, socks and panties. Wendy followed me down, squeezing next to me in the space between his knees. Joe pulled up his coat and undid a button, then put his hands to his fly. I could see his cock bulging in his trousers and it looked quite big, either that or already half-stiff.

He pulled it free, flopping his balls into a tuck of his underpants to let his cock loll out to one side. It was large, if not huge, with dark, wrinkled skin and a heavy foreskin from which the tip had just began to peep. I can never be indifferent to the sight of a man's cock, which I find both obscenely ugly and utterly compelling. Joe was no exception, and even as I caught the scent of man mingling with the bacon and cooking fat I knew I was going to enjoy sucking him enormously.

'Big, aren't I?' Joe announced. 'I bet you don't get many like that with your bankers and what not. Come on, suck me.'

I rocked forward on my heels, took his cock in my hand and kissed it, then just gulped it in, overcome by the whole beautiful dirtiness of the situation. Wendy giggled and Joe sighed as I took him right in to the back of my throat. I put my spare arm around her shoulder, drawing her close and sucking on Joe's lovely cock, feeling it swell in my mouth.

He was almost hard when I decided I was being greedy and pulled back, leaving his cock glistening with my saliva. Wendy gave me a last look, both excited and nervous, leaned forward and took him in her mouth, just inches from my face.

It was lovely to watch Wendy suck, with her pretty, ever so slightly chubby face full of swollen, dark-skinned, dirty penis. She had her cheeks sucked in and her eyes wide, watching his shaft as she sucked on it, moving her mouth slowly up and down. He was soon fully erect, really straining as she started to use a new trick, coming off his cock and then pursing her lips to let him penetrate them as she went back down.

'You're a fucking good cock-sucker,' he groaned. 'How about a feel of those big knockers?'

Before she could answer he had leaned forward, reaching down for her breasts and pressing his gut to her face. I though she would stop him but she didn't, allowing him to grope her and pop her left breast from her bra. Feeling slightly left out, I pushed my head in close, kissing his balls before sucking them into my mouth. They tasted of male, bacon fat and ketchup, just as Wendy had predicted, but it was perfect, wonderfully rude, while my change of position had left my bum sticking out behind, doubtless giving him a fine view of the rear of my knickers.

I was getting seriously aroused, but hardly expected a man like him to offer me a lick in return. In fact, an element of the pleasure was that he wouldn't, and that if I wanted to come, I was going to have to masturbate in front of him. With that thought I reached down and slid a hand into my knickers, letting my knees come apart as I did so. My pussy was wet and the first touch to my clit set me on what I knew would be a long, slow rise to an exquisite orgasm.

Wendy gave him back to me, moving slightly aside so that he could keep feeling the plump breast that he had lifted out of her bra. I took him in, deep, as I began to rock back and forth, stroking my clit to the same even motions. I do love sucking men's cocks, it's just such a dirty thing to do, to take a man's penis in my mouth and suck on it until he comes in me or over my face. I wanted that now, as I came, a faceful of sperm, splashed in my mouth and across my cheeks, dribbling down to my naked boobs.

I began to tug at his cock, masturbating him into my mouth, determined that he would come as I did. Wendy giggled and her hand found my back, tracing a line down my spine to my bum and slipping into the back of my French knickers. As she began to feel my bottom I was sure the timing would be perfect. Joe's breathing was deep and punctuated by little grunts. I knew he was coming and jerked harder, full into my mouth, keen to come at the instant I got my mouthful of sperm. Wendy had pulled a little back, nervous of getting her face soiled but eager to see it happen to me, still feeling my bottom.

He grunted and grabbed at his cock, jerking it free of my mouth to bring himself off with a flurry of rapid tugs. I saw the sperm erupt, right at me, a thick streamer erupting full in my face, catching the bridge of my nose and then my eye, right in it. I had been right on the edge of coming. With a messy face and a mouthful it would have been perfect, but getting it in my eye completely broke my orgasm.

He did say sorry, to be fair, but that wasn't really the problem. I so badly wanted to come, but instead had to make a run for the little wash area at the back to get my eye clean. Wendy helped, and I was soon fine, but I wanted to come.

'Lick me,' I demanded. 'It won't take a second.'

Wendy hesitated, glancing back to where Joe could undoubtedly hear us.

'I don't care,' I urged, 'just do it.'

'A girlie show, eh?' Joe's voice came from the door. 'You might have done it before giving me my suck. Come on then, get your face in your little friend's cunt like she asked.'

'In front of you?' Wendy answered. 'Look, I'm not sure . . .'

'Please, Wendy,' I begged. 'I'd like him to watch.'

'But . . .'

I couldn't let her get prissy; I just needed to come too badly and the idea of her licking me with greasy

Joe watching was too good to miss. She was nothing like as turned on as I was, but if things weren't quite to her taste I could try and make them. There was stock piled on all sides, including a tray of big plastic bottles of ketchup, mustard and mayonnaise.

Wendy was adjusting her bra over the boob he had been fondling. It was too good to miss, especially as she already had spunk on her bra. I grabbed a bottle and squeezed. A great jet of ketchup shot out, only not over her breasts but full in her face. She squealed and I quickly lowered my aim, sending a line of it full across her neck and both breasts. Joe yelled a complaint but I ignored him, laughing at the look on Wendy's ketchup-smeared face as she stood staring at me, eyes wide and arms held out in a gesture of disgusted amazement. I squeezed the bottle again, close up, depositing a thick blob of ketchup into her cleavage. A lot went on the floor too, and as she made a grab for the bottle she stepped in it, slipped and sat down hard, right in the mess.

I was laughing so hard I could barely stand, and when she lunged at my knickers and tugged they came down to my thighs and I came with them. She grabbed me as I landed on top of her and we rolled over, my arm going into the sticky mess. I fought back, knowing she could beat me but thoroughly enjoying the feel of her slimy, sauce-smeared skin as we grappled. I had dropped the bottle and my hand touched it as Wendy rolled me on to my back. She rose, straddling my body, only to get a stream of ketchup full in her face. Joe called out again, telling us to stop and calling us dirty little bitches, but I was in no mood to take any notice.

Wendy had grabbed the bottle and we wrestled with it, sending sprays of ketchup over both of us, but mainly in my hair and face. I bucked my hips, trying to unseat her, but failed and the next moment the nozzle of the bottle had been pushed into my open mouth. She squeezed, her dirty face set in a sadistic leer as my mouth filled up with ketchup. Most of the rest of the bottle went in, forcing me to swallow frantically to stop myself from choking. When I finally managed to push the bottle away she had emptied most of it, leaving me too busy spluttering and gagging to defend myself.

She rolled me over as I tried to spit my mouthful out, grateful only that it tasted better than Joe's come. Wendy sat on me, settling her weight into the small of my back. With my knickers half-down my bum was showing and I heard Joe's grunt of surprise at the state I was in, repeating his opinion that I was a filthy bitch. He was enjoying himself though. As I looked up I found him with his limp cock in his hand, stroking it over the sight of us wrestling, or rather, of me being beaten, as I had neither the strength nor the will to get Wendy off me.

I tried to kick, but it was futile. Her weight was on the small of my back and I was too far gone to really fight anyway. All I could do was lie there and hope she would make a proper job of dealing with me. She did, reaching for a fresh bottle and squeezing the entire contents over my naked bottom. I felt it land, sticky and wet and disgusting, running down between my cheeks and soiling my pussy. She gave me a slap, spattering herself with ketchup, but only one. I knew why too: spanking would be too much my thing, even with a bruised bum. Wendy, filthy with ketchup, her bra probably ruined and her jeans in a disgusting state, would make sure I got worse.

Sure enough, I felt her hands on my bottom, hauling the cheeks apart and showing him my anus. Once more I struggled, but more to try to seem unwilling than anything, given that I was having my bumhole shown off and I was pretty sure what she was going to do to me. Sure enough, I felt the nozzle of the ketchup bottle touch my hole and screwed up my eyes in disgust. Wet sauce oozed out on to my ring and I knew she had squirted some out to lubricate me. The nozzle prodded my bumhole and I tried to clench tight but it went up anyway, sliding past my ring and inside me as I gave a low, despairing moan.

Wendy was going to give me a ketchup enema in front of him and there was nothing I could do, only grovel on the filthy floor and let it happen. Her boobs were pressed to my back, slimy with ketchup, slipping against my skin as I wriggled in my pathetic attempts to break free. I felt something up my bum, pressure, then a disgusting spluttering noise as she squeezed. I cried out as my rectum filled with ketchup, swelling and bloating as she emptied as much as she could inside me.

When she took the nozzle out I could feel the load up my bum and was clenching my ring in a desperate effort not to utterly disgrace myself. The nozzle went up again and she squeezed, putting more up me, then even more. I began to plead for mercy, knowing I could take only so much before I let go, but she kept on, spurting it out inside me, until I could feel the extra weight in my gut.

She sat up, her full weight on my back. Straining my neck around I saw her reach for another bottle. Joe was beyond protesting, his complaints forgotten, half-stiff penis bobbing in his hand. Wendy touched a mayonnaise bottle, hesitated and took up a mustard one, a full litre of hot, English mustard. I squealed in protest, but it was half-hearted and she knew it. Down it came, the fat barrel of the bottle rubbed between my slimy buttocks, then raised, the nozzle burrowing down between my legs.

I tried to clench my cheeks. My eyes were screwed up and my fists were balled, but it was no good. As I felt the mustard squeeze out on to my flesh my dirty little mind got the better of me and I relaxed, allowing Wendy to press the bottle down between my thighs and squeeze. I felt it fill my vagina, a sensation so exquisitely disgusting that I could have come over that alone. Next she did my pussy, laying a long worm between my sex lips as I lifted my bum in meek acceptance. It started to burn as she did that, both what was in my vagina and over my vulva. I gasped, quickly starting to pant with the pain even as the nozzle probed my greasy, slimy bumhole. It went in, and I cried aloud as the contents of the mustard bottle were squirted into my rectum with a revolting burbling sound. My pussy was burning, my anus too. It hurt, burning like fire, but I needed to come too badly to make it stop.

'Here, how about a frankfurter stuck up her cunt?' Joe's voice sounded, followed by a giggle from Wendy.

A sound came from behind me, a meaty splat. An instant later I felt something fat and round touch my vagina, like the head of a small cock. It went up, filling me and pushing mustard deep up me until the end bumped on my cervix. Joe laughed and a picture came to me of my pussy with the last few inches of the sausage sticking out and a collar of ketchup and mustard around it. It was an image both obscene and ridiculous, and masturbating in the mess as he watched would add the final touch. I tried to get my hands back, but Wendy wouldn't let me, clamping her thighs around my body and laughing at my futile efforts.

'Stuff one up her arse,' Joe growled, his voice hoarse with effort.

'Dirty bastard!' Wendy answered, but a moment later I felt the rounded tip of a sausage nudge between my bumcheeks.

I was too slimy to stop it, and too turned on anyway. It went down between my cheeks, pressing to my filthy bumhole and pushing in. All I could do was groan and lift my bottom, submitting to it. My rectum was full, and I could feel the mustard bubbling out of my anus as I relaxed. The sausage pushed in, plugged me, making my ring burn worse than before. Again I tried to reach back to masturbate and again Wendy stopped me. I was beating my fists on the ground in helpless frustration as she fed the sausage up my bottom. My legs were moving too, my thighs sliding in the mess on the floor. I felt it go, every inch, sliding up my straining bumhole as I whimpered and squirmed on the floor, begging to be allowed to come. It was in me, and she had begun to fuck me and bugger me at the same time, sliding the two sausages in and out of my holes. The pain was rising, burning me as the fat tubes of meat worked inside me. I should have been coming, but I couldn't, and suddenly it was just too much and I was screaming out my stop word over and over.

Wendy got off immediately; Joe just laughed. I jumped up, dancing on my feet and babbling about hoses and water. Joe was laughing so hard he couldn't talk, but managed to jerk a thumb at a door to the rear of the shack. I ran for it, not caring if it did lead outside, at that moment I'd have flushed myself in full view of the road, anything to dull the pain.

It wasn't that exposed, an area of mud and grass within a fence but open to the sky and the hillside. The hose was obvious, attached to an upright tap. I grabbed it and twisted it on, spraying water between my legs, beautiful, cool, soothing water. I shut my eyes in pure bliss as the burning faded and the sausage in my vagina squeezed slowly out to fall on the muddy ground. I douched myself, feeling the mess inside me fall out in clots as the water ran. That was the feeling that got my head back. My whole underside still stung, but I just had to do it.

Sitting down, I let my bottom ease into cool mud, squashing it out around my buttocks, back up my bottom-crease and over my pussy. I leaned back, against the fence, parting my thighs wide and rolling up until I could get at my pussy and bum. My bottom was caked with mud and still slimy with sauce as I began to rub myself, exploring my dirty pussy. Wendy appeared, standing in the doorway, just watching me with her mouth open as I took two handfuls of muck and smeared them over my breasts. I blew her a kiss and slid my hands back down.

One sausage was close and I took it, sliding it back up my pussy and starting to fuck myself with it. The other had gone up my bum, adding to the glorious bloated feeling in my rectum. I let a finger stray down, touching my stinging anus, easing inside as a thick worm of mustard and ketchup came out with an obscene bubbling sound. With one thumb on my clit I began to masturbate towards orgasm.

My bumhole was greasy with mustard, stinging crazily and gaping wide. Two fingers went in easily, deep, until I could feel the head of the sausage in my rectum. I put a third in, stretching my ring between them as the mustard started to ooze out and the sausage with it. It stung crazily and I screamed, but I was coming, my thumb flicking over and over on my clit. My pussy tightened, squashing the sausage and pulping it inside me. My anus began to pulse, squeezing the sausage out in one long, ecstatic motion as my head went dizzy and my back arched in orgasm. It fell from my buggered hole at the very peak of my climax, followed by a thick spurt of mustard. I jammed my fingers in deep and spread myself, letting the whole filthy, slimy mess ooze out as I rode my orgasm on and on until at last it began to fade and I slumped back, exhausted.

I sat there for maybe a minute, ignoring Wendy's questions, indifferent to the cold, filthy mud, numb to the mustard. Finally I found the strength to get up and wash, making a thorough job with the hose. Having the cold water against my burning bum was bliss. Up it, too, when I gave myself a much needed enema, which set Wendy giggling, but having come I had started to worry about being seen. After all, the enclosure was no more than six feet high and overlooked by a fair bit of the hillside, so any lucky farmer might have watched my whole, filthy display.

Wendy took her turn to wash and we went back in. The inside was a mess, filthy with ketchup, mustard, grease and several squashed sausages. Joe told us to clean it up, naked, and to my surprise Wendy stripped meekly. He stood there gloating as he watched, occasionally reaching out to squeeze a boob or pinch a bottom. By the time we were done he had his cock out again, and insisted we help him come before we could go. We obliged, posed with our arms around one another and our bums stuck out to give him a good, rude view of our pussies and bumholes. It took him a while, and when he did come he wiped his hand on Wendy's bottom. Far from objecting, she gave her head a rueful shake and sat down on the stool, thighs wide. We watched her masturbate, quite shamelessly, plump ginger pussy spread wide as she rubbed her clit, one chubby boob cradled in a hand with the nipple bobbing under a thumb.

We left munching our bacon sandwiches. I was washed, tidy and outwardly respectable even if I did have no knickers or bra on. Wendy was another matter, with her jeans filthy with ketchup, particularly across her bottom. There was another car, a black Jaguar, parked behind ours, but I thought nothing of it. The door opened and as the occupant climbed out I realised who it was – Sir Rhys Mintower.

He just stood there, smoking a cigar and watching us, until we reached our own car. It seemed more than likely that he knew what we'd been up to, and I could think of nothing to say that would cover the situation. I contented myself with a nod, to which he responded, taking the cigar from his mouth.

'Before I wasn't sure,' he said slowly. 'Now I am. Genuine sluts.'

Nine

Amy's article came out towards the end of term. It was magnificent, a masterpiece, blending what she wanted to say with the style of the magazine, angrily demanding the right of women to be spanked if they wanted to be, yet never giving an inch to the involuntary surrender of control.

It started as a vigorous indictment of all forms of physical chastisement, denouncing judicial punishment, especially in schools, as little less barbarous than hanging. Domestic discipline was given the same treatment, set out as an abuse of women by men and totally unacceptable in any form. By the time she got on to spanking as sex play I really thought she had tricked me, extracting my most intimate thoughts by pretending to enjoy her own punishment.

I was wrong. Only then, when she had every reader, including myself, nodding in thoughtful agreement over her remarks, did she change direction. Leading carefully into the subject, she explained the use of erotic spanking as a cathartic pleasure, much like smoking or eating, only without the respective dangers of cancer or putting on weight. Spanking, she explained, could be given with care and understanding, providing sexual stimulation through endorphin release as foreplay, as long as the partners understood that it created no true inequality. It could also help to conquer one's fears, erasing them by turning each into a source of pleasure.

She went on to explain the physical limits that should be set to avoid any chance of damage, and that nobody should ever spank another person without being prepared to take it from her partner in turn. That was the point at which her argument became not merely persuasive, but splendidly cheeky. Men's ability to be involved at all was cast into doubt, the idea being that they were simply too insensitive to understand the subtleties of a woman's enjoyment of a smacked bottom. That wasn't really fair, but it made me laugh because I knew that it derived from Amy's preference for girls and distrust of men. By the time I finished it I was grinning from ear to ear, as was Amber, who had had her remarks on safety and limits repeated almost verbatim.

I could just imagine Beth reading it, soaking up Amy's words with her mouth hanging open. When I said as much to Amber I got turned over her knee and given fifty hard slaps with my skirt turned up, a punishment that I'm sure Amy would have classified more as domestic discipline. It was done to cut off any thoughts I might have had about continuing my relationship with Beth, but only succeeded in giving me a warm bottom and putting me in a still better mood.

It was impossible not to be happy, for several reasons. First there was the release of tension now that the article was out and my anonymity had been retained. Second was the fact that Amber was up for the weekend and she, Wendy and I had shared my bed the night before. Third, and maybe best, was the delicious and wicked thought of numerous female bottoms across the country, bare, round and rosy as they were smacked to a warm glow, and all because of me. Just how many sets of panties had been pulled down into a tangle around how many pairs of girlish thighs I would never know, but even if only one *Metropolitan* reader in ten thousand took Amy's advice the figure would be in the hundreds.

Amber's suggestion was that I should be spanked for every girl I'd caused to be spanked, which sparked a fine but sadly impractical fantasy of spending years travelling around the country for punishment, getting a spanking a day, each with its own special style. We enlarged on this as we drove out to the moors for a picnic, imagining the great queue of spanked girls, some vengeful, some tearful, but every single one turned on and eager to get me across her knee.

It was a glorious day, so we drove well north, up to the high moor and found a comfortable place among the heather. We ate salad and drank Riesling, each reading the article again and again, thoroughly happy and thoroughly pleased with ourselves. We had seen nobody all day, and inevitably I ended up getting spanked again, along with Wendy. We kneeled together on the rug, bottoms up and hands crossed behind our backs as Amber used the straps from the picnic baskets to fasten our wrists.

With us both tied and helpless, Amber undid our jeans and tugged them down, then made a big show of lowering our panties. Once we were bare, with our backs pulled in to make our pussies pout and flare our cheeks to show our bumholes off, she spanked us, taking us around the waist in turn and delivering a hundred hearty smacks to each quivering pink bum. I was on heat by the end, and ready to masturbate or get in a tangle with Wendy and come under her tongue. Of course I couldn't, not with my wrists strapped together, and Amber made me beg, all the while tickling my pussy with a piece of grass. I was nearly demented by the time she condescended to untie my wrists, and I put my fingers straight to my pussy.

I hadn't got in more than five good rubs before Amber called out in alarm. When I looked up it was to find over a dozen hikers approaching us through the heather. Wendy was still strapped up, and while I managed to get my jeans and panties up in good time, she was still struggling with hers when they came close enough to look down into our hideaway. All they saw was a little tummy as she did her button up, but she was scarlet with blushes, much to my amusement.

We finished off later, in the shelter of a little gully, taking turns to lick pussy while the third person kept look out. It was a lovely orgasm, and afterwards I felt utterly content with the world, bringing the outing to a beautiful close.

The last part of term was fairly dull, with my research on hold as I helped invigilate and all the other tasks of the examination season. As a student I had always imagined that there could be no easier job than walking between lines of desks, each with its tight-faced incumbent, eager or thoughtful, worried or just plain baffled. In reality it is both tedious and frustrating, as one wants all the students to do as well as possible and it is pretty heart-rending to see a well-liked tutee state that the chimpanzee has fewer chromosomes than man.

By the end of it all I was badly in need of something more light-hearted and looking forward to returning south. As usual I intended to spend most of the summer with Amber, coming back north only when I had to. Two days before I left she rang, saying that Amy had called and wanted to put together an article called *Endorphin Junkies* which she hoped would include interviews and such with us.

As before, I had my reservations, but we were assured of privacy and Amy had played fair with us before. It also sounded far too much fun to miss, with Amber suggesting the creation of a new fantasy to give them something to get their teeth into. Inevitably that made me think of Beth's reaction when she saw the finished product and I accepted, subject only to being allowed to read the thing before it went out. Nor was I the only one who was going to be in it. They wanted photos and Vicky, who has no reason to care what people think of her, had volunteered.

By the time I got down to Hertfordshire, Amber had Vicky's part all worked out, a fantasy at once strange, visually effective and designed to play to their tastes. Amber had found some reference to 'the female as exotic prey', which she considered an inspiring phrase. It had also irritated her, as it was part of some supposed high-brow art criticism object-ing to this and dismissing it as a purely male fantasy. As Amber has been indulging her taste for exactly that for years she took the remark personally and had determined to use the *Metropolitan* piece as an opportunity to set the record straight.

What she had done was blend the fox-hunt and pony-girl fantasy to create a new image, the zebra-girl. This was, in fact, not entirely new, but new enough, especially when the zebra was due to be hunted, roped and caged. Amy was delighted with the idea, and full of enthusiasm, promising to come out and see it herself. All they needed were a few posed shots, but this was less than satisfactory and it was agreed that we would do it for real once the photographer had finished.

The problem was where to do it. We needed woodland, or ideally parkland, several acres of it, on which we could guarantee to be able to play without disturbance. With the *Metropolitan* crew present neither Michael and Ginny, nor Henry, nor his gay friend were willing to let us use their land, which made things rather awkward. Amy was willing to drop the actual hunt if necessary, contenting herself with pictures taken in Anderson's garden. Neither Amber nor Vicky were prepared to do this, arguing that it would make the whole thing false if we didn't do it in reality. Amy seemed to regard this as naïve, but eventually Amber won the day.

Unfortunately, after what had happened to me at the fox-hunt nobody wanted to risk public land, which left us in something of a quandary. It was me who suggested asking Morris Rathwell if he had anything on his books, which earned me a threatening look from Amber. Unfortunately nobody else could come up with a better suggestion, and so she was finally forced to call him.

Amber's relationship with Morris Rathwell and the twins goes back a long way. It is also fairly fraught, involving a lot of competition and some fairly painful sexual escapades for Amber. In the long run she has undoubtedly benefited, yet to hear her talk you would think he was a demon in human form, an attitude I can sympathise with although she does rather make a fuss.

This occasion was no exception, with Amber trying her best to find out what she wanted without him getting involved and failing miserably. Rathwell happily admitted to having suitable land on his books, an overgrown airforce base in Norfolk, now a jungle of small trees and weeds. It sounded ideal, but inevitably he refused to even let us know where it was unless we gave him the full story and promised that he and the girls could come. With little choice in the matter, Amber gave in.

Not that it was Morris who was the main enthusiast. He wanted to come and promised to dress suitably and behave himself, perhaps sipping a glass of something cool in the shade. Melody took a far less casual attitude, especially when she heard that Vicky was to be the prey. Proving that she is stronger and fitter than Vicky is something of an obsession with her, and she was desperately keen on the idea.

That left me feeling pleased with myself for solving the problem and also for adding a more genuine element of competition to the fantasy. Melody scares me sometimes, but seeing her try and capture Vicky was going to be great fun, just so long as I could keep up. Only then did Amber point out that my own contribution to the piece was best done after the zebra chase, which was going to leave me the prime object of Melody's attention and Vicky's revenge on an abandoned aerodrome.

The day we had chosen was blazing hot, which was certainly going to help in our attempt to create an African atmosphere. Amber and I drove up separately, rising early to make good time and reaching the gates of the base before anyone else. It looked ideal on the map, entirely surrounded by farmland with a road on only one side and this minor. Even at the gate we could see very little, with dense stands of birch and hazel obscuring the view and a twelve-foot fence of rusting wire to prevent intrusion.

The Rathwells arrived close behind us, including Harmony, who was posted at the gate to let the others in. The interior was huge, a great wide space of flat land dotted with the mouldering remains of barrack huts and other buildings. There were even a couple of old aircraft fuselages, rotting slowly in the open air but still with their American markings discernible. To me it seemed ideal, but Rathwell was less enthusiastic, explaining that he was unlikely to have access for more than a few months and that it was too far from London and too run-down to be used as a venue for his clubs.

Anderson and Vicky arrived as we were looking around, along with Ginny, and lastly Amy and her crew: a photographer, Claudia, a make-up artist, Paulette, and Isabel, whose curiosity had got the better of her. Together we chose one of the hangars for our base, largely because most of its amenities were intact, if without water or power. Once settled, we began to prepare, Amy asking who was and was not prepared to appear in photographs.

Amber couldn't: there were just too many of her respectable clients who were likely to read *Metropolitan*. Vicky was not in doubt, nor Anderson, neither of them caring in the least for public opinion. Ginny volunteered, with no real risk in being recognised, as did Melody, with enormous enthusiasm, Harmony also.

It took two hours to put Vicky's body paint on, with Amber painting the stripes on with an eye-pencil while Isabel and Paulette filled them in with black and white paint. She started nude, elegant and muscular, but not dramatically different from any other six-foot woman with no clothes on. By the end she was truly wonderful, an exotic beast in black and white camouflage. Every stripe had been done exactly, from the fine detail on her face to the broad, bold bands that accentuated her hips and chest and the subtle tapering lines that made her legs seem longer and her waist slimmer even than reality. The lines swirled together on her bumcheeks, creating a subtle irregular target pattern that drew the eye to their firm roundness. White extensions had been plaited into her own glossy black hair, giving her a magnificent stripy mane that fell almost to her crease. A white tail bobbed over her bottom, seeming to sprout seamlessly from her spine, with the stripes following what looked exactly like natural contours. The final touch was her boots, her sole item of apparel, thick-heeled, ankle-length pieces in black leather, shaped like hooves at the toe and high at the ankle to make her calves, thighs and buttocks tense. Also to stop her vanishing into the distance so fast nobody could hope to catch her.

If Vicky was impressive, the twins were not far behind. They love their Amazon look, Melody especially, and this was the perfect opportunity to indulge it. Both were close to naked, their dark skin oiled and gleaming, black running shoes their sole concession to modern style, body jewellery their sole concession to modesty. Their heavy, powerful buttocks were nude, their big breasts also. Both had their hair in gold and turquoise beads, Rathwell's colours, a feature Harmony had extended, beading her pubic hair and with her pussy otherwise quite bare. Melody was no more decent, with an elaborate collar and arm bracelets in the same colours but her pussy shaved and marked with brilliant yellow paint, as were her cheeks and breasts. Personally just looking at them made me want to grovel at their feet, but all they got from Vicky was a disdainful glance. Paulette was more impressed, fussing around them to help and asking endless questions, until finally they teased her into stripping off and joining them. Amy made no objection as long as it didn't interfere with her work, and we ended up with three glorious black Amazon girls, although Paulette was smaller and kept a pair of tiny black panties on, which slightly spoiled the effect.

Anderson had been persuaded not to wear khakis and a pith helmet on the grounds that it might cause offence, and had gone for a less obviously colonial look, with light white trousers and a white shirt. Unlike the twins he had thought to bring equipment and had a bolas tucked into his belt. Ginny was also equipped, with a lasso, but was still less African-looking, with leather chaps that left her gorgeous bottom bare and a minuscule blue bikini top that struggled to confine her huge breasts.

The official photo-shoot went off well, with the girls behaving themselves and even Melody doing as she was told. They mocked up the chase, carefully keeping bits of aircraft hangar and so forth out of the shoots and plenty of flesh in them. With Amy's enthusiasm for women's right to show off, no objection was made to nudity, even with the girl's pussies showing, and plenty of shots seemed likely to be pleasantly rude, even if they weren't likely to be the ones published.

Vicky was chased, caught, roped and put in a wooden stockade, all very mild stuff with the tying obviously purely ritual and not a smacked bottom or a licked pussy to be seen. Despite the contrived way it had been done, all those involved were hot and flustered at the end, and ready to go for real as soon as they'd taken in a little water. With the cameras safely away I volunteered to join in, as did Amber. The rules were to be the same as for the fox-hunt, save only for the mad scramble at the end. When we caught Vicky, or rather, if we caught Vicky, her fate was to be more carefully accomplished, with first rights going to her captor and none of the make-believe that had characterised the photo-shoot.

Although I lack any real pretension to athleticism, I hoped not to be a mere spectator and had put a few useful items in the back of the car. Vicky didn't know this and I was hoping she'd see me as a weak link in the hunt and so improve my chances. I waited until she had vanished among the scrub before going to the car and extracting a weighted net and two big rolls of sticky tape.

Back at the hangar I stripped quickly, feeling embarrassed in front of the magazine crew despite their indifference to all the surrounding nudity. Unlike those who had been photographed, I made no attempt at exotic costume, going for practical running shorts and top in a mid-green I hoped would blend with the foliage. Amber had made slightly more effort, choosing military shorts and singlet in grey and green which had much the same effect on me as the twins' more revealing outfits. She also had ropes and a swagger stick, typically making sure she had something with which to dish out a bit of corporal punishment.

It took a moment for Amber to get the twins to follow instructions, so Vicky had plenty of time to get clear before we spread out into a wide crescent and came in pursuit. Melody and Harmony took the flanks, running ahead in the hope of scaring her into the centre where the rest of us would be coming up more slowly. It was the same tactic that had been used to hunt me, but the base was bigger, with more ground cover. Also, Vicky's markings, although striking close-up and a clash with the green and yellows of the foliage, actually broke up her outline remarkably well.

I had soon lost sight of Amber and Ginny to either side. As we crossed the broken tarmac of a runway I glimpsed them again, moving forward into the next belt of young birch. I ran on, picturing the map of the base in my mind and wondering what I would have done in Vicky's shoes, or rather hooves.

She'd want to get caught, eventually, but not quickly. Her pride would see to that, and if it was either of the twins who came up with her first she could be guaranteed to put up a genuine fight. She would want to be caught by Amber, maybe Ginny and myself, while it would also be a matter of pride for her to avoid Anderson. Undoubtedly she would guess that he and the twins would be on the flanks, probably Paulette also, who looked quite fit, and so would try and take cover in the centre as the first sweep passed her. If I was right she would be concealed in the scrub roughly in front of me.

I began to zig-zag, peering into the denser copses with my eyes peeled for the vivid black and white pattern of Vicky's skin. Several times I was deceived by shadows thrown in bright sunlight, and after crossing a great area of barren tarmac where two runways met I began to wonder if my logic was right. At that moment I saw her, or rather her lower leg. She was crouched among a dense stand of birch at the apex of the scrub opposite me, where the runways divided, a clever psychological choice as anyone approaching was likely to take the easier path to either side of her hideaway before pushing into the trees.

As I was fifty yards away and out in the open I walked on, doing my best to pretend not to have been seen. She stayed still, although I was sure she could see me, making no sound whatever as I walked past her and behind a stand of hazel. I pulled my net free, turned back on my tracks and dashed straight at where I assumed she was. Her reaction was instant, breaking through the birches away from me, towards the open ground. My small size and head start were a help for only a moment, but it was long enough. A moment before she gained the tarmac I had flung the net over her, and myself a moment later.

I threw my arms around her and held on for dear life as she went down, full length on an area of grass between the trees and a gorse bush. Her arms were trapped but she still managed to throw me off, only to find the net tangled in gorse. I climbed on again, felt my bare arms slide in her grease paint, grappled her and tried to get at my tape. She was impossibly strong, kicking her legs up to lift my full weight with ease and turning me back on to myself. Her legs closed on my waist, catching me as if in scissors and throwing me to the ground.

Her thighs tightened on my body, long and hard, pinning me in place as she struggled with the net. I was face down, pulling a tape roll from one arm. The tab gave and I pulled myself in to her, slapping the tape on to the coarse surface of the net and wrenching out a length.

If she had pushed me away with her legs she would have been free, but she closed, trying to grapple me through the net with her fingers. She caught my singlet and I felt it tear, but my arms were around her and my fingers fumbling for the tape roll. I found it, pulled and wrenched myself back. My singlet came away in her fingers, leaving me topless, but the tape was around her, pinning her upper body into the net. She went back, preventing me from making another turn, rolled up her legs and pushed. I fell hard, dropped the tape roll and landed with a squeak.

Vicky was on her feet before I was, running, but still in her net with a twist of tape hampering her movements. I came after her, ignoring scratches in the heat of the chase, breaking out on to the tarmac and putting every ounce of strength into it. With her fancy hoof boots and the net she had to be slower than me, but it wasn't by much, and as we sprinted across the runway I wondered if I could actually catch her.

I thought she would take off down the runway, but she dodged into the scrub at the far side, stopped, struggled with the net and threw it off as I reached her. We grappled, her arms locking around me. An instant later I had been thrown to the ground; she had turned me and swung a leg across my back. My wrist was caught and twisted high into the small of my back and I was helpless.

Quite casually, she tied me with my own tape. My protests that I was supposed to be hunting her were ignored as she pulled the roll off my arm and lashed my wrists together in the small of my back. With that done she settled her weight on my shoulders, took hold of my shorts and tugged them off, my panties coming with them. That was it for me. Having my bum stripped was just too strong a feeling for me to try and hold whatever vestige of dominance was left to me. I stopped trying to struggle and lay limp, resigned to the humiliation of being stripped and tied up. My singlet was already gone, torn free and discarded somewhere out on the runway, leaving me bare with my front pressed to the warm ground and the grass tickling my nipples and between my thighs.

I could feel her painted bottom sliding on my back, with her hot, damp pussy right on my spine. She taped my ankles up, rendering me completely helpless, then rolled me over and stood up, smiling down at me. Her body paint was a mess, the black and white stripes smeared into grey where we had wrestled, while a good deal of it had come off on me. She was sweating, too, plastering her mane to her skin, while her beautiful tail was a bedraggled mess and hanging at an angle. For all that she looked magnificent, and I felt beaten and submissive, ready to be taken advantage of. Sticking my tongue out, I wiggled the tip at her, making my willingness plain.

She nodded, glanced around, cocked a leg across my body and calmly sat on my face. I had a moment to take a gulp of air, another to admire her zebra-striped bottom as she squatted down, and then it was in my face, queening me. Her pussy was over my mouth, my nose pressed to her bumhole and her slippery buttocks spread across my face. She wiggled her bum, making my nose press into her sweat-slick bottom-hole as I began to lick, tasting pussy and grease paint.

It felt great, and verging on the surreal, queened by a girl painted as a zebra, captured and tied by someone who was supposed to be my prey, which made my helpless submission all the stronger. With my tongue lapping at her clit she was soon breathing hard, then moaning and at last coming with a long sigh of ecstasy as she squirmed her bottom in my face.

Even when she had come she stayed sat on my face for a while, indifferent to the fact that I could only breathe by gulping in air past my lower lip. When she finally did condescend to rise she made me kiss her bumhole, then took my own discarded panties and put them to my mouth. Knowing that once gagged I'd be unable to call for help, I tried to struggle, but she just pinched my nose until I was forced to gape and stuffed them in. I could taste myself as the little scrap of cotton was wadded into my mouth and tied off with tape, and tried to plead with my eyes, hoping she would at least bring me to my own climax before leaving.

She just laughed, fully aware of what I wanted but choosing not to give it. Instead she moved me into the shade of a birch stand, gave a cheery wave, checked that the runway was clear and loped off, heading back towards the buildings. There was absolutely nothing I could do, not even masturbate over my fate, which I badly wanted. Being taken unawares, handled so forcefully, tied and made to lick pussy, then gagged with my own panties was so right for me, and if I knew that being left helpless would make it all the better in the long run, then that was very little consolation at the time.

I lay there for what seemed an age, listening and hoping somebody would come across me. There was birdsong, noises that might have been the others, once the distant rattle of a train. Given the size of the base I was quite likely to lie there until evening when the game was over and Vicky came back for me. By then I would certainly have wet myself, maybe worse, and while having Amber find me like that would be no more than pleasantly humiliating, for it to be any of the *Metropolitan* crew would be unbearable.

My bladder was beginning to get tight when I decided I'd have to try and get free. The base was on chalk, with occasional flints, although none near me. I managed to get to my knees, but with an effort that left me sweaty and panting through my nose. Movement was hard, as all I could do was shuffle along on my knees, and I had to keep them spread to make any headway at all. This meant keeping my pussy wide and my bare bum against my bound ankles, adding to my feelings of sexual exposure and frustration. I was close to tears before I'd gone ten feet, in an agony of self-pity and erotic humiliation, not really sure if I wanted to be free or caught by one of the men, pushed forward and mounted from behind, even buggered as I squirmed in my bonds.

The need to pee was getting worse, too, and I realised I should have done it while I was on my back, rolling up to let it spray out clear of my body. Now if I went it would almost certainly go on my legs, and if I lay back down I'd have trouble getting up again. Wishing I'd drunk less water before setting out on the hunt, I pressed on, making my painful way through the scrub.

After maybe another fifty feet I stopped again, deciding to just let my bladder go and spare myself the growing pain in my tummy. I set my knees as far apart as they would go, relaxed and at that moment heard the sound of somebody coming through the foliage. I turned, trying to squeal through my panty-gag, to snort, anything to attract attention. It wasn't necessary. Melody was coming straight towards me, grinning from ear to ear at my predicament.

'You should have stuck close to Amber, little one,' she said. 'Oh dear, I do wish I had the camera.'

I responded with a muffled grunt, the most noise I could make. She walked around me, her eyes sparkling with merriment as she took in the state of my body.

'You've got big black and white targets on your face, you know!' she laughed. 'Vicky sat on it, did she? I bet you asked for it. There's nothing you like better than licking another girl's bumhole, is there?'

All I could do was nod my head and let in hang in shame.

'I suppose I should untie you,' she went on, 'although I've not seen Vicky, so it might be an idea to get off on your face myself. Anyway, I'm not sure I've got anything to cut the tape. It's strong stuff, and if I pick at the end I might break a nail, which would never do.'

I looked up at her, wide-eyed, hoping she would make me lick her and then set me free. She frowned, scratched an ear and nodded.

'I'll be back,' she said suddenly. 'Don't go away.'

She ran off, leaving me. As she had gone towards the base I was hopeful she was going to fetch a knife.

Certainly she hadn't just left me, not without taking the opportunity to tease me or humiliate me in some way. Sure enough, she came back within minutes, only not with a knife but with the heavy machete they'd used to make the stockade for Vicky. In addition she had the ball of thick string used to tie the stakes and a bag which chinked as she walked. She was grinning and I knew I was in trouble.

'I'm fed up with zebra hunting,' she announced. 'Vicky's too fast.'

I wanted to point out that the last time she'd wrestled Vicky she had ended up with her own monster-size strap-on dildo up her bum. The gag stopped me, which was probably just as well.

'I fancy something more tender anyway,' she went on. 'Zebra's so tough. Spit-roast girly should be just the thing.'

She had to be joking, but her jokes tend to go a long way and I felt my stomach tighten. I was hers to use, after all, and if I could be sure she wouldn't actually kill and eat me, then that was about all. There was also the question of why she hadn't alerted Morris to my plight. If she had he'd have taken over, which meant she wanted me all to herself and for something very private.

I squirmed a bit as she ducked low and put her shoulder to my tummy, but she picked me up with ease, taking my weight on her shoulder with my legs to the front and my bum stuck up in the air. Two playful slaps set my bottom quivering and she set off, holding the bag in her free hand and ducking low so we wouldn't be seen.

It was impossible not to be impressed by her strength. I may be little, but she carried me clear across the base, walking or even running at a slow lope, and never once putting me down. Twice she stopped, once to make sure the runway was clear and once when somebody passed close by us, but I never saw who it was. Only when we were just yards from the far fence did she stop.

There was a wood beyond the fence, with thick green foliage hiding us from view. A dense birch stand cut us off from the base, thinning in the shade of the bigger trees to form a secluded clearing. Melody dumped me on the ground, gave my bottom another slap and stood back.

'This I'm going to enjoy,' she said, addressing me and then looking up. 'I wonder where Harmony's got to?'

Once more she loped off, leaving me without a word. I tried to get up again as there was a rusting iron structure nearby that I was sure could be used to break the tape on my wrists. I nearly made it, too, getting to my knees and reaching the object, all the while listening to curious calls that were presumably from Melody. I had even managed to get my bonds against a rough edge when she came back, her sister running behind her. They accelerated as they saw what I was doing, and I was pulled back into the open space.

'Naughty, naughty, Penny,' Harmony chided. 'You wouldn't run away and spoil our fun, would you?'

I shook my head miserably. They tied me to a tree, low down and under my armpits, also with my thighs roped tight around my middle so I was forced to kneel with my bare bum stuck up as I watched them prepare. Melody took the machete and began to cut birch, choosing straight, thick saplings and lopping off the side branches. Harmony gathered these and began to tie the finest into a bundle, making a long but delicate birch, clearly for use on my bottom, maybe all over me.

Melody soon had a half-dozen short, thick stakes and one longer one. Using the string, she made two squat pylons and set them some five feet apart. Laying the longer stick along the top she gave a thoughtful nod, then turned to me, grinning. She had made a spit, and not a joke one either, but a solid construction on which a pig or lamb could perfectly well have been roasted.

With her birch rod finished, Harmony had begun to gather dry wood and bark, perfectly seriously, as if it was for real. Melody joined her, piling the wood beneath the spit before arranging larger pieces on top. It was entirely functional, and only the absolute certainty that they could not really be intending to cook and eat me kept me from going into a blind panic.

It was bad enough, though, just from the casual way in which they were going about their preparation, as if spit-roasting their friends was a perfectly normal way to spend a sunny afternoon. My position didn't help either, naked and tied with my bottom spread to the air, nor the way they looked, with their rich brown skin gleaming with oil and sweat and not a stitch of clothing between them. Had I been able to speak I would have given my slow-down word, at least to give myself a chance to set some limits for them. I couldn't, or more than mewl and make muffled grunting noises, all of which I tried, but to no effect.

The fire was built up to Melody's satisfaction, along with a big pile of spare wood, certainly enough to roast a good-sized pig without collecting more. She gave the horrible construction a critical nod and lifted the long pole off the top. Harmony dump a last log on to the woodpile and picked up the machete, then began to stroll towards me, swinging the thing in her hand.

'Lunchtime, I'm afraid, Penny darling,' she said, and brought the machete hard down on the rope running between my chest and the tree.

I felt it jerk as it cut and rolled to the side. A second cut freed my wrists and she pulled the tape away as Melody joined us. My arms were taken and pulled to my front, tucked in under my ankles and tied off, leaving me trussed. Harmony cut my ankles free, only to immediately replace the tape with rope and tie it off to my wrists.

With me safely hog-tied she stepped back, smiling down at her handiwork. I was more helpless than before, and more exposed, with my thighs tight up to my tummy and my pussy and bottom spread wide. The pain in my bladder was worse, too, with my legs squashed so firmly against it.

I knew it was a joke, albeit an elaborately prepared one, but I was still trembling and having trouble getting enough air in through my nose. Melody was standing over me beside her sister, leaning on the six-foot stake, both of them grinning as their eyes wandered over my helpless body. I saw Harmony reach out a foot and felt the toe of her shoe on my bum, prodding the meaty bit as if to test how succulent I was going to be.

Melody bent, catching me by the ropes around my legs and pulling me fully on to my back. Holding me in place, she slid the pole in, between my thighs and under my hands, then up between my breasts and out at my neck, forcing me to throw my head back. The birch bark was rough in places and scratched, but I barely noticed, aware only of the significance of being staked and thinking how I would feel on the spit.

They lifted me easily, one at each end of the pole, and walked to the spit, lowering the pole into place until I was hanging over the fire, trussed and bound, completely helpless, just as if I were in reality to be roasted for their midday meal. They left me like that, shivering and with the muscles of my middle jumping in reaction to what was being done to me, as Harmony fetched her birch. She began to whip me, gently at first, on top and whisking the twigs up underneath me to catch my back and bottom, including my pussy lips, where they poked out from between my thighs. It tingled, bringing the blood to my skin and making me jerk each time a twig caught my sex. My breathing got harder, until I was puffing and snorting through my nose, while I was sure that if she went on I would finally lose control of my bladder.

I did, just as she brought the birch down across my bum. The stream just burst from my pussy, spraying out in every direction, including over both the twins. Harmony squeaked and jumped back; Melody just laughed as my pee spattered out on to the stake, then in a long arch behind me as my wiggling bottom changed its direction. I was sobbing into my gag as it happened, the pee running out of my pussy and down between my bottom-cheeks to drip from their crests and the small of my back.

Neither girl spoke, but just watched me piddle until it dried to a trickle and finally stopped, when Melody shook her head in disapproval. Bringing a bottle of water from her bag, she rinsed me down, then cleaned both her own legs and her sister's where my pee had splashed on them. It was pretty humiliating to have wet myself so blatantly, but all part of the over-whelming feelings building up inside me. It might have been pretend, but I was trussed on a spit for real, and I had only my trust in the twin's humanity to let me be sure they wouldn't do it.

As Harmony finished the beating with a few firm birch-strokes to my legs and bum, Melody went back to rummage in her bag, bringing out a big, green pepper grinder and a bottle of fancy olive oil with two chillies and some cloves of garlic floating inside it. She shook the bottle, making the contents bubble, stepped back to me and unscrewed the lid. I could only stare as she poised it over my naked body and began to pour. I felt the warm oil on my skin, dribbling down my limbs and on to my tummy, then my breasts and neck. Harmony came close, sliding her hands in to rub the oil over my body, basting me like a suckling pig.

It began to tingle, then burn where the birch had hit my skin, making my whole body hot. Plenty went on my pussy, the chillies making my flesh swell and burn until I was squirming ineffectually against Harmony's hands. She just laughed at me, easing two oily fingers up my pussy, then three and at last her whole hand, working it inside me as my vagina stretched, hot and oily around her fist.

'Stop playing with your food,' Melody chided.

Harmony giggled and pulled her hand free, leaving my pussy gaping and tingling from the oil. Melody turned me, back-up, and held me as her sister poured fresh oil on to my skin and rubbed it in, also on my whipped bottom and the sensitive groove between my cheeks. As the oil began to burn against my bottom skin she slipped a finger deep into my anus, rummaging inside. As she fingered me my ring began to sting, pulsing as if I was having an orgasm.

She laughed as she pulled her finger out, then tickled the little hole with her nail, bringing fresh contractions to my muscles. My body seemed to be on fire, my pussy and anus swollen and pouting as each hole dribbled oil on to the fire beneath me. The panties in my mouth were sodden with saliva and I was panting so hard I was scared I would go into a fit, but they kept on, basting me thoroughly and then grinding pepper over my skin to worsen my woes.

When they let go I swung back down, removing the awful sight of the firewood beneath me but not taking the image from my mind as they peppered my chest and legs and pussy.

Melody was whistling some pop song, so cool, so nonchalant as she bent to her bag and pulled out a big box of cook's matches. I could only stare, my whole body already burning, my lungs bursting for more air. She kneeled, put a match to the box, struck it, let the flame rise on the wood and put it to the firewood beneath my squirming, helpless body.

I panicked, losing all control and twisting my body so hard that the spit upset, sending me to the ground. I heard Melody's yell and saw her jump back, and then she was laughing and I saw that the firewood had been pushed away from beneath me as I was turned on the spit.

Ten

I've never felt inclined to vegetarianism, but I couldn't face a single mouthful of the roast pig for which the spit had really been intended. It was just too close to home.

Amber wasn't too pleased with the twins for roasting me, but with the *Metropolitan* crew around she couldn't really say much. After all, it was way beyond anything Amy would have considered acceptable, even in jest. What did happen was that Rathwell spanked the twins for leaving him out of the fun, side by side with their bare black bottoms turned up and everything showing as he gave each of them a dozen firm slaps. Amy objected, Isabel also, but were forced to back down when not Morris but Melody defended the punishment.

Personally I was so high on both endorphins and adrenalin that I could barely stay still for a second. With my panties a soggy rag and my other clothes scattered across the base I had nothing to wear, but for once it didn't bother me. I wanted my indulgence and I wanted it heavy, although I was quite happy never to see a roasting spit again.

They'd caught Vicky, running her to ground at the southern tip of the base. She had tried to break for it, running straight at Paulette, only to have Amber cut her off. They'd tussled, but unlike me Amber had managed to hold her own, at least long enough for the others to come up. Once tied, Vicky had been given a dozen firm swats of Amber's swagger stick across her zebra-striped bottom, then had been made to lick first Amber, then Ginny, all in front of the wide-eyed Paulette.

Anderson had finished off by mounting her, from behind, much as a zebra should be mounted, with Vicky kneeling and spread in the ecstasy of capture. She had come under his fingers with her pussy still full of cock before he rolled her over and came across her stripy face and breasts while she rubbed the mess of sperm and grease paint into herself. That had been too much for Paulette, who had fled back to the base, although I was disappointed not to have seen it happen.

They had brought Vicky back hung upside down from a pole, just for the look of the thing, and only then ended the fantasy. Rathwell had announced that he intended to stand everyone lunch, and they had eventually found the twins and me, disturbing us just as I was being persuaded that instead of calling them demented bitches, psychotic tarts and so forth I should be licking their pussies in gratitude for the thrill. They didn't get it, but nor did I, leaving me on my hormone-inspired high.

Those of us who'd been in the chase were all at least fairly grubby, while Vicky and I were a real mess. Most of us were scratched, too, but in no mood to stop, especially after reviving ourselves with lunch and plenty of water. Rathwell had had the sense not to serve out anything alcoholic, or we'd have just spent the afternoon asleep, but as it was the majority of us were keen for more.

Amber and Anderson had both enjoyed Vicky and were relatively cool, standing together and discussing bolas technique. Ginny was with the twins, giggling happily with pork fat running down her chin and into her ample cleavage, clearly ready for whatever fun came her way. Morris Rathwell was carving the pig with the machete and chatting to Claudia, apparently content but I guessed keen for his pleasure.

The other three *Metropolitan* girls were talking together, doing their best to seem cool about everything but not really succeeding. Amy had been fun on the beach, but nobody except Amber and I knew about that, and now she was being far more detached and professional than I'd expected. Paulette seemed more fun, as she had at least had the guts to join the hunt, for all her shock at watching Vicky being made to service her captors. Isabel was the worst, holding herself aloof with a pretence of purely detached, investigative interest that I was sure was false.

I was supposed to be interviewed about my love of spanking, but from a far more personal perspective than before. They would have photographed me, from behind, in a lacy camisole that left my cheeks bare. Amber would have punished me, and my smacked bottom would have been photographed to make a comparison with the first picture. It was pretty bold for them, I thought, but Amy seemed determined and apparently Mintower had no objections. The crucial thing was the context, and that excused printing a picture better suited to the sort of specialist spanking magazine that would normally have been anathema to the *Metropolitan* editorial line.

All that would have been fine, had I not been smeared with chilli oil, dirt and black and white grease paint, not to mention the effects of the birch and a good deal of rolling around on the ground. The pictures had to be postponed and Amy made me promise not to let anybody punish me so that my bottom could return to pristine condition. I did do the interview, describing not just the pleasure that came with the physical aspect of spanking and erotic teasing and torture in general, but also the rush I got from largely mental stimuli such as having my panties pulled down. By the end I was more turned on than ever and desperate to play.

Anything would have done, so long as it involved my utter degradation and a mind-wrenching orgasm. I was even happy about the crew watching, my embarrassment having turned to a positive desire. A full-blown birching would have been good, perhaps hung from my hands with just my toes on the floor, or a nettle whipping to leave my bottom bloated and throbbing as I masturbated in front of them. Neither was practical, nor any of the other corporal punishment options the base provided, simply because it would take more than a week for my bum to return to an even pale pink suitable for Amy's purposes.

They were pretty shocked by the state I was in anyway, even Amy, who for all her belief in a woman's freedom to express her sexuality was finding it hard to handle in reality. That made the idea of them watching all the better, and a sense of mischief was added to my arousal.

I could wait no longer, and persuaded Amber to declare open season on me, anything which marked my skin excepted. With the deal made I ran for the buildings, leaving them to finish their lunch. I was keen to be caught, quickly, and thoroughly used, but also anxious not to upset Amber, who had put up with about as much of my sluttish behaviour as she could be expected to. Not that what Vicky and the twins had done to me had been any fault of mine, but I wanted to show her that at the end of the day she was the one I was in love with. As I kissed her before running off I whispered the word 'barracks', which suited her vaguely military look and with luck would provide the right conditions to play.

The conditions were right, not exactly the satin sheets and candlelight ideal of romantic love, but right for me in a dirty mood. Each hut was a long half-cylinder of corrugated iron, closed at each end by now heavily decayed plywood set with windows and doors. Most were empty, their floors littered with broken glass and green with algae. Only at the end of the line did they become less utterly derelict, many still with cheap, iron bedsteads in place and even ancient mattresses. The best was second in from the back corner. Both the door and the windows were intact, with a thick growth of brambles shielding them, and peering inside I could see the rows of beds almost as the departing servicemen must have left them. That alone was stimulating in its way, although laddish army types are not my thing at all. They were still men, and single, some twenty of them to judge by the beds, and would doubtless have been hungry for girls.

I found a suitable stick and slashed my way to the door, taking a few scratches and nettle stings in the process. Inside it was better still, with the male atmosphere heavy on all sides, at least in my imagination. I tried one of the mattresses, making the rusty springs inside creak as I pressed down and thinking of what might have happened to any girl foolish enough to allow herself to be lured back to such a place alone. Possibly she would have been taken into the back, to what had evidently been the washroom, perhaps with a bed. They'd have taken turns with her, one after another, mounting her, humping away and coming up her pussy or over her belly until she was soggy with sperm. Once she was too slimy for fun the cruder among them might have buggered her, making her kneel with her dress up and her big white panties pulled down around her thighs. Others would have expected her to suck and swallow their come, or done it over her pretty face until she was dripping with it, her hair soiled and her make-up running in the mess.

If all twenty of them had burst in at that instant my thighs would have come open of their own accord, welcoming the lot to their share of pussy or whatever else took their fancy. When they'd finished with me I'd have come in front of them, sat in a pool of their sperm with my thighs up and fingers in my pussy and anus, just to show what a dirty little tart I was. At orgasm I'd have stuck my fingers in my mouth and come to their chorus of lewd or disgusted remarks, revelling in the taste of my body and theirs as I frigged myself into oblivion.

I was going to do it for real if I wasn't careful, which would have stopped me from getting my full pleasure when I was caught. Trying vainly to blank all thoughts of sex from my mind, I crossed to the door and peered out, finding only the long lines of huts and the broad space between, quiet and sultry in the afternoon sunlight. It was so tempting to put my fingers to my pussy, to bring myself to climax with just a few, well-placed touches while my army-boy fantasy ran through my head. They'd make me come anyway, even if I did, but it wouldn't be as intense, so I held back.

A figure appeared, far down the line of huts, not Amber, but Isabel, walking fast and being decidedly furtive. She was peering into the huts as she went, and I wondered if the erotic atmosphere had not finally penetrated her prissiness. The thought of her sneaking into one of the huts for a crafty frig delighted me, and I wondered if it would be over what had happened to Vicky, or maybe the sight of the twins getting their spanking, or else some private fantasy of her own.

It was impossible not to be curious, and the thought of watching Isabel masturbate was too good to miss. She, after all, had taken the most self-righteous tone over my love of spanking, denying me the right to my own feelings. Watching her with her hand down her panties as she came over some dirty mental image would be just perfect. Doubtless she'd be guilty about it, just as I had once been, but if I caught her at just the right moment then all sorts of things might become possible.

Once more I peered from the door, keeping back in the shadows. Isabel was some two hundred yards down the line, looking into a hut window. She was in black jeans, very tight over her trim little bum, and a loose blue top that hinted at large, or erect, nipples. Doubtless she would pull it up while she masturbated; in my experience most girls do. I'd see them and watch her play with them, tweaking each to erection, stroking them as she teased herself . . .

My voyeuristic need and sense of mischief were warring with my need for submission. I badly wanted punishing, but I told myself that Amber would doubtless get me anyway. Watching Isabel was a more immediate need. She was coming closer, and moving faster, her nervousness becoming more pronounced as she rejected each hut. It seemed likely she disliked the idea of the broken glass that littered most of them, and so was likely to take one close to my own.

In the end it was the one two down from me she chose, the first with dry mattresses. As she pulled the door open she gave a last look around, her face set in an expression of unmistakable tension. Undoubtedly she was planning to masturbate, and maybe be pretty rude about it, given just how nervous she was. With luck she wanted to smack her own cheeks, or finger her bumhole, but even if she just sneaked a quicky with her hand down her jeans I was desperate to watch.

As soon as I was sure she was not coming back out I slipped from the door. Knowing full well the nervous thrill of masturbating outdoors, I could guess what she would do. First she would find a place of absolute security, where she could relax and maybe have a chance to cover herself if somebody did come. Second she would do whatever was needed to bring herself to climax, growing bolder, and hopefully ruder, as her pleasure rose. Third she would cover up quickly and leave, feigning nonchalance but probably with a pink face.

I wanted to see as much as possible, to feel her excitement and embarrassment, to indulge my voyeurism to the full. Afterwards I would admit it, if not to her, and doubtless the crime would be considered when I was finally punished. Running quickly to her hut, I peered inside. She was not in the main dormitory area, despite the presence of two mattresses she could have used. I would have used them, taking the chance of someone peeping in at the windows; not Isabel, which argued for a wonderful sensitivity and shyness that would make watching her all the more fun.

The back was better anyway, as at the front I would have been visible to anyone coming along the line of huts, and Amber was bound to arrive soon. After running light-footed to the back of the hut, I peered cautiously in at an algae-encrusted window. It was the washroom, and Isabel was standing with her back to me, apparently listening, with her hands at the buckle of her belt.

I knew the moment, the point at which decency is finally abandoned. The trousers come down, or the skirt up, the panties follow, and any chance of feigning innocence is gone. I always hesitate, feeling nervous and rude before exposing myself, and Isabel was the same. She tugged the buckle, her hands actually shaking with her emotion. It came open and she popped her button, her fingers fumbling and slipping. Her zip was down and she was struggling the tight denim over her hips, revealing a pair of tiny pink cotton panties. Down they came, jeans and panties at the same time, pushed to her ankles. One shoe was kicked off and she pulled the trouser leg clear of her clothes, leaving her legs free.

She sank down, squatting, her pretty little bottom stuck out towards me with the cheeks fully open, the back of her pussy just visible, her bumhole stretched and blatant, a view of exquisite rudeness. Rude yes, but an awkward position for masturbation, and I realised that it was only my own dirty mind that had thought playing with herself her intention.

I watched anyway, feeling dirty and thoroughly bad but unable to turn my eyes away. She began to pee, a thick yellow gush running out from beneath her on to the floor, quickly forming a big pool. It would have gone on her jeans and panties, but she noticed in time and quickly pulled them away. Her shoe went in it, though, and with her face half turned I saw her grimace at the sight.

It was hard not to giggle, and I was hoping she'd lose her balance and sit in her puddle. She kept it, pushing her bum further out as her pee died to a trickle. I felt a stab of disappointment that there hadn't been more, only to find my jaw going loose as

I realised there was more, much more. Her bumhole had pushed out as she peed and her muscles relaxed, everting as if she was expecting something up it.

She wasn't. What she was expecting was something to come out. Her hole opened, along with my mouth, gaping, stretching, to form a taut pink ring as it all started to come out. I felt awful, my sense of intrusive intimacy stronger by far than when she'd been peeing. Not that I looked away, but stayed right where I was, my eyes glued to her bottom as piece after piece extruded from her hole and dropped to the floor beneath her. Even when she was finished I stayed still, feeling so dirty for watching that I was weak at the knees.

Only when she moved did I regain my senses. It was just too much. I had to come, and come over the thought of punishment for what I'd done, for being a dirty little peeping Thomasina. I ran out from behind the hut and back to the first one I'd been in, throwing myself down on to a mattress. I was face down, bottom stuck up, the way I wanted to imagine myself beaten. My hands went down, one under my tummy to my pussy, one back to my bottom, feeling the swell of my cheeks and the damp crease between. After what I'd seen it had to be anal, and my fingertips found my clit and bumhole at the same time.

My anus was greasy, wet with a mixture of my own juice and the oil the twins had rubbed in. The ring felt hot as I circled it, deliberately teasing myself, but only for a moment. I popped the first joint of my finger it, toying with my hole and thinking of how I'd watched Isabel's open. It had been such a rude thing to do, so dirty and so intrusive, especially when I could have left at any moment.

I began to rub my clit, dabbing at her and tickling the mouth of my bumhole at the same time. My mind drifted, focusing on what I had seen and what the consequences of my act should be. A punishment was undoubtedly in order, something severe, something to really put me in my place. Spanking was too good for me, although it would make a start, right after I had been made to announce my disgusting behaviour to everyone, out loud, standing on something so they could all see me. After that I'd get my spanking, in the classic position, head down across Isabel's lap, stark naked because I didn't even deserve the privilege of having panties to pull down.

Once I was red-bottomed and snivelling I'd be made to apologise, then to stand to one side with my hands on my head and my red bum showing. I'd need to go myself, but only when I was so desperate that my toes were wiggling and my bumcheeks clenching would I have the nerve to ask. They would laugh at me. They would tell me it was time I learned how poor Isabel had felt, that I should suffer the same sense of being intruded on, violated. They would say I was welcome to relieve myself, in front of them all . . .

I was right on the edge, holding back to make my climax as good as possible, running over and over the awful moment when I would squat down in my misery and shame. So lost was I to my surroundings that it took a second to register the creak of the door and another to stop what I was doing. I turned with a gasp, my cheeks flaring red, expecting to see Isabel standing in the doorway. She wasn't, but Amber was, looking at me with no great surprise. In her hand she held a single, large stinging nettle, grasped in a cloth.

'You couldn't wait?' she asked coolly.

'No,' I admitted. 'I'm too turned on, Amber: I want to be punished. I know you can't whack me, but sit on my face, please, now; let me lick you; make me kiss your bumhole,'

'Patience, darling. Roll over.'

I obeyed, hastily, happy to be in whatever position she wanted, just so long as I was properly punished. She had to be told why, of course, but I found my cheeks reddening at the prospect.

'I'm glad you're so contrite,' she remarked. 'You have been a bit of a brat lately.'

'I know,' I answered, 'and I'm sorry. It's you I love, though, you know that. There's something else too, another reason why I need punishment.'

'Oh, yes? Who else have you had sex with without asking me? A gang of dockers? A horse or two?'

'No, nobody.'

'Then why so remorseful? What could you have possibly done since lunch?'

'Did you see Isabel just now?'

'Yes. You didn't have her, did you? I thought she was the last one who'd let herself go!'

'No, but I watched her. She was two huts along, in the back, relieving herself.'

'You watched Isabel pee? That's naughty, yes, but . . .'

'No, not pee.'

'Ah, and you stayed to watch?'

'Yes. I didn't mean to; I thought she was going to play with herself. I thought she'd been turned on and needed to come in private . . .'

'And you were turned on by it?'

'Yes . . . No . . . I mean, yes, but not like that, just because it was so rude.'

'You are a disgrace, Penny Birch, a dirty, wanton little slut, a tart, a trollop.'

'I know.'

'The filthiest little tramp I've ever met, which is why I'm so glad you're mine.'

'Won't you punish me?'

'Oh I'll punish you, be sure of that, and for real. Still, it's a shame you didn't have a camera. She's so self-satisfied, more than Amy. It would do her good to have a big colourful print of her dropping her load stuck on the notice-board at their offices.'

I laughed in response as she smiled, only for her hand to close hard in my hair. She twisted and pulled me back on to the decaying mattress, holding me down as she delivered two quick, stinging slaps to my inner thighs. I yelped and closed my legs, then spread them wide, expecting more. She had put her nettle on the bed next to mine, and now moved it, making space to lay out four ropes she had tucked into her belt.

'I shall tie you,' she announced, 'and tease you a little with this fine stinging nettle, just your front. After that we shall see, but at the least I think we should make sure Isabel sees your nettlerash. Now relax.'

She chose a rope and turned to me. I lay limp, my breath coming in long, deep drafts as I allowed her to do exactly as she pleased. My wrists were taken, each pulled up and roped to the bedstead, securing me. I expected to be spread-eagled, allowing her to use my face, boobs and pussy at will, but my exposure was due to be worse still. A rope was tied to each of my ankles, and each rope was led to a peg high on the wall above the beds to either side of mine. This left my legs rolled high and wide, lifting my bum, sticking it out and spreading my cheeks. My pussy and anus were gaping, utterly exposed and vulnerable, while my boobs and face stayed available. Four pieces of rope and I was utterly restrained, powerless to defend myself and sexually available in every orifice.

Amber gave a satisfied smile at her handiwork and picked up the nettle. It was useless to protest about marks. She knew as well as I that only my rear view needed to be pristine for the photographs. Besides, I deserved punishment and had no right to choose what form it took.

She held it up to me, letting me see the long stem and the jagged leaves, each with its array of tiny stings. My nipples were straining upwards, and it was impossible not to push my chest out as the wicked thing was moved closer to my skin, a foot, an inch, and touching, brushing the under-tuck of my breasts with a sharp, tickling sensation that quickly grew to a fiery stinging.

I groaned at the pain, pushing my boobs up for more. Amber obliged, laying a long trail of stings over my upper breasts, circling each nipple and finally touching them as I squirmed and writhed in my bonds. I was squealing like a pig, arching my back and gasping for air, feeling each tiny stab of pain, then the warm, throbbing ache as my whole chest seemed to swell and expand.

She kept on, heedless of my cries and pleas, stroking my belly and flanks, my inner thighs and pussy mound, and lastly, most agonising of all, my vulva. I had shut my eyes and my back was in a tight arc, straining my ankles against the ropes and pressing my hips into the mattress. My breath was coming in short, ragged pants, interspersed with whimpers as the awful hot tickling moved closer to my sex. My sense of abandoning myself, of being used, grew as each new piece of my flesh was turned to a field of angry red spots, my tummy button, the swell of my belly, my outer lips and at last my wet, swollen, puffy little cunt.

I really screamed at that, not at first, but when the poison began to work. My pussy was on fire, and seemed huge, a great, wet mass of sex-flesh burning and throbbing with the pain. I couldn't take it, and found myself screaming out my stop word and begging over and over, then apologising, in broken sobs as the tears filled my eyes, to Amber for being a slut, to Isabel for watching her at toilet, even to Beth.

Amber stopped immediately, dropping the nettle. Her hands went to a rope but I was already shaking my head, still mumbling apologies and then begging once more for the privilege of having her bottom in my face. She answered me with a single, understanding nod and climbed aboard the bed. To mount me she had to climb over the ropes, straddling my body and then turning so that I could look up her legs.

Her bottom looked glorious in her army shorts, full and meaty, unmistakably feminine despite the male garment, swelling out the material in two plump balls of flesh. Her hands went to the front, just as Isabel's had done. She tugged open her belt and stuck her bottom out, again as Isabel had, squatting as she stripped her bottom and lowering it towards my face, just as if she intended to use me as her toilet. My eyes were fixed on the plump swell of her pussy and the puckered, muscular ring of her anus, knowing I would soon be kissing and licking both with abandon. Her shorts were at thigh level, and pressed to my neck as her bottom settled comfortably on to my face, smothering me in chubby, girlish rear. My view went, from the full rudeness of her sex and bottom, to two round arcs of pink flesh, to blackness as she settled on my face.

She wiggled her cheeks to spread them across my face, rubbing her pussy on my mouth and her anus against my nose. I kissed her pussy lips, nuzzled her and began to lick, in heaven as my beautiful Amber allowed me to lick her and my bound body throbbed to the pain of nettlerash. For a while she let me lick

222

her pussy before her weight shifted, bringing her bumhole over my mouth. I felt the motion and knew she intended to come, her favourite way, queened on my face with my tongue up her bumhole. She started to masturbate, her bottom moving on my face to the rhythm of her fingers and I probed the tight, soft muscle of her ring with my tongue, teasing, burrowing inside, licking the hot flesh.

She squirmed with pleasure, rubbing it in my face, forcing me to probe her yet deeper. It was so rude, and so right for me, with my tongue up my lover's bumhole as she sat, poised and cool, on my face. Being tied and covered in hot, angry nettlerash made it better still, making me feel punished and forgiven, thoroughly disciplined, then allowed to apologise by licking her anus.

Had I been able I'd have been masturbating and we'd have come together, but I couldn't, forcing me to put everything into her pleasure. She paused and I knew she had pulled her top up, freeing her big breasts to the air so that she could cup one and stroke a nipple as she frigged. Again she began to masturbate and I knew she was near orgasm. She began to grind herself on my face, rubbing her pussy against my chin and wiggling her open bumhole over my mouth. My tongue was pushed up as far as it would go, straining, deep in, so deep I could feel the hot, soft flesh beyond the ring of tight muscle.

Amber started to come, calling out my name as her anal ring tightened on my tongue and began to spasm. Her bottom was squeezing my face, pushed down so firmly that I couldn't breathe or move, just lick and lick as she took her pleasure of me. For a moment I was lost to everything except the joy of having her come. I was her servant, pure and devoted, happy to lick her bottom or whatever else was demanded of me just for the sake of her pleasure. I didn't even care if she smothered me, until the pain in my lungs finally overcame my servility and I twisted my head to the side in desperation.

She sighed, a sound of immense contentment, as she lifted her bottom enough to let me suck hot, pungent, but wonderful air into my straining lungs. I gasped until my head had cleared, admiring her bottom, inches from my face, her pussy wide and moist in a nest of dark gold hair, her anus a wet, open hole between the full curves of her cheeks.

'Pop your tongue back up, Penny, it's your turn,' she said from above me.

I sighed in pleasure, a sound abruptly cut off as her bottom settled back on my face. My tongue found her bumhole, probing deep once more and I began to lick. Her hands touched between my legs, two fingers splaying my smarting pussy lips wide to get at my clit. A thumb entered my vagina, a finger pushed down on my greasy bumhole and in.

She began to masturbate me, so skilfully, manipulating my clit with the touch of long practice and understanding. I knew it wouldn't take long and I let my mind drift as I licked her bottom and her hands worked my sex. She was on my face in a squat, as she often was, but not naked. Her shorts were down, pushed around her thighs to bare her bottom, just as she might have done to relieve herself, just as Isabel had done.

It was a glorious image: Amber, Isabel, any girl, bum bare, squatting, exposing every intimate detail of her sex and bottom, hasty, embarrassed as she relieved herself on the ground. I wished I'd caught Isabel, startled her, made her lose her balance, sit in it, cry out in horror and shame and embarrassment. Then I'd have really deserved my punishment, from both of them, Isabel overcoming her inhibitions through sheer outrage. They'd have put me in bondage, the same humiliating, exposed position. They'd have nettled me thoroughly, then beaten me with their belts, strapping my out-thrust bottom until I begged for mercy, whipping my pussy-lips and laughing as I writhed under the blows. Isabel would have mounted my face, made me lick her bottom clean. Then it would have been Amber, queened on me as she now was in reality, my tongue deep up her bottom. Not for my pleasure, though, but to punish me, to punish me in a way that fitted my crime, squatting over my face, and doing it in my mouth . . .

I came, every muscle in my body locking tight as it hit me in one long, glorious climax that went on and on. Although my lungs were bursting, although my wrists and ankles burned against the straining ropes, just on and on until at last I went dizzy and my filthy fantasy broke. I nearly blacked out, not quite, but as Amber lifted her weight off my face with a happy sigh all I could do was slump in my bonds.

Eleven

My photo-shoot went smoothly, with Amy and
Claudia at Amber's and the suitably neutral and
domestic background of the bedroom wall. Having
gone all week without more than a gentle spanking,
my bottom was pristine. I'd used plenty of skin cream
and powder as well, producing two soft, pink hemi-
spheres of which I felt justly proud. I bought a new
camisole to show off in, pure silk in a delicate yellow
to suit my dark hair, trimmed with fine lace and two
sizes too small to make my bottom look fuller and
extra spankable.

Amy was impressed, going into raptures over the
name tag on my camisole, although it meant nothing
to me. She was more circumspect about admiring my
bum, at least in front of Claudia, contenting herself
with a squeeze when no one was looking, and asking
first, to do credit to her manners.

Claudia used a whole film on my unspanked rear
view, asking me to make endless subtle changes in my
pose and adjusting the lighting almost as often.
Despite this I enjoyed it, both because it was nice to
have my bum the main focus of attention among
three attractive women, and because I knew it would
get better once it was time for my spanking.

Even though it was for the magazine I wanted it
done bare, and had told Amber that she was to undo

the poppers on my camisole. I knew Amy would like to see my pussy as I was punished, and it was only fair after the way I had done her. Claudia might or might not enjoy it. Even at the airforce base she had remained pretty cool and unreadable, and she gave away nothing about her underlying emotions.

Amy asked if she should leave the room while Amber spanked me, but was told it was unnecessary and that it was unimportant whether I was watched or not. She smiled at that, possibly getting the hang of my sexuality enough to know that the humiliation of being done in front of her and Claudia would greatly increase my pleasure.

That decided, I was put across Amber's knee as she sat on her bed, bum towards the door where the girls were standing. My camisole was unpopped and lifted, exposing my pussy, and Amber lifted her knee, forcing my bum into greater prominence and making my cheeks flare to show by bumhole. All this she explained to the girls, adding to my emotions. Even as the spanking started she went on talking, explaining that she was using her fingertips to make my skin sting and bring the blood to the surface quickly.

It was a gentle spanking, and nice, making me sigh and start to moan as my bum warmed and pinked. Amber kept going, ignoring me and making sure my bottom was turned an even colour, with no blotchy areas to spoil the photo. She explained this, but to my surprise Claudia objected, pointing out that if my cheeks were too even a pink it would look as if the picture had been enhanced.

Amber suggested a long-handled hairbrush, which was resting on her bedside table for exactly that purpose. Claudia agreed, and to my surprise picked it up herself and gave me a meaty smack on each cheek. I yelped, not surprisingly, but was told not to be a baby by Amber and Claudia simultaneously. Another dozen were applied to my bottom, making it bounce and drawing further futile protests from me, until at last Claudia was satisfied with the effect.

I was allowed to look in a mirror, finding my bum pink and blotchy, quite clearly properly spanked, then photographed once more. Again Claudia made me pose in a dozen slightly different positions, and again she adjusted the lights virtually every time. Only for the last six did she change her routine, quite casually tugging open my poppers from behind. The pictures were taken with it dangling loose over my bum and with me bent enough to ensure the show of a good bit of crease and at least a hint of fur between my thighs, maybe more.

Afterwards I would have been more than happy for the three of them to take full advantage of me, perhaps completing my beating, then queening me one by one as the others watched. It didn't happen, despite me dropping a couple of not so very subtle hints, and the only submissive thrill I got was to serve them lunch in just my camisole, all rather tame. When they left Amber took me to bed, which made a pleasant finish to the session although I would have preferred to get the others involved.

For all their acceptance of our behaviour, they still seemed to be having trouble really letting go, at least when not alone. I said as much to Amber, who replied that I should be pretty happy to have managed to achieve as much as I had. This was true; in fact I had seldom felt more pleased with myself, barring one or two little things to mar my cat-that's-got-the-cream satisfaction.

Beth was the first of these, because I still found it irritating that she thought she understood me better than I did myself. At the least I wanted to talk over the *Metropolitan* article with her and make her eat her words about the pleasures of erotic spanking. Ideally I wanted her across my knee for a while before thanking me and returning the favour, but I was prepared to go without. Unfortunately Amber had threatened to keep me in the cellar for a week if I went within ten miles of Streatley, so at the least I would have to postpone my visit.

Second was the twins, and in particular Melody, who had scared me and badly needed to be dealt with. True, Morris had spanked them in public, not for spit-roasting me, though, but for not inviting him to join in! Their argument was that I should have known full well that they wouldn't hurt me, and it was true, I should have. After all, as Melody had remarked, if they'd really been going to cook and eat me they'd have stuck the spit up my bum. Easy to say, but hanging trussed, tenderised and basted over a fire I hadn't felt so sure.

Had I been Vicky it would have been easy, or at least feasible, as both the twins enjoyed wrestling and made it plain that female friends were always welcome to try their luck. The condition was that the winner did as she pleased with the loser, and if I tried it I was just going to get my head sat on again. I would have to wait my chance for something more subtle.

Another irritation, albeit trivial, was Isabel, who was just annoyingly prissy. She made me feel like a specimen under a microscope, although some might have argued that this was simply poetic justice for a biologist. I had also suffered a rare twinge of guilt, for watching her without her consent, so my feelings were mixed.

As it happened, it was Isabel who gave me a chance to get my own back on Melody. From the conversations while we were at the airbase she had gathered that a fair bit more went on among my friends than girly spanking play and games of pursuit, capture and punishment. Most of all she wanted an interview with Melody, who was not only female and had an exceptionally strong personality, but was also from an ethnic minority. That made her ideal magazine material, apparently.

She rang to ask for the Rathwells' number, but I was not allowed to give it. Isabel wheedled but I refused, promising only to talk to Melody myself. Melody agreed, happy to get a chance to put her personal philosophy across. Only when she started to tease me about getting in a temper over the roasting incident did I decide to try and use the opportunity to take my revenge on her.

I had pictured Isabel living in a smart central London flat, rather like Natasha. It would have been in an up-market yet fashionable area, airy, convenient for work, and doubtless purchased with Daddy's money, again like Natasha. The truth was somewhat different, in that she lived in a cottage near Liphook, which she had inherited from an aunt. This I discovered when I rang to arrange the interview with Melody. She suggested it as a venue rather than the *Metropolitan* offices, apologising for the distance but pointing out that it would be a lot quieter and also promising lunch. After a few calls back and forth it was agreed, and a plot was beginning to form in my head.

It needed some time, so I set the date for the following week and the venue for Isabel's cottage. On meeting Mel I was as friendly as anything, kissing her, squeezing her boobs and apologising for throwing a tantrum just because she'd put me on a spit. We chatted merrily all the way to Liphook and I told her about watching Isabel, which she found hilarious and not shocking at all.

By the time we got to Isabel's we would have been quite happy to follow lunch and the interview with a threesome. After the interview Melody even suggested it, quite calmly, as if proposing that we open another bottle of mineral water. Isabel declined, politely but with an all too obvious unease. We left soon after, with Mel complaining that Isabel had forced whatever she said to fit her own preconceptions. I had to agree, but pointed out that it isn't always easy for people to get over their inhibitions.

'She's a typical rich white girl,' Melody snapped. 'Full of crap about how liberated she is and how she's in control of her own life, but when it comes down to the real thing, she can't handle it!'

'She might be intimidated by you,' I pointed out. 'Or maybe she just doesn't fancy you.'

Melody shrugged, indicating her total indifference to Isabel's preferences.

'I'm game, anyway,' I assured her. 'How about a drink and then we can go in the woods.'

'That I like,' she answered.

I'd have been amazed if she'd said anything else. We found a nice pub somewhere to the south of Haslemere and shared a bottle of wine, one glass for me as I was driving, the rest for Mel. After that she was more ready than ever, and teasing me about how she was going to make me strip to my shoes and streak, or even persuade any men we might meet to let me suck them off.

I chose a wood I'd been to before, an obscure stretch of forestry land cut off from the road by a railway with access beneath a high arch of red brick. It was one of Anderson and Vicky's pet places, but I was sure Mel had never been there. We walked in,

231

and as soon as we were out of sight of the car I ran, knowing full well she would chase me. Sure enough, she did, and caught me, inevitably. I was made to strip, stark naked, by which time she was too excited to do more than give me a brief slapping before telling me to get on my knees. I went willingly, kneeling on my clothes as she tugged down her jeans and panties. With her seated on the thick trunk of a fallen pine I began to lick, kissing her pussy-lips and inner thighs in an attempt to tease, only to be taken by the hair and pulled in hard.

As I licked her I put my hands down, only not to masturbate. Her breathing had begun to change, getting deeper and faster, signalling her approaching orgasm as I lapped at her clit. The grip in my hair tightened; her thighs squeezed together around my head, and I snapped cuffs to her ankles and heaved with all my strength to send her sprawling backwards over the log.

I was already diving beneath the pine trunk, which was well clear of the ground, snapping a cuff on to one wrist as she struggled to right herself. A chain led back to her ankle cuff, fixing her around the log. She had recovered before I could get the other wrist cuff on, and I had to fight. Normally she would win easily, but upside down, half drunk and already restrained she was hardly at her best.

Eventually, despite a few bruises, I had her where I wanted her, lashed kneeling under the log with chains running over the top and connecting her ankles to her wrists. She had laughed at me for bringing an anorak on such a hot day, but now she knew why. The pockets were stuffed with bondage equipment.

I added a few more ropes for good measure, pulled up her top and bra to let her big breasts loose and took her jeans and panties down as far as her bonds would let me. Only then, with her helpless and exposed, did I pause to get my breath back.

'I think that counts as a wrestling win, don't you?' I puffed.

'Sure, Penny.'

There was amusement in her voice, not really the right attitude for a girl in bondage with everything showing.

'So I shall amuse myself with you,' I went on. 'A good spanking would be a start.'

'Nice,' she answered. 'Make it a hard one. Have you brought your little hairbrush?'

'No, but that's the good thing about a wood: there are so many things that can be applied to a girl's bum.'

'Sure, spank me good, Penny. Make me notice.'

'I will, the question is, what with? There are twigs of all sorts for a start, and not just birch, although it might be appropriate. Hazel shoots are good, or ash, nice and heavy, that would really get you squealing. Plaited willow stings like anything. Then there are nettles. I could tickle your pussy and boobs with them, maybe whip your bottom. Now, let me see. I don't want to keep you waiting. What's handy?'

Weeping willow was the answer, or at least the best. There were several just a few yards down the slope, by a piece of marshy ground. Making sure that Melody could see me, I broke off three long, whippy twigs and plaited them together, making a springy, three-foot whip that I knew would sting nicely and bring the blood to her pussy.

She kept her cool, watching as I made the whip. I recognised her attitude, taunting me into trying to break her because she knew full well she could take anything I would be prepared to dish out in the way of corporal punishment. She was right, but it would have been a shame not to whip her when I had the chance. There was amusement in her eyes as I swished my home-made whip through the air, almost contempt.

It was deserved, because the whipping I gave her would have had me howling and blubbering if it had been the other way around. All she did was grunt a little, while I ended up sweaty and flustered with a sore arm and a piece of broken willow in my hand. Her bum was marked, with long purple welts on her dark skin, but as a punishment it was pretty feeble. Not that I was going to admit my failure, and at least her pussy was even more swollen and wet than before.

'I feel better for that,' I declared as I threw aside the remains of the whip. 'So do you to judge by the state of your pussy. You're dripping!'

'Get your face in there, girl. I know you want to.'

'Not yet, Mel, you don't get off that easy.'

'Oh no, Penny, what are you going to do? I suppose you're going to fuck me?'

'You wish. Not that it wouldn't be fun to slide a nice, big strap-on between your chubby pussy lips, Mel, or even up your bum. The trouble is, you would like it more than me.'

'I'd love it. Come on, girl, get your strap-on. Fuck me. Push it up my arse. Anyway you like.'

She was taunting me, showing how the beating hadn't done anything more than excite her. I made a face, feigning uncertainty and a little irritation.

'Admit it, Penny,' she went on. 'You're too nice, too much the little middle-class white home-girl. You wouldn't do anything I couldn't handle easily. You couldn't.'

'No,' I answered. 'I couldn't, probably. Still, I've got to try. Have you ever been fucked by a dog?'

'A dog? Get real.'

'Oh good, then at least the experience might be new for you, even if you do handle it easily.'

'Quit joking around, Penny. Come on, make me lick you or whatever you want to do . . .'

She shut up because I had pushed my panties into her mouth, or at least tried to. It was a struggle to get them in, and I had to hold her nose for ages to make her take them. It worked in the end, leaving her glaring at me with just a little piece of white cotton sticking out at one corner of her mouth. I tied them off with my bra, which made a suitably absurd sight with the two cups bulging out over either cheek.

'There we are,' I told her. 'Enjoy the flavour. Now, where was I? Oh yes, dogs, or more exactly one dog, a dog to fuck you. They love to mount girls, you know; in fact, I'm surprised Morris has never taught you the trick. Maybe he's just never thought of it. It'd make a great cabaret, don't you think? You and Harmony on stage, mounted by a couple of Great Danes? No? Oh well, perhaps not. Dobermann pinschers might be better, more you, or Old English sheepdogs. Wouldn't you look funny, with a pair of great big woolly sheepdogs mounted up on your bums, humping away with their tongues lolling out? No? A giant poodle then? Tall, plenty of leg to let him get at you, a big cock I dare say and surely the most humiliating choice? Still no? My, we are a fussy one!'

She had been shaking her head vigorously as I spoke, so vigorously in fact that I wondered if I hadn't touched a nerve. Certainly she was shivering, and possibly beginning to think I was serious.

'For now,' I went on, 'I doubt we'll be able to be choosy about breeds. Still, I imagine this is Labrador country, so we should be OK. I would think most owners will be happy to let their pet hump you if I ask nicely. Obviously they can have a go first. How would that be, a nice country gentleman in your pussy before his doggy has a turn? Nice?'

She was still shaking her head, genuinely worried, but I could see in her eyes that she was thinking I'd never really be able to persuade a dog owner to go through with my filthy scheme.

'Maybe you're right,' I admitted. 'Men can be funny about these things. Odd really, you'd think anyone with a cock in their trousers would leap at the chance of having you from the rear, and any gentleman would surely not wish to deprive his dog of his own share. Yobs would be better: they'd fuck you, then cheer the dogs on. No, it's not really worth the risk of rejection.'

I patted her bottom, just firmly enough to make her cheeks quiver, then sat down on the pine trunk, directly over her back.

'Another animal perhaps, something lewder than a dog, something with a dirty image. Hmm, yes. Did you see the piggies just before we parked? With their cute little piglets? They were all sows, of course, the big ones. The boar will be kept in a little field well off the road, maybe an orchard, that's how they used to keep them. He'll be bored, and very frustrated, what with several hundred females the other side of the hedge. I'm sure a nice, plump human girl would be just his thing. After all, you're in the right pose for a pig, bum up, pussy sticking out behind. You even look a bit like one. You're nice and juicy too; he'd be able to smell you. I doubt I'd even have to lead him; he'd probably mount you of his own accord. After a good snuffle at your pussy that is, they like that. He'd poke his big, rubbery nose in, nuzzling it between your pussy lips. He might get right in, with his snout stretching out your hole while he gave you a good lick with his fat, piggy tongue. At the least you'd get your pussy and bum licked, just for the salt.'

I trailed a finger up between her legs, touching her pussy, briefly burrowing inside the wet hole and giving her bumhole a tickle. There was serious consternation in her face, and I knew I was getting to her. I continued.

'Once he'd made sure you were ripe and ready, he'd mount you, just as if you were a real sow, climbing on your back and prodding at your rear until it went in. They're not very large, pigs, cock-wise, but big enough, and spiral. Imagine it, Melody, his weight on your back, his trotters resting either side of your neck. The cock prods at you, bumps twice, slips in the crease of your bum, finds your pussy and he's in, a big, fat pig, rutting between your buttocks, in your pussy, up you, with the long, spiral cock working in and out of your vagina as you're fucked. That's right, Melody, fucked by a pig.'

She was squirming a bit and her breathing was coming hard, just like mine had done when being prepared for the spit. Panting through the nose is less than dignified, but when trussed up with everything showing it's no more than a minor detail. I gave her a happy smile and went on.

'I'd do it, too, only I'm not sure you'd notice much difference between the boar and Morris. A horse might be better. We passed a riding school on the way down, didn't we? I'm sure we did. I wonder if they've got something suitable for you. Did you know Catherine the Great is supposed to have been fucked to death by a horse? So I believe, anyway, a charger I imagine. Don't worry, I'd go for something calmer, a nice, sedate old cart horse with a cock three feet long and as thick as my ankle. Still tricky, of course, I'd have to keep hold of him. I could rub him on your pussy until you're really dripping, then see how much will go up, then jerk him off all over your bum. No? You are a fuss-pot, Mel. It'll have to be something, you know: you're not getting away with it, and I mean that.'

She was getting in a fine state, much as I had done on the spit. Logically she might be sure I either wouldn't, or couldn't, carry out my threats, but logic is hard to maintain when you're tied up, effectively in the nude and under someone else's power, as I well know. I gave her bum another gentle pat.

'I wonder if there's a zoo nearby,' I mused. 'A baboon would be perfect, a mandrill rather. Imagine his little bright-blue buttocks slapping up and down on your big brown ones! What a sight! No, I must stick to practical ideas. Hmm, dog, pig, horse, what else might there be? There must be deer in these woods, but I imagine they'd be too shy, even with you helpless. A bull would be fun, but I doubt I could handle one, a ram likewise. Oh well, it looks like it'll just have to be a dog, and it will be a dog, Melody Rathwell, even if I have to kidnap one.'

There was real worry in her eyes as I dressed, without my bra and panties, of course, but outwardly respectable. I ignored her, saying nothing and finally putting my anorak over her head and tying it in place with an arm dangling down in front of her face like a ridiculous trunk so that she could breathe easily. With her helpless and deprived of both speech and sight, I left, feeling thoroughly pleased with myself.

It was just as well she knew nothing about the country, because a fair bit of what I'd said had been made up. With her background in London, New York and San Francisco I had felt sure I was on safe ground, and it seemed to have paid off. Not that she could have challenged me with her mouth stuffed full of my panties, but no doubt had shown in her eyes.

The thing was, she would probably have done it to me, had she been able. So when I had her helpless she naturally assumed I would go through with it myself. I couldn't, unfortunately, although I had turned myself on so much that had a friendly farmer appeared as I reached the track and offered the loan of his pig I would have accepted and let him have Melody first into the bargain.

No farmer appeared, nor anybody else, and as I ran back to the car the sole evidence of humanity was the rattle of a train from the far side of the wood. In the back of the car was my masterpiece, hastily constructed with only minor assistance from Amber.

She had a pair of tight leather shorts with a ring behind the fly into which a dildo can be fitted. I had borrowed both the design and the dildo, creating a garment of which I felt I could be proud. Essentially it was a furry body-suit, made of synthetic brown fur and cut much like an Edwardian bathing costume. With it on I was furry from chest to knees, while a fly allowed the dildo to be fitted as needed. I had even used longer fur on the belly piece and around the crotch, just like a real dog, while a pair of paw gloves added the final touch of realism. The dildo was a fine object as well, designed not for two girls to fuck together as with a normal double dildo, but very definitely for one girl to fuck another. It was as thick as a good-sized cock, eight inches in length and moulded in loving detail to resemble a particularly grotesque erection. It also had balls, currently filled with single cream which could be ejaculated to order. The final touch was a ribbed area that pressed to the wearer's crotch, allowing her to bring herself off on it while she fucked her partner.

While no more indecent than a leotard, at least until the dildo was fitted, the costume was hardly normal country wear, so I bundled it quickly into a plastic bag and started back to where I had left poor Melody. Going back I had an awful vision of her having got free, waiting for me with her mind seething with a whole range of awful punishments. Fortunately she was where I had left her, very still, listening. It was impossible not to grin. Her pose left her bum stuck right at me, her pussy so blatantly flaunted that I doubted if any man coming across her could have resisted fucking her.

I stripped off and put the doggy suit on, quietly, but deliberately breaking a couple of twigs to make Melody start. When ready I did a little listening myself and began to walk towards her. I have had a lot of practice at being a dog, having played at puppy-girls with Amber often enough to bark and pant realistically and put in yet more practice while making my outfit. As I approached Melody I gave it my best effort, panting, snuffling and giving a pleased yip, all interspersed with my own voice, making friendly remarks to the dog. It must have been a fair performance, because it had poor Mel squirming in her bonds.

'Hi, Melody, I'm back,' I announced as I reached her. 'This is Fido. I don't know his real name, but Fido will do. Good boy, Fido. Fido is a very friendly Alsatian whose owner is somewhere across the wood, and doubtless worried, so we mustn't be too long, must we?'

She squirmed her bottom and shook her head, or rather my anorak, with the trunk like sleeve waving wildly as she moved. I ignored her and went back to my doggy imitations before starting to speak again.

'OK, Fido, Melody. Melody, Fido. I always feel it's polite to be introduced before you fuck. Yes, that's right, Fido, you can smell pussy, can't you? Nice plump pussy. Come now, don't be shy: you can have

240

it, you know. Come on, up you come ... My, you have got a beauty.'

I mounted Melody, pressing my furry tummy to her rear. She gave a little, despairing grunt deep in her throat and tried to wiggle her bottom, but I was already probing with the dildo.

'You should be pleased, Mel,' I continued. 'He's got a lovely big cock. I can see it, right up between your pussy lips. I bet that feels nice. Come on, Fido, in we go. Do stop wriggling, Mel!'

Writhing would have been a better word, but she was tied too tightly to stop me. I kept prodding, sometimes missing on purpose just to string out the fun but finally finding her hole and slipping easily inside.

'There we are,' I chided. 'That's not so bad, is it, now it's up? Good boy, Fido, enjoy your fuck.'

Melody had stopped struggling, presumably resigning herself to a doggy fuck now that the cock was actually in her. I began to hump her, using quick, urgent pushes the way Henry's Rasputin did it. My intention had been to come up her like that, but she was so acquiescent it clearly wasn't enough. I was going to have to bugger her. I let the dildo slip out and rubbed it in her crease, smearing juice over her anus, just a few times before entering her again.

'Good idea, Fido,' I remarked. 'Bumholes are just that little bit tighter, don't you think? Good boy, come on, let Auntie Penny help.'

I had quickly flicked my paw glove free, and put my hand to the dildo, guiding it out and pushing it to her bumhole. She squeaked and thrashed, frantic to keep it out of her anus, tensing her hole as I prodded and lifting up so the dildo would slide back into her pussy. Each time it happened I fucked a little more, only to take it out and once more press it to her anus. She kept fighting, and I could imagine her feelings, resigned to the fucking but determined she wasn't going to suffer the added degradation of buggery.

'Sorry, Mel, but it's bumhole time for you,' I told her. 'Come on, Fido, she'll be ever so tight in her bottom. That's it, good boy, push.'

She kept fighting, but I was determined, and as her anus became more and more slippery with her juice she found it harder and harder to defend. Finally it happened, my knob jamming in her ring, opening it, slipping once, then finding the hole and popping inside to ease a good two inches into the slippery cavity of her rectum. I jammed the rest in, keeping up the quick, purposeful thrusting motion and ignoring the peculiar noises Melody was making as what she fondly imagined was a dog's cock worked its way up her back passage.

'Good boy!' I crowed. 'Oh that does look nice, Mel. Come on, enjoy it, feel his nice big prick in your bumhole. Squeeze on him, he'll love that. Good boy, Fido, come on, give her a good bumfucking and come up her pretty rear-end. Push a bit more, that's right, all the way in, so your balls slap her pussy. She'll like that.'

Once I was in I began to bugger her, keeping my pace and rubbing my pussy against the ridges of the dildo. With the glorious sight of her bottom spread bare in front of me and the dildo protruding from my furry belly and into her hole I knew I would soon come. It was even worth getting into the more human position, just to watch her anus move as I buggered her.

I held it there for a long time, watching her shiver as I buggered her, feeling my front slap on her full bottom with each push, hugely enjoying my power over her and the knowledge of what would be going on in her head. Nude, on her knees, being buggered by a dog. Melody, beautiful, strong, dominant Melody, tied and gagged with a pair of my panties, beaten and teased, now with a shaggy, rutting Alsatian on her back, first in her pussy, then up her bottom, her glorious, big, round, dark bottom, with the hole straining on an animal's penis, a dog's penis . . .

As my climax hit me I bit my lip hard, determined not to cry out despite the waves of overwhelming ecstasy that were flooding through my brain. For the peak I held myself deep up her bottom, imaging my doggy alter-ego about to come. Melody grunted through her gag and I jammed myself hard against the ball sack, squashing it flat and spurting a half-pint of ersatz dog sperm up her bottom.

She made the most extraordinary noise as her rectum filled, a great pig-like snort that may have expressed a helpless surrender to pleasure, perhaps disgust, or may just have been the effect of the air being knocked from her lungs as the cock was jammed to the very hilt up her bum. I held myself in for a long time, letting the cream fill her as my orgasm died slowly away. Only when the last faint echoes had died did I start to pull back, easing the dildo slowly out so as not to hurt her and leaving her bumhole gaping wide as the cream began to ooze back out.

I sat back on my haunches, watching as the creamy white mess spurted and bubbled from her anus, in pulses as her muscles struggled to recover from the stresses of sodomy. It was dribbling down her pussy, filling the open hole and clotting in her hair, running down her labia and dripping from her clit. Her buttocks were moving, too, clenching and spreading in time to her breathing.

It was only fair to let her come, especially when she was probably too far gone to realise that it wasn't a dog licking her. I put my face to her pussy and dabbed my tongue into the cream. It tasted nice, sweet and rich and also of girl, and I began to lap, cleaning it from her lips. She wriggled at first, as much as she could, trying to push my face away. Not for long though, and I knew she had abandoned even the decency of pretending to resist as she groaned deep in her throat and pushed her bottom up and back, opening herself to my tongue.

I could see no reason to keep her anguish short, and made a thorough job of her bottom, licking up the cream as it dribbled from her sodden anus, and cleaning her ring when it had finally managed to close properly. Her pussy lips came next, with my tongue burrowing in among her hair until I had cleaned all I could reach. Finally I took mercy on her, lapping out the pool in her vagina, slurping the full length of her sopping pussy, lower and lower, until at last I was licking her clit.

She immediately began to grunt through her panty gag and tried to rub her bottom in my face. I kept licking, feeling her muscles clench as she started to come. As it hit her she began to writhe her bottom about, sobbing deep in her throat and bucking up and down in a crazy fucking motion. She was grunting more and more loudly, then out came the most abandoned, doleful groan, the noise of a girl who has let a dog lick her to orgasm and enjoyed every second of it despite herself.

Perfect timing was needed, so I waited just long enough for her to come off her high and start wondering what was going on before giving her a playful slap on the bum and telling her it had been me all along. I expected some anger, but was prepared to argue my case about the spit-roasting. She did call me a bitch, a sadistic ass-bandit and a number of other expressions she'd picked up in the States, most of which I didn't understand. She wasn't cross though, more menacing, the way she was before wrestling matches.

I explained that I'd done it to her to make things even after the spit-roasting incident, but she was less than impressed. My suggestion that she should take her feelings out on Harmony and so balance things between the three of us was even less well received. Rather than accept my reasoning she told me I had a choice. Let her go now and she would content herself with rubbing my face in the dirt while she beat me with a willow switch. Leave her and she'd spend the next year training up a litter of giant poodles to mount girls, just for me.

As I was already in it up to my neck I asked her if she planned to train the poodles on herself, removed my anorak, unfastened her wrists and skipped quickly back before she could grab me. Revenge would come, but not until I'd had the chance to savour my victory.

Revenge came faster than I expected. Only two days later Amber and I were chatting calmly in the kitchen when the bell for the gate went. She answered it and presently I heard the crunch of tyres in the yard and saw the big, golden nose of Rathwell's appalling Rolls-Royce outside the window. The sight put my heart straight into my throat, and I seriously expected the door to open and half-a-dozen giant poodles to be let out. None came, only Melody, which was nearly as bad.

She played it very well, because if she had demanded the right to punish me Amber would have thrown her out. Instead she was perfectly reasonable, suggesting that I had gone a lot further than she had and that it was only fair for the balance to be restored. We discussed the comparative traumas of thinking one is about to be spit-roasted and thinking one has been buggered by a dog, but I knew I would have to give in at the end. Melody's argument was that it was completely ridiculous for me to think they would actually have cooked and eaten me, which I had to concede. On the other hand she had genuinely thought she was being mounted by a dog, or at least she swore she had.

I conceded defeat myself, demanding only that the revenge be in proportion and that I be allowed to punish Harmony at some future date. Melody happily agreed to her sister's fate. My own came immediately.

Amber gave her a riding-crop and said to take me into the paddock and have fun with me, taking no more than twelve strokes. An instant later Melody had me by the ear and was leading me outside. I expected a whipping, doubtless getting my head sat on. What I had forgotten was that Amber had agreed to let a local farmer graze three young Jerseys in the paddock.

Melody laughed when she saw them and I knew exactly what she was going to do. I was frog-marched across the paddock and forced to kneel, with my face inches above the largest, most glutinously disgusting cowpat imaginable with her hand twisted hard into my hair. I begged and pleaded with her, promising to do anything as long as she spared my face, but she just held me there as my dress was turned up and my panties yanked down, baring me.

I never said my stop word. I could have done, maybe she would even have taken notice, but my own masochism betrayed me, making me hold it back. Then it was too late. Melody gave a sudden shove and my face went in the cowpat. I shut my eyes just in time, but it went in my mouth and up my nose, warm, sticky filth, oozing up around my cheeks and into my hair, soiling me utterly as a great bubble of utter, abject humiliation rose in my throat.

She beat me like that, face down in the cowpat, bum up with my pussy and anus showing, twelve hard strokes of the riding-crop in quick succession. It hurt crazily, and I could hear her laughter as she thrashed me, the swishes of the crop and the smacks as it hit my skin, also the squelching noises as my face moved in the cowpat. I couldn't breathe, let alone scream and howl, but I kicked my feet and beat my hands on the grass, as pathetic as ever.

I thought it was over when the twelfth stroke cracked down on my naked buttocks and my head was pulled suddenly up, only to be pushed straight back into the steamy filth as I gasped for breath. My mouth was wide open and I got it filled with dung, leaving me spluttering and coughing as she at last let go of my hair. She took me about the waist; her hand found my pussy and she began to frig me, forcing me to come over my own degradation.

It was more than I could resist, and I let her do it, gasping out my pleasure as she worked my clit with expert fingers. I tried to stop myself, to hold back and salvage a last, tattered remnant of pride, but I couldn't and as I started to come I committed the final act of self-debasement and put my own face back in the cowpat.

I walked back with my head hung, Melody leading me by the hand. She helped me wash at the outside tap and took my dress off as it had suffered a bit. Inside I left her to talk to Amber and went upstairs, intending to change. I only got as far as stripping before I flung myself on the bed, not sure if I wanted to cry or masturbate to a second orgasm. The bell went before I could decide and I was about to rise when I heard a voice I recognised, Beth's. Amber's voice answered, calm, friendly, not in the least surprised, which I certainly was.

'I'm glad you made it,' Amber was saying. 'I wasn't sure you'd come.'

'I wouldn't miss this, not for anything,' Beth answered. 'She'll accept it, won't she?'

'Oh yes, she'll accept it. She's been after it for months.'

'Good.'

'She's already had twelve, from Melody here,' Amber went on, 'but another few won't do any harm. She's in the bedroom, right opposite the top of the stairs. You'll find a cane in my wardrobe.'

'Thanks.'

I heard Beth's footsteps as she started to mount the stairs. I pulled a pillow down the bed and rolled on top of it, raising my bum into a convenient position for punishment. With a heavy sigh I rested my chin in one hand, waiting for Beth to come and give me the whacking I so richly deserved.

NEXUS NEW BOOKS

To be published in September 2005

SCHOOL FOR STINGERS
Yolanda Celbridge

Tomboy Caroline Letchmount enlists at Furrow Weald finishing school in Cornwall – motto 'Bare up and obey!' An institution with a military regime of merciless corporal punishment, and flagellant girl gangs – the Swanks and Stingers. When accustomed to pepper panties, bare-boxing and canings from 'sixpence' to 'five shillings', she is ready to be auctioned as a girlslave to rich voluptuaries. Meeting her school friend Persimmon, now an adept of the naval birch, in a lust-drenched tropical island, Caroline must decide if she is truly submissive.

£6.99   ISBN 0 352 33994 2

DEPTHS OF DEPRAVATION
Ray Gordon

Belinda fears that her sixteen-year-old daughter may be falling for Tony, her handsome but cruel new neighbour, and resolves to do everything in her power to keep the two apart. She believes that by giving her body to Tony she'll be able to preserve her daughter's innocence, but she soon finds herself hooked on debased and perverted sexual acts as she plunges deeper and deeper into the pit of depravity.

£6.99   ISBN 0 352 33995 0

THE BOND
Lindsay Gordon

For some like Missy and Hank, the bond is an extraordinary passage from innocence to extreme passion. It is a need for sensual freedom and an ability to journey beyond the body. For the Preacher, the bond is a curse; responsible for a broken heart that will never heal and can only demand vengeance. Pursued by this spectre from their past, Missy and Hank flee to an uncertain future in New Orleans where the greatest mystery of all – the origin of their secret life – waits in the dark. Along the way their journey is fuelled by the hunt, seduction and domination of their lovers – the way of the bonded.

£6.99   ISBN 0 352 33996 9

If you would like more information about Nexus titles, please visit our website at www.nexus-books.co.uk, or send a stamped addressed envelope to:
Nexus, Thames Wharf Studios,
Rainville Road, London W6 9HA